Pop the CLUTCH

Pop the CLUTCH

*For my parents -
Thanks for raising me in an area that seems totally weird to me now
that I've lived in other places.*

CHAPTER ONE

VIOLET

Second chances were like zombies—rotting from the inside, reeking of death, and a total waste of time seeing as how they were going to die again. Nothing made it through death unscathed—not people, pets, or even cities. Which was why the changes made to my hometown seemed almost impossible to accept. The place had been transformed.

Steel mills and auto factories had ruled the horizon when I'd lived there, and everyone you knew drove an American car because a family member or friend had worked for that company. But many of the mills had closed, and the auto industry had laid off workers, instigating the shuttering of the support businesses in a factory town. I hadn't expected people to adjust to that, but they had. Adjusted and profited. A different sort of suburbia had emerged from the ashes. A fact proven by the view as I looked across the overpass at the skyline baking under the summer sun.

The flat patch of asphalt leading to the stamping plant where half the town had once worked had morphed into something else, sprouting buildings and looking more like a shopping center than the industrial complex I remembered. A couple of department stores, a home improvement center, a handful of restaurants, and a huge exercise facility dominated the view that was once owned by blue steel walls and a logo you could see for miles. The same logo I'd seen on the majority of cars driving past me as I rolled into Downriver, Michigan.

I tapped my fingers on the steering wheel as I waited for the light to turn green, trying to remember the last time I'd looked out over that particular piece of land. Graduation… College… Chicago. Eight years? No, nine. Wait, ten. It'd been ten years since I'd last driven down these roads. Not nearly long enough, to be honest, but enough for the place to come back from certain death after the plant closed. Enough time for the city to rise again, though whether like a phoenix or a zombie, I had yet to determine.

The light turned green, and my stomach dropped right along with my foot on the gas pedal as I turned onto the main road through town. There were reasons I'd left and reasons I'd stayed away, but the reasons to finally come home had outweighed them all. I didn't want to be there, but it was time to cross that border and head inside the battle zone known as my hometown. It was time to come home.

After a short drive and a couple of turns, I pulled into the driveway of my grandma's house. Long and low, the brick ranch sat nestled behind a lawn of bright green as it always had. Nothing appeared out of place, though my memories seemed to have faded over the years. Had that flowerpot on the porch always been blue, or was it red when I'd lived there? Had the storm door always been tan? I'd thought it was white. And I could have sworn the house numbers had been brass and not the dark bronze decorating the brick.

"It's a house, not a spot-the-differences puzzle," I mumbled as I opened the car door. The sudden pressure against my chest made my breath catch, the humidity giving heft to something that should have been weightless. We were too far inland to catch a lake breeze, and the heat of the day practically radiated off the concrete beneath my feet. Or maybe, just maybe, that inability to breathe came from something internal. Being here, looking at this neighborhood where I'd spent the majority of my life, made me both nostalgic and completely out of sorts. I could feel the force of eyes on me, could sense the judgment my very presence would incite. The tidy, suburban homes with secrets inside the walls and big windows to hide behind closed me in. Made me itch to get on the road and head back to the anonymity of the city two states away.

But some things were bigger than my personal comfort, and one of them was waiting for me. So, I took a deep breath, and I squared my shoulders. And I opened the door to my past.

Almost literally, because stepping inside the house was like opening some kind of time capsule.

The kitchen looked the same as it had every day when I'd come home from school. Dark cabinets, light countertops, and braided rugs brightening up the floor screamed home to me. Memories of baking cookies for bake sales and holidays jostled to the forefront of my mind, overpowering any of their not-so-sweet brethren with their silliness and warmth. This place had been home for so long, had been where I'd fallen in love with food. Had been my entire world.

The smell of fresh-baked bread and the vanilla of the beeswax candles Grandma had always burned pulled at my heart, made my earlier worries almost disappear. That smell was pure childhood magic, and my God, had I missed it. I hadn't known how much until right at that moment. There was nothing better than the smell of home.

"Is that you, Vee?"

"No one calls me Vee anymore." My lips curled up almost of their own volition as Grandma walked into the kitchen from the hallway with a bright smile on her face. Looking at me with the same amount of love in her eyes as she had since I'd been a tiny thing playing dolls on the floor beneath my feet.

"That's because you scold anyone who dares to cross your *'Don't call me Vee'* rule. But I changed your diapers—I'm allowed a little lenience."

Her arms wrapped around me like a blanket, creating a fortress of safety that settled my soul in a way nothing else could. It'd been months since I'd felt her embrace, since she'd been able to meet me in one of the coastal towns on Lake Michigan for a girls' weekend. I hated coming back here, and she hated Chicago, so the lake was our compromise. But she'd had to cancel our regular trips when she'd started feeling a little under the weather, and I'd had to make the decision to return when "a little under the weather" had been diagnosed as cancer.

"How're you feeling?" I asked, holding her tight. She'd lost weight. Her shoulders were definitely bonier than the last time I'd seen her, and her hair seemed thinner and much grayer. Something she hid well, but I noticed. I saw.

"Oh, honey, I'm fine. Quit worrying over me." She patted me on the back and pulled away, her smile a little less bright, her eyes a little more watery. All signs of her lie.

"Grandma." I gave her my best family glare, the one she'd taught me. The look that said both "Don't mess with me" and "You'd better tell me the truth right now, young lady."

"Violet," she mimicked, cocking her head in rebuttal. "I'm fine today, and I'll be better once all this is behind me. So quit worrying so much. Come on now, let's go sit and catch up."

Lies, all of them. But I let her tell them, and I let myself believe them if only for a few moments. Tomorrow, we could deal with the truth. Cancer, chemo, radiation, surgery...all the not-fun things that needed to be picked apart. Nothing was going to change in the next twenty-four hours.

I followed Grandma into the family room, sweeping a glance across the mantel. My high school graduation pictures dominated the left side, while pictures of my cousin Dahlia took up the space on the right. The two of us could have been sisters in those pictures—our reddish-blond hair and light eyes a perfect match to one another. Not anymore, though. That color had been too striking, too unusual. Too easy for strangers to recognize. I hadn't been a strawberry-blonde since my freshman year of college. Since the first time someone had told me they'd seen me in a clip on the internet.

"You brought your swimsuit, right? We should get you a pool pass since you're here for the summer and all." Grandma kept her voice light and almost innocent, but I knew her better than that.

"I'm not staying the whole summer. I'm here until Dahlia finishes her training classes, then she's taking over."

"What's your hurry?"

"I'd prefer to be in a more populated area when the zombie apocalypse starts." I kept my voice deadpan flat as I gave her a much-practiced, casual shrug. "Safety in numbers, and all that."

Grandma tried to tsk at me, but I could see her fighting not to smile. Being on the receiving end of her fake glare was totally worth that bit-back grin.

"Gotcha," I said, leaning against the couch cushions. "No, really. I've booked a huge catering gig for a popular event in August, and I've been picking up as many shifts as I can at the restaurant. I need to save more money if I have any chance of opening my own bakery within the next decade."

"Why you choose to live someplace so expensive is beyond me."

The adult side of me fought the urge to roll my eyes like the teenager I'd once been, having argued this point too many times to count. "I like it there."

"You don't like it there—you like that you can *hide* there."

I lost my battle against the eye roll on that one. "Grandma—"

She interrupted me with a wave of her hand. "Besides, you don't have to work so hard. I'll help you."

Different day, same argument. I hadn't expected it so early, though. "You know I won't take your money. Plus, I like the restaurant and the catering business. They both give me chances to work on things I wouldn't normally get to do. They stretch my skills."

It was her turn to roll her eyes, which only showed me where I'd gotten that particular habit from. "Please. You had skills before you even went to culinary school. How much stretching do they need?"

"If I want to open my own business, lots. Which is why I take every job I can—word of mouth is vital in this industry."

"Stubborn child." She tempered her words with a soft smile, no less beautiful to me with gray hair than with the red I remembered from my childhood. She'd been the one to clean up my scratches and soothe my aches, the one who'd raised me and taught me right from wrong. The one who'd picked up the pieces when I'd messed up over and over again. The only mother I'd ever known, the person who'd stepped up when a plane crash had stolen her own daughters and their husbands. Who'd been practically my only family for my entire life. Who'd taught me to love the science of baking the perfect cake and cookies from the time I was too short to reach the counter. And she was sick.

"Of course I'm stubborn. I take after you." I shrugged, fighting to hold back the fear her illness instilled in me, fear of losing my favorite lifeline making my throat tight. "I should grab my bags before my luggage melts out there."

"Oh, sure. I could help you—"

The ringing of her phone interrupted her, breaking the oncoming argument over what she should and should not do barreling down on the little ranch house. Grandma sighed and rose to answer it, giving me the perfect opportunity to escape outside before she could stop me. I needed to be alone for a few minutes, to remember why staying once Dahlia didn't need me anymore was a bad idea. A really bad one—a horrible, no-good, awful, terrible idea. As much as I missed this house and what was left of my small family, there was no future for me in the enclave of Downriver. Not with my past. If I moved home, the rumors and lies people had once loved to spread about me would rise from the dead. I'd be Vee all over again...the favorite subject of every gossip mill in the area. I couldn't see setting myself up for another round of betrayal and abuse by returning, so I needed to stay gone. As soon as I fulfilled my commitment to Grandma and Dahlia.

Determined to make the best of my few weeks home, I dragged my suitcase inside to what had once been my bedroom. The space hadn't changed much, if at all, which was more of a curse than not. Pink walls, tan carpet, white furniture. It screamed teenage girl and was practically a shrine to the life I'd had. The one I'd run away from.

I fingered the edge of the lacy curtains, remembering the times Jace, my high school boyfriend, had crawled through the window that first winter we'd been together. How he'd grab me with his cold hands and kiss me senseless. All the times he'd sneak into my room, into my bed, and I'd warm him with my blankets and body. He'd set me on fire with a touch back then, and I'd happily burned for him. For a while, at least.

"Violet?" Grandma called from down the hall. "You want lunch, honey? I can make a fresh pitcher of lemonade."

Lemonade. Of course.

"Yeah!" I yelled. "Be there in a second."

Fighting back the urge to rip down the cheery fabric—especially thankful I didn't have matches to start a blaze so I could vanquish the demons haunting me—I pasted on a smile and headed for the kitchen. A couple of weeks, maybe a month, and then I could escape once more. I just needed to ignore the spider webs wrapping themselves around my heart and mind, the ones trying to trap me where I didn't want to be.

EASTON

If ever there was a moment to regret opening my own auto repair business, it was whenever some armchair-mechanic customer tried to talk me into doing something I didn't want to do. Especially one who liked to throw my family history in my face.

"I don't know about the timing," I said, staring down at the piece of shit taking up space in my lot. "This is a big job, and your deadline's close."

Rick, my dad's former boss, wasn't one to give up easily, though. "I get that, I do. But I need this thing running, and you're my last hope."

Last. That word rankled more than it should have. Rick hadn't come to me because he thought I had the skills or the talent to fix his neglected, beat-up piece of garbage. He did it because every other shop around had probably already said no. As should I.

"If you'd have gotten it to me a week ago, I could have done it. We've got a few too many projects coming in that are going to take up time and space. I can't take over a lift when I've got work on the books to do, especially when we don't even have any idea what's wrong with it other than the engine doesn't turn over."

"I'm begging you as a family friend," Rick said, pushing that so-called family friend connection to my dad for the third time since he'd shown up. "I have to get this beast ready to head out west. If I had any more time, I'd give it to you, but I'm stuck. I'll even pay you extra. Just...please. I need this thing running. Besides, it'll be a cool project."

Cool project? Who was this guy kidding? A forty-year-old, seized-up rebuild on a foreign car was not a cool project. It was the epitome of banging your head against a brick wall as you dealt with the ins and outs of shitty design made worse by lack of proper care. The bastard had been a foreman at the stamping plant. He had to know something about cars, which meant his comment was a blatant lie.

I was already shaking my head to refuse the job, but Rick wasn't done.

"Though, I mean, if you can't do it, I understand. These older trucks aren't easy to fix. Even your dad had a rough time with them, and he was the best mechanic around."

Was…before he'd left town on a whim. And before I'd come into my own. "I'm a far better mechanic than that man ever was."

I realized my mistake the moment Rick grinned. He'd gone in for the low blow but had come up swinging high instead. And I'd totally fallen for it.

"Then you can handle this job." Rick reached out and grabbed my hand as I dealt with the fact that my mouth had just written a check my ass—and that bastard known as time—might not be able to cash. "The wife's at the bowling alley." He jerked his finger over his shoulder, as if I didn't know there was a bowling alley fifty yards from my front door. "I'll leave this here so you can get right at it. Thanks, Easton. You guys are the best."

Best, my ass. If he thought we were even close to the best, I wouldn't have been his last hope. But it was too late to back out of the deal. Unlike the sperm donor linking Rick and me together, I always followed through on my word, which meant my life was about to become one long workday focusing on a vehicle I wouldn't buy with other people's money. Wonderful.

Silently cursing myself for not being more careful with my words, I trudged over the hot asphalt and into the icy coldness of the shop office. There was no air conditioning in the garage, so we kept the office close to freezing to be able to cool off when needed. Bonus was that the cold air seeped into the customer waiting area, so we didn't need a second AC unit for that. Win-win in my book.

I wiped the sweat from my brow as I double-checked the weekly log for incoming jobs. Each one represented a chunk of time and needed a spot inside the work area. With only three lifts, one of which was being taken up by a custom muscle car build that wouldn't be ready for delivery for at least another three weeks, space was at a premium. Every job on that list was a promise, though. Ones I intended to make good on. Ones that needed to run smoothly and stay in a reasonable sense of order.

I dragged a finger over the notes, calculating time and staff as I went from one job to the next. Hour, three hours, four hours, could be bumped, six hours, overnight… Shit.

I tapped the note on the log and opened the door to the garage to find one of my two business partners. The more reliable one. "Hey, Brogan. You think you can flip that radiator replacement and body work for Ms. Foster in two days instead of four?"

Brogan backed away from the Thunderbird he'd been bent over, wiping his hands on a rag and frowning. "Maybe. Depends on what else I've got on the books."

"That's what I figured. I was just looking over the schedule, and we've got a conflict. I'd like to move her up to this week instead of next to alleviate it. If we work the schedule right and I put in some extra hours, we'll finish hers just in time to bring in that Mustang engine upgrade we've got booked and make an even swap."

Brogan shrugged. "Yeah, sure. Fit it in wherever. I've got nothing to do this week outside of work. I'll get it done."

He always made my life so much easier. "Great. Thanks."

I headed into the office and grabbed the note I'd left myself with Ms. Foster's information. I'd have killed for that phone number when I was in high school, though not to call Ms. Foster. Her granddaughter, on the other hand…

The phone barely rang once before she picked up. "Hello?"

"Hey, Ms. Foster. This is Easton over at Second Gear Auto Repair."

"Oh, Easton. How are you? Did you and the boys get the cookies I sent over?"

Yeah, that made me grin. Ms. Foster made sure we were well taken care of. Especially Colton, the third partner in the shop. I think she had a soft spot for the guy, which was pretty shocking, considering his history with one of her granddaughters. "We sure did. Thank you for sending them." I was going to have to work out hard for a month to burn off those cookies. Worth it, though. "I'm calling because we've got you scheduled to come in for service on your Oldsmobile, and we've got a block of time available this week. You think you can bring the car over here on Wednesday so we can start working?"

"Oh, sure. No problem. It's not like I have a rip-roaring social schedule or anything."

Jackpot. "Great. Thanks for being so accommodating."

"Anytime. And you let me know when you want some more cookies. I can have my granddaughter bring them over to the trailer park for you."

"I will, and thanks again."

When she disconnected, I hung up but fiddled with the phone cord. She said she'd send her granddaughter, which meant Dahlia. Star soccer player, math whiz, and ex-girlfriend to Colton's twin brother, Wyatt. That relationship hadn't ended well, and even though it'd been a number of years since they'd dated, Colton still seemed to hold a grudge against the woman who'd almost sidelined his brother's hockey career. I'd have to make sure he wasn't around or was at least prepared to face her again. Last time...well, it hadn't gone well. Those two running into each other *never* went well.

Thinking of Dahlia got me wondering about Ms. Foster's other granddaughter. Violet. Cheerleader, bake-sale champion, and my high school crush. Man, what I wouldn't give to see her again. To know how she grew up and what sort of person she was. Was she married? Did she have kids yet? Did her hair still hit at just the right length to tease her breasts the way it had when we'd been in school? Did her eyes still light up whenever someone made her laugh?

Was she still the sweetest, most beautiful girl I'd ever met?

"Shit." I rubbed a hand over my face. Violet fucking Foster. I'd been obsessed with her, been completely in love from the time I'd realized girls didn't have cooties, even though we hadn't ever really spoken. But at that time, kids from my side of town didn't mingle with kids like her. All that rich-versus-poor shit that got handed down from generation to generation tended to muck up things like getting the most popular girl in school to go out with you when you were the kid from the trailer park. I'd wanted her, but I'd never acted on it. In high school, she'd gotten a boyfriend, Jace, and I'd gone on with my own life and my own relationships. Until that night in the rain, the first time we'd ever been alone together. After that...

Well, there'd been the video taken in the bowling alley, inside the same business I could see through the front window of the shop, and it had seemed as if the whole town had flipped its collective wig. By that time, I'd been used to judgment—being from the only trailer park for miles around didn't exactly lend itself to mingling with the kids of the middle managers at the plant. Two-bedroom houses on wheels couldn't compete with quaint ranches and colonials or five-bedroom brick minimansions. Especially when you were using a government aid card at the local grocery store to keep your family fed since your father had decided to move on to greener pastures.

Violet, though, had been one of the good kids. I remembered her as kind and funny, easygoing. Hot as hell in a soft, approachable sort of way too. Everyone had loved her...until the video. She'd gone from everyone's best friend to the town slut in the space of a sitcom rerun. At least to those who'd supposedly been her friends. That girl had gotten worked over in the rumor mills like nothing I'd ever seen. Why the whole town had made such a big deal out of her doing exactly what every other kid had been doing never did make sense. Neither had why she'd never defended herself. Of course, that was during the darkest time in my life, so I could have missed something along the way. Probably had. Your family falling apart had a way of stealing your attention.

"What's happening?" Colton, the artist of the group and the one business partner who sometimes needed to be reminded of what his job was, barged into the office with a bag of chips in hand. I was glad for his presence at that point. I needed to get my mind off the past and back on the job at hand. I had shit to do.

"Got Ms. Foster's car coming in this week," I said.

Colton nodded, obviously not seeing where I was going with my information. "Cool."

"Dahlia might be bringing it."

He tossed his empty bag in the garbage and wiped his greasy hands on his coveralls. "When is she coming?"

"Wednesday."

"Get a time from her if you can, and I'll take a long lunch."

"Good call." I hopped up and followed him into the garage, into the heart and soul of Second Gear Auto Repair. We had two cars up on lifts and one on the floor with the hood up, all ready to be worked on. All promises to customers that we had to keep. All money to be made if we could just get them running right.

I headed for the muscle car at the end. That one was the least of my worries, but I needed to finish some prep on the driver's side quarter panel before closing her up. If I worked double shifts for a few days, I might even be able to finish the body work and get her out for painting. I needed that bay, which meant I was about to have no life outside of the shop. That was okay, though. This place had always been my dream, ever since my dad had let me crawl underneath his old Chevelle and taught me where the oil plug was. I'd do whatever it took to make the shop a success.

"All right, gentlemen," I said. "Let's get to work so we can bring in the next round. These bays are going to be busy for a while."

"Turn and burn," Brogan said. He flipped on the music and

turned the volume up loud before ducking under the hood of the Thunderbird he'd been working on all morning. Colton headed for the little hatchback in the middle spot, ready to change out the brakes. I grabbed the parts I needed and dialed in on the job at hand.

Time to get shit done.

CHAPTER TWO

VIOLET

"I need a favor, honey."

"What's up?" I finished my pencil stroke and looked up from my notebook. Not baking for the past few days had left me antsy, so I'd spent a lot of my time planning instead. Sweets tables, cakes, chocolate collections…my notebook was almost filled already. But doodling icing designs for a fall season of petites fours was better than staring at the television set.

Grandma set the phone on the charger as she walked past. "That was Mary. She's having computer issues and needs to borrow mine to make a slave of her hard drive, but I have an appointment to get my car looked at. Can you take the car in for me? The shop owner will bring you back home."

My heart paused for a second, then sped up to an almost painful beat. I'd been at Grandma's for three days and had so far successfully avoided walking out the door for anything more than mail retrieval or taking out the trash. Apparently, my hermitting time inside was up. I'd agreed to stay for a few weeks while Dahlia was at her yearly work retreat. I'd known I was going to have to leave the house eventually.

"Sure," I said, my voice nearly hoarse.

"Great. I'll get you the keys." She hurried into the kitchen, looking far more pleased than I'd have expected over such a simple thing.

"Where am I taking it?"

"Second Gear Auto Repair."

I drew a blank. "Where's that?"

"Over on Van Horn. You know, the business complex right behind the bowling alley?"

My stomach sank. The bowling alley…Jace's dad's bowling alley. Where Jace and I had made out in the black lights after cosmic bowling nights. Where our group of friends had spent so much of their time during and after business hours. Where we'd all felt comfortable just hanging out.

Where I'd learned a tough lesson about closed-circuit surveillance cameras.

My throat grew tighter as I mumbled, "I thought that auto shop was Mr. Cooper's place?"

"Oh, that's right. You wouldn't know. Mr. Cooper sold the business. The new owners seem to be doing a right job of it, and they have a senior discount. I've been taking Betsy there for her service calls and repairs for about a year now."

The back door opened. Gram's neighbor, Mary, came walking in without knocking, just as she'd been doing since I was a little girl. She might as well have lived here with us those few years after her husband had left.

"Oh, hi there, Violet." Mary hustled into the kitchen, a laptop and knot of cords in her arms and her reading glasses askew. She fit the bumbling professor stereotype to a tee. "I was wondering when I was going to see you. You haven't stopped over to say hello since you've been back."

"Hello, Mrs. Michelson." Her eagle-eyed stare was, as always, harsh and appraising in a way that made me feel like a kid who'd gotten into trouble in her classroom. "Sorry I haven't stopped by. I've been working on menus for a big catering job and trying to organize them into some sort of workable, profitable plan."

"I could have helped you with that. I'm pretty good with a spreadsheet and research." She peered over her glasses right into the most secret places in my brain. Okay, probably not, but it sure felt that way. "I believe you remember that?"

Remembered... I still had nightmares. Mrs. Michelson had been the high school computer science teacher, one of the most feared teachers in the district. There were no breaks for anyone in her class and no second chances. Scraping by with a B was considered an accomplishment. The other kids had been terrified of her, but she'd been friends with my grandma since the two were the only young mothers on the block. That didn't mean she hadn't scared the crap out of Dahlia and me back in high school, but it had been different for us. She wouldn't just mark our grades lower if we'd screwed up—she'd tell Grandma before we'd even had a chance to walk in the door. But she'd also fought for us when we'd needed her to during those tumultuous teenage years, and she'd stepped in to try to help me when my life had hit the proverbial skids.

"The internet is forever, Vee. There's no erase, no way to shred the evidence. You're going to have to figure out a way to live your life around it."

Grandma dragged me away from that particular memory. "Violet's going to take my car over to Second Gear while you and I figure this issue out."

Mary stopped short, the movement harsh. "You are?"

I shrugged. "Yeah, why?"

Mary ran her eyes down my body and back up before darting a glance at my grandma. "No reason."

I had a sudden urge to cover myself, though I didn't get the chance to.

"Ignore her," Grandma said, pushing me toward the door. "Take my car. Someone will bring you home. No rush, though. We'll be here. Working." She grinned and turned away, totally focusing on an equally absorbed Mary. Something about computer crashes and data backup companies and the latest game they both wanted to be able to play. Things more their speed than mine, seeing as how I avoided computers as much as possible.

I left without another look back, trudging through the humidity toward Grandma's gold sedan. Dark clouds hung heavy above, ominous and threatening, forcing the air to feel even hotter and thicker than earlier in the day. It was going to rain. Scratch that...it was going to *storm*. I needed to get to this shop, drop off the car, and be back before it started. I hated storms and always had. Storms in the Midwest were unpredictable, dangerous things that could swoop in and destroy everything in their path. Everyone, too.

I drove hard and fast, nearly going airborne over the train tracks cutting the town in two when I hit them. A five-minute drive took less than three...I considered that a win. Pulling into the lot behind the bowling alley, I immediately spotted the Second Gear Auto Repair logo at the far end of the multi-unit building. I headed toward it, driving along the back of the bowling alley. The shadows had built up between the buildings, the darkness settling into the corners and across the black asphalt. The stretch of driveway felt so much more ominous than it should have. The storm was blowing in faster than I'd expected, bringing a heaviness with it that seemed almost impossible to shake. Same as that day. I'd walked home from the bowling alley as it had poured, as the sky had lit up with lightning bolt after lightning bolt and thunder had shaken the ground. It'd stormed so hard and so fast, in fact, that the streets had flooded. That was what I remembered. Cold, wet, and water everywhere. In my boots, soaking my clothes, running down my face and mixing with my tears.

Refusing to let that memory take hold in my mind, I parked in front of the glass door with the same logo as the overhead sign. Bright and colorful, the place didn't quite look like an auto repair shop. The windows were filled with swirls of paint advertising oil changes and brake jobs, the logo a modern take on a vintage circle design. Classic but updated, a new twist on an old standard. It was as if an artist had become a mechanic and used the windows to display his talent. And maybe one had. I'd never know if I didn't get off my butt and actually walk inside.

You can do this. I took one last deep breath to calm my nerves before stepping out of the car. It was just an errand, a simple, quick transaction that would be over in minutes. I hoped. I clenched my jaw and walked inside, trying to convince myself that whoever ran the place had moved in to town after I'd left. Hell, they probably didn't even know who Vee Foster was.

Or Cowgirl.

Cowgirl Vee. God, I still hated the name my classmates had given me. That name and the feelings it brought up in me were the reasons I couldn't let people call me Vee any longer. I wanted nothing tying me to what I'd done, nothing to make people associate that moment with me. I never wanted to be her again.

"One second," a deep, male voice called when the bell dinged overhead. I let the door close behind me, welcoming the almost icy chill of the place. Someone liked their air conditioning…and their mineral spirits—the metallic scent of it permeated the air and took me back to mornings spent following Grandma's second husband around. Of time spent at his side while he'd worked on his car in the garage.

Posters in the same bright style as the logo covered the walls at rakish angles. Advertising engine rebuilds, custom paint jobs, tires…they were beautiful, and they made the small space seem lively and alive, which really was an odd thing to think about in regard to this type of business.

Looking away from the walls adorned with artistic efforts I almost envied, I walked to the counter and took another deep, shaky breath. I needed to calm down. This was no big deal. Just drop the car off and head home. It wasn't as if I'd recognize anyone here. Not as if Grandma would send me to a place where I'd run into people I knew without warning me.

A man walked through a door in the back, and I immediately began plotting how to seek my revenge on the neglectful old woman.

Easton Cole. My middle school crush. The guy I'd almost fainted on when he'd asked me to dance at the eighth-grade graduation party. As a boy, Easton had sucked all the oxygen out of the room simply by walking into it. A trick that had apparently grown right along with him after high school, seeing as how my brain had forgotten to tell me how to breathe. He'd always had a presence—something about him had made girls turn, stare, or simply go brainless as they'd watched him walk by. Hell, even when I'd been completely, madly wrapped up in Jace, I'd noticed Easton. Not that I'd ever acted on that—he'd been the epitome of bad news to my teenage thoughts and assumptions. Or so I'd thought at the time. He'd even asked me out once before I'd been with Jace, but I'd said no.

Stupid woman.

"What can I do for..." Easton's words trailed off and his eyes went wide when he looked up. When he spotted me standing in the colorful waiting room.

I practically melted under that sky-blue gaze. He was one of the most attractive men I'd ever seen in real life. How did that happen? He'd been good-looking in high school, but the man had grown up into someone way taller, broader, and hotter than I remembered. Rougher, too, by the looks of him. And he was a mechanic, which meant he was good with his hands. He even had a grease smudge on his forearm. His muscled, tanned, ridiculously attractive forearm. He definitely hadn't been sporting those muscles when we'd been in school.

Thrown off-balance by his very presence, I waved in a completely awkward and absurd way. "Hi, Easton."

He glanced at my hand, his dark brows pulling together in what I could only guess was confusion. I quickly forced my arm down and gave him a smile, hoping he didn't think I was an idiot for waving to someone fewer than five feet away.

The pressure of needing to fill the silence grew, pushing me past my comfort level faster than I'd have thought possible. Why was he so quiet? What did I need to do to get him to speak? "Uh… I'm dropping off a car for my grandma."

Nothing.

"Beverly Foster? Gold four-door sedan with a bobblehead cat in the back window?"

The tick of the clock seemed way too loud. Was it supposed to be that loud?

"She said she had an appointment. Though, I guess I should have asked her what she was getting done." I pursed my lips and nodded, completely unsure of what the hell to do next. "I can… call her. To ask. If you need me to."

He stared for a moment, looking surprised, but then his lips turned down in a frown. Something that made him even more attractive, oddly enough. With his mop of curly, black hair and a constant smile that was near-deadly, the not-too-bad boy had been a secret star in just about every good girl's fantasies. But this man in front of me was a little badder than the teenage version had been. And so much more dangerous.

"We're replacing the radiator and fixing a crack in the bumper from where she backed into a light pole," he said, wiping his hands on a red rag he pulled from his pocket. "Let me get you the estimate."

"Sure." I tried to take a step back but bumped into a small table. The abrupt stop caused me to stumble, and I nearly fell into a plastic chair.

"Are you okay?" Easton grabbed my arm, his hold tight. His hand warm and rough around my elbow.

But old habits died hard. Especially ones you fell into for self-preservation. I yanked my arm out of his hold, retreating until I felt there was enough of a safety zone between us. Until I could almost breathe again. "I'm fine. Sorry."

His pause was noticeable, his expression inscrutable. Something in that look, the way he almost examined me with his stare, made my throat feel tight. My neck ached and my heart pounded as I waited for him to yield. To leave me alone. When he didn't—when he continued to watch me as if waiting for something I had no idea how to give—I crossed my arms over my chest and broke eye contact. Hiding in plain sight from that blue-eyed stare.

"I'll be right back." His soft voice scratched at my senses, but I couldn't say anything back. Instead, I waited silently for his retreating footsteps before I finally took a deep breath and forced my arms to relax. *Way to humiliate yourself, Violet.*

"Here you go." Easton appeared beside me, too quiet to break in to my thoughts before he was right there. He handed me an envelope, keeping his eyes down. Definitely not looking at me. Wonderful. "Tell your grandma it'll be a couple of days. I'll call her as soon as we're done."

"Yeah, all right." I floundered for a second before backing away. Carefully, this time. Pressing the envelope against my chest as if holding my heart in place. And maybe I was. I wasn't sure what I'd expected from him, but it wasn't this complete and utter dismissal without a glimpse of the kind soul who'd probably saved my life that day.

Desperate to escape, I hit the door too hard. The bell smacked into the glass, tolling loudly before making a weird thunking sound. At least I didn't break it, though. Still, I rushed outside in an effort to escape, then froze as the wall of humidity slammed into me. I'd thought being outside would ease the pressure in my chest, but I was wrong. So very wrong. The late-afternoon storm had finished blanketing the sky, and rain was just starting to darken the concrete. The air hung heavy—thick and hard to breathe through—as the first wave of water fell from the clouds.

Hot, wet, and sticky…exactly like that day. When a young Easton, dealing with his own tragedies and without any knowledge of my actions, had given me permission to do what I'd needed to do to survive. The day I'd found myself slipping into a situation I hadn't seen coming, one that had haunted me ever since.

The walk to Grandma's was going to suck.

"You got a ride back?"

I jumped at Easton's voice, turning to see him holding the door open. "Ah, no. Grandma said—" I stopped, stuttered, unwilling to imply he should give me a ride home. "Never mind, I can walk."

He peered up at the sky. "It's gonna storm."

I shrugged, playing casual, ignoring the way his blue eyes seemed to peer right inside me. "Not the first time I've had to walk in the rain."

And just like that, the energy between us went from tense to electric. Easton knew I'd gotten caught out in a storm before. He'd been the one to pick me up and take me home that horrible night. But not right away, not until after he'd taken me someplace to calm down. Not until we'd shared a moment. One that had apparently meant nothing to him, seeing as how he didn't seem to remember it.

Easton frowned, wrinkles forming around the corners of his eyes. Sexy wrinkles that hadn't been there ten years ago. "Hang on," he said before disappearing back inside. A few seconds later, he walked out the same door with a set of keys in his hand. "Let's go."

"Go where?"

"I'm taking you home."

Easton rushed across the lot, his long legs taking strides twice the length of mine. I sighed, frustrated, but I followed him. I'd like to say he didn't really give me much of a choice, but the truth was, I wanted to follow him. Wanted to see how he'd changed, if he remembered that night. Wanted to remind him of what he'd done to help me.

Plus, I really, *really* wanted to get out of the rain.

"You don't have to do this," I said as we reached his car. Low-slung and wide, the thing screamed speed and power. Apparently, he was no longer driving the old truck I remembered. The one with the bench seat and the heater so strong, it had nearly burned my legs through my wet jeans when he'd flipped it to high. That fact shouldn't have made me as sad as it did.

"I know I don't have to." He unlocked the big, black beast of a car with the tinted windows and the shiny rims. It reminded me of a wild thing, of some kind of predator made of steel. The epitome of sex and aggression on wheels that probably had cost more than some people's homes. It didn't look like something the Easton I'd known would drive. Which probably meant I knew nothing.

Easton held the passenger's side door open for me, an act that took me by surprise. That was the move of a gentleman. As if we were on a date or something. The boy with the badass car, charming me with his half smile and tempting me inside.

"Get out of the storm, Vee."

I paused for just a moment, staring into those blue eyes of his. The same ones I'd secretly swooned over for years as a teenager. But I wasn't a teenager anymore, and neither was he. He was a man. A handsome man who apparently had a bad memory but some serious manners. Who stood with his arm on the door, waiting for me to make my move. Giving me a choice.

"Thanks," I whispered as I slipped past him and lowered myself to the seat. My decision easier than it should have been. "But, please, don't call me Vee."

Easton shut the door without a word to me, though I heard

him yelling something toward the shop. When I looked up, Colton Bearn stood in an open garage bay, arms crossed, staring back at the car. He was Easton's friend—both having grown up in the trailer park—and brother to Dahlia's ex-boyfriend from high school. He'd been the playboy of the school by the time he'd graduated, screwing his way through the female student body, or as much of it as would accept his advances. Honestly, that was about half of them. Not bad odds. But at my lowest, when every guy in the school had been grabbing me in the halls, thinking they had the right to touch what they'd seen on their computer screens, he'd stayed away. Whether that was out of respect for our connection through Wyatt and Dahlia or because he'd been disgusted by what I'd done, I never knew for sure.

As much as I'd once liked Colton—his wild hair and easy smile had always been hard to ignore—I'd ended up hating him a little bit, too. He'd screwed half the female student body but had been seen as nothing more than a teenage boy sowing his oats. I'd had sex one time that anyone knew about—and they *all* knew about it —and had been labeled the town whore. Not Colton's fault, but maddening quite the same.

Easton opened the driver's door, which let me catch the last of what he was saying to Colton, who'd been joined by another man. One I didn't recognize. "—right back. I need to finish that brake job before the end of the day. Keep Jude busy for me." Easton slid into his seat, his eyes on the ignition. But Colton was still looking toward the car. Staring right at me, to be precise. But it was the other man, the one I couldn't quite place, who stole my attention. The one with the slicked-back black hair. The one who smiled at me in a way that made my stomach sink.

"Good to see you, Cowgirl," the man who wasn't Colton yelled, his smile turning more toward a smirk. And just like that, every day since I'd graduated high school disappeared. I was back in my senior year, being ridiculed by the people I'd thought were my friends. Humiliated again and again because of a stupid, reckless decision I'd made.

I turned toward the door, ready to escape. Ready to run if I had to. But Easton's warm hand settling on my bare thigh made me freeze.

"Don't," he demanded.

I sat back, still shaking, still breathing too hard as I watched him. Waiting for something more, some sort of direction. Some way to make my heart stop pounding.

"Stay in here. I'll take care of it," Easton said as he threw his door open wide.

He hopped out of the car and disappeared into the shop, following Colton, who was literally shoving the darker man through the large bay door. I took the few minutes Easton was gone to get a grasp on the tsunami of emotions swirling around me. Whoever that guy was had just given me a huge reminder of why I never came home. There was no way to grow here, no chance to restart or get a second chance. The world of Downriver was stagnant, forcing you to stay what you'd always been...or what those who lived there had decided you were. Even if that thing was the furthest from the truth.

I lost track of time as I stared at the bowling alley through the windows. I'd experienced so much heartache from that one building, so much hate. I didn't want to be near it. Hell, I'd never wanted to see those walls again. Yet there I was, sitting thirty feet away. Looking right at the door I'd used the night I'd killed the Vee everyone had thought they'd known.

"C'mon. It'll be okay. No one will find out."

I'd been so stupid.

What could have been seconds or hours later, Easton slipped into his seat with a scowl on his face. I jumped and spun toward him, letting the bowling alley go. Breaking the spell it seemed to have on me. But I still couldn't speak.

Easton's white T-shirt clung to him—wet and basically see-through. His hair and shoulders glistened in the dome light, the scruff on his jaw dark and shadowy. He looked pissed off, which only added to his attractiveness for some screwed-up reason. I never had liked to play it safe. "Sorry about that. Jude's an idiot with a mouth bigger than his brain. It won't happen again."

I knew better than that—once an asshole, always an asshole—but I let him lie.

Easton slammed his door and turned the key in almost a single, smooth move. The car came to life, the engine rumbling in a way only true muscle cars could. Not waiting for a response, Easton pulled out of the lot, heading toward Grandma's side of town without asking where he needed to go. Taking me away from the bowling alley at last.

"So," he said as he carefully passed the railroad tracks I'd flown over earlier. "How've you been?"

"Fine. Good." I nodded, staring at the road ahead, wishing I could teleport home. "Grandma said you guys opened the shop last year."

"Yeah, back in May."

"A mechanic and a business owner. Good. That's good." I bit my lip and looked out the side window, trying to think of anything to say that would break the awkwardness and make the ride seem faster.

"And you?" he asked, sounding unsure.

"Pastry chef."

"Really? You always did make the best treats for the bake sales, but I thought you wanted to be a teacher."

My shoulders curled in by habit, and I had to fight to keep my tone even. "That became impossible."

He hummed but didn't push for more details, something I could appreciate. That topic wasn't one I liked to remember, let alone discuss.

"You look different," he said as he turned into Grandma's neighborhood. "The hair color and...stuff."

I shrugged, fighting to keep things casual, not wanting to go into all the details of why I was no longer a redhead. "I needed a change."

"I liked the red, but the brown is just as...nice." He pulled into Grandma's driveway, leaving the engine running as I sat staring at him.

Did Easton Cole just compliment me? "Uh... I... Thanks for noticing. And thanks for the ride home."

"Yeah. No problem." He nodded as he tapped his thumbs against the steering wheel. "I really am sorry for Jude's mouth. It's hard to control him some days."

"I seem to remember Dahlia saying the same thing about Colton once."

"It's *impossible* to control Colton," he said with a snort of a laugh. "Dahlia and Colton. Yeah, they had a...thing after Wyatt left."

"Yeah. 'Thing' is the polite way to describe it." Rage-filled year of battle was a much less polite version. Those two hated one another.

"Right." Easton grew quiet, staring out the front windshield.

"So...thanks for the ride. Again." I opened the door and stepped outside. He looked up, his bright eyes meeting mine as I stood in the open door. The rain pelted me, soaking me in seconds, but that look held me captive. His expression piercing a piece of me and making me stay. But then he nodded.

"See you around," he said.

"Yeah, maybe."

Desperate to escape the intensity of his stare, I slammed the door and hurried inside. Easton didn't pull out of the driveway until I'd walked into the house, something that struck me as unusual. He was definitely a man with manners. A car-fixing, dirty-job-having, gorgeously broody man who held open doors and waited to make sure women were safely inside their homes before leaving. But with a bad memory. Damn him.

"Was that Easton Cole's car?" Mary asked from where she sat at the counter in front of Grandma's laptop.

"Yeah. He gave me a ride back." I pushed my wet hair out of my face and kicked off my sodden shoes.

"You should have called," Mary said, pulling me from my own head. "I could have come and picked you up."

"He didn't mind."

"Obviously." Those four syllables dripped with sarcasm, and her soft smirk was positively wicked when I looked up.

"Oh, Violet. You're back." Grandma hurried into the room with a big smile on her face. "Mary's taking us to Fergie's for the fish fry tonight. Go get changed out of those wet clothes. Those shorts are a little—" She frowned

"What?" I glanced down at my shorts and tank top. They'd seemed fine when they'd been dry, but with as wet as they'd become, I could see why they were no longer appropriate. The fabric clung to my every curve, nearly see-through due to the light colors. Just like Easton's shirt, but all over my body.

"You have got to be kidding me." I pulled one side of my shorts away from my hip, frowning when they smacked back into place with a wet, squelching sound. "I was practically naked in front of Easton Cole."

"Well…" Grandma started, looking me over. She seemed concerned at first, but then her lips twitched.

"Don't think I'm going to forget you sent me in there blind, old lady," I warned, pointing her way. "You could have told me I'd know the owners from school. And don't laugh at me."

She put her hands up, fighting back a grin. "Wouldn't dream of it."

I cringed. "I'm never leaving the house again."

"Those are the shortest damn shorts I've seen in an age." Mary closed the lid to the laptop. "I bet he took a good look at you out there even before you got wet. Now go dry off and cover yourself a bit more so you don't give the old geezers any heart attacks. I've got a taste for hush puppies."

"But—"

"I said go." Mary pointed, her strict teacher face firmly in place. The one that made it clear I really had no choice in the matter.

"Yes, ma'am. Full coverage coming up," I said, resigned to the fact that I'd basically given Easton a show as I'd run inside. And as much as I shouldn't have wondered, as much as I should have left it alone, I couldn't help but picture him sitting in that beast of a car. Watching me. Following me with his eyes. Wanting me.

Impossible.

CHAPTER THREE

EASTON

There was something almost wrong about watching Violet Foster walk through the rain in clothing that left not a damn thing to my imagination. Wrong, and yet I couldn't stop myself from staring. Jesus, she'd grown up. A lot. In ways that made me want to see even more of her than I already had.

I pulled out of her grandma's driveway and headed for the shop, my mind spinning every which way. Violet Foster had come back to Downriver. She'd always been unbelievably pretty in that wide-eyed, appealing sort of way I couldn't resist. She'd also been one of the kindest, most open-minded chicks I'd ever met.

And the star of a salacious sex tape before graduating high school.

Nothing about her had ever quite fit. Not the crowd she'd hung out with and definitely not the scandal that had rocked the community our senior year. Of course, I hadn't really known her then. I'd known of her—the whole damn town had known *of* her —but our crowds had never mixed. Not really. I'd wanted to— even gotten up the nerve to ask her to dance at our eighth-grade graduation party—but nothing more had come from that. I'd asked her out at some point that next summer, but she'd said no. Something that had broken my little teenage heart and ego. She'd been with Jace by the time we'd gone back to school, and I'd come to the conclusion that I'd missed my chance to spend time with her.

At least until one stormy night when I'd been driving around trying to get my new reality off my mind. When I'd seen a soaking wet, pre-sex-tape-release Violet walking down the side of the road. She'd been shivering, her face red and tear-stained, looking so damn small as she'd huddled in her jacket. I'd stopped the truck to pick her up, and when those sad eyes had met mine, I'd known I'd made the right decision.

Two car rides, a pizza, and some conversation were all we'd shared that night, but it was a moment I'd thought about a thousand times since, just like that dance. The next day, the rumors had begun, kids talking about Jace and Violet and a security camera at the bowling alley. The video had spread to every home, every computer, within a few days. But by then, I'd lost my father, which had left me as nothing more than a spectator to the crash and burn of one Miss Violet Foster as my own life had spun out of control in a completely different way.

"Fucking hell." I ran a hand through my hair before dropping it to downshift easy as I came up on the tracks. Once I'd crept over the roughest railroad crossing in the area—cursing myself for driving the Hellcat when I should have just taken my truck—I revved the engine and raced down Van Horn. The car may have been impractical for about a million reasons, but I needed the speed and craved the adrenaline rush it brought me. Driving hard, racing even, usually cleared my head when things went sideways, but not this time. My fast car was no match for the swinging of Violet's hips in soaking wet cotton. For the curves and legs and dark hair framing those light eyes. Nope, speed wasn't even close.

Brogan stood waiting in bay one when I pulled into the lot.

Watching me. Ready for a conversation I really didn't want to have. I parked in my normal spot and took a minute to resettle myself. Brogan could wait. Besides, it wasn't him I was planning on hunting down.

When I was ready to focus on work, I adjusted myself through my pants to hide the half hard-on torturing me. *Must stop thinking about wet cotton. Must stop—*

"You planning on working this afternoon?" Brogan hollered. I glared through the window before turning off the ignition. Was I planning on working… Did I do anything else? Was I ever not either at the shop or at my trailer? Shit, I hadn't taken time off or even been on a date since we'd opened the place because I worked so much. Brogan knew this—he was usually right at my side, but that didn't stop me from huffing an irritated breath because of his mouth.

Damn it, I needed to jerk off and take a nap, but those would both have to wait.

Ready to confront Jude, another one of the guys we'd hired to help during our busy times, I slammed the car door and stormed inside. My temper grew the more I thought about what he'd said. About him calling Violet…that name.

Brogan caught me first. "Was that really Violet Foster?"

I grunted as I walked past him, not ready to deal with his opinions. Not when I needed to straighten out Jude.

"Easton," Brogan said, trying to sideswipe me as I headed for the office.

"Get the fuck out of the way."

"Man, wait." Brogan placed his hand against my chest, stopping me. I stared him down, growing more pissed with every second he held me up. "Colton dealt with it."

I pushed his hand off with a snort. "Colton wasn't the one watching Violet panic because of what Jude said. Where is he?"

"Yo." Jude appeared from the office, a red rag in one hand and a half-peeled banana in the other. "What's up, man?"

I shoved past Brogan, closing in on the man I saw as a little brother of sorts. The man I was ready to throw down with because of his mouth. "What the fuck were you thinking, calling her that name?"

"What's the big deal?" Jude asked, his brow pulling down in confusion. "Are you honestly heated over what I said to that chick?"

"Yes, you dumbass. You upset her. Her grandmother's a customer here, and that shit was years ago. Why'd you have to bring it up?"

Jude shrugged. "Like it matters anymore? You said it yourself. That shit was years ago. She has to be over it by now."

I shook my head, staring up at the ceiling for a second to keep from throttling him. I'd seen Violet's face when he'd called out that name, had practically felt the way her entire body had gone stiff before she'd started staring at the door like she'd been desperate to escape. That girl wasn't over anything, not by a long shot.

"Easton." Colton crept up beside Jude, putting his hands up, giving me a serious stare that meant he wasn't screwing around. "He's an idiot, but he meant nothing by it, man."

"Hey—" Jude started, glaring at his cousin.

"Shut up, dumbass," Colton replied, not looking away from me for a second. "Violet got a raw deal on that whole video thing, but Jude only meant the name as a joke. I made sure he's aware that he is never, ever, to joke that way again."

Jude practically fell forward as Colton smacked him on the back of the head, straightening in time to give Colton a pissed-off look. "Right. I'm sorry. It won't happen again."

I let out a huge breath and clenched my hands into fists, wanting to punch something but not wanting that something to be one of my friends. Jude was younger than the rest of us and needed more guidance than discipline, but he wasn't a bad guy, usually. Colton was an ass with a big mouth he tended to open without a lot of forethought, but he wasn't a liar. Never had been. If the two of them claimed they'd dealt with this, then I had to believe they had.

"Just watch your mouth, yeah?" I said, giving in to Jude and Colton the same way I always did, just as I had since we'd been kids running around the trailer park. "I don't want to lose a customer because you sometimes mistake your mouth for your asshole."

"Understood." Jude nodded once before the concerned expression on his face morphed into a sarcastic smile. "Want to go watch that video she made? I think I still have a copy burned on a DVD at home. Probably tucked inside an old Jenna Jameson case with a sticker that says 'Ride me, Cowgirl.'"

"Jude," Colton said, dropping his voice in warning.

Jude backed away, laughing. "Joking…just joking."

But that was a joke Violet wouldn't appreciate, which made it one I didn't want to hear. "Joke like that again, and I'll fire your ass." I swung around and headed for the office, needing a few minutes to get my head on straight. Violet Foster had come home. I hadn't thought it possible. She'd run so hard and so fast, I'd been sure she'd never come back. Not that I blamed her. Shit, after the way everyone had turned on her, after the bullshit had blown up with that bastard Jace, even I'd have told her to leave and never look back. In fact, I might have done just that the night I'd bought her a pizza. And I never ran from a fight.

"You okay?" Brogan stepped into the office, closing the door behind him.

I sighed, dropping into the chair behind my desk. "What the hell was he thinking?"

"He was thinking that it's been a lot of years, and that, in his world, that shit doesn't matter anymore."

"It certainly seemed to matter to her." I grabbed the stress ball I kept on the desk and squeezed, letting my mind wander. Violet Foster: cheerleader, member of the orchestra, soccer player—

she'd done it all. But she hadn't been cocky or arrogant. No, she'd been a nice girl with a pretty smile and a way of walking that had turned guys' heads. Our crowds hadn't mixed, our social circles had never overlapped, and she'd remained this odd sort of celebrity who'd been close and yet not.

Until the day I'd picked her up from the side of the road, soaking wet from the rain and looking completely broken. Something that had haunted me for years.

"Easton." Brogan's single word broke me from my thoughts. "You can't fix her, man."

"I'm not trying to fix her." Those words tasted like a lie, though.

Brogan leaned against the door with his arms crossed over his chest, watching me. Inspecting. Waiting to see which way I'd take this. Violet's fall had come just after my dad had decided he didn't want to be in our family anymore. Those events would forever be tied together in my mind, and he knew it.

One selfish decision made by another person had thrown my world into disarray, just like one video that had gotten out when it shouldn't had done the same to her. Different events, same conclusion. Our lives had shattered in our senior year, but I'd had Brogan and Colton to help put me back together. I'd had a mom and a younger sister who'd needed me to take over as the man of the house. I'd stayed and fought to resume what I'd seen as normal, while she'd run away as fast as she could.

Brogan would tell me to walk away from her, to ignore Violet's sudden appearance and stay on firm ground instead of grabbing hold of that anchor and jumping into the sea. I probably should have listened to him, too. Let Violet go about whatever business she had and wave goodbye when she left town again, because she would leave. There was no way the girl would want to stick around. But the expression on her face when Jude had called her Cowgirl was already eating at my resistance, and something about the lost look in her eyes wouldn't let me turn her away. She wasn't over anything. She was just going through the motions to get through the days.

And damn, did I remember what that was like.

Brogan sighed, shaking his head. "I know Violet Foster has always been some sort of fantasy for you, but the reality of her won't live up to your dreams."

"She's not my fantasy."

"I call bullshit. You've been humping the mattress for her since middle school. Don't try to lie to me of all people."

I leaned back in my chair, keeping my eyes on his, trying to convince both of us. "Yeah, well… I'm not chasing after her now. We're just fixing her grandma's car."

"So long as that's all we're fixing. She's chaos in a tight T-shirt, man."

Tight...wet...see-through... "Fucking chaos."

"Exactly."

But still, thoughts of her fear and sadness tugged at me. "Her mistake is old news."

"Old news with a rotting smell to it that some of the locals just aren't going to let stay buried. Fair or not, she's a lightning rod for gossip, and you can't fix that for her. You work eighty hours a week and find time to help your mom, do maintenance at the trailer park, and deal with everyone else's bullshit. You don't need another weight on your shoulders."

He wasn't wrong. "I don't need the distraction."

"Exactly," Brogan said with a nod as if I'd agreed to his plan to distance us from Violet. "We fix her car and send her on her way."

"Totally." I looked him in the eye, knowing that was a lie, understanding he knew it too. Some things were irresistible. Colton couldn't see a skirt without chasing it, Jude couldn't pass up the opportunity to be a smartass, and I couldn't see a mess without stepping in to clean it up. But Brogan was all of our wingman. He couldn't watch any of us falter without swooping in to rescue us from ourselves.

Still, this wasn't about my need to repair the broken. This was about Violet...a girl I'd secretly crushed on for most of my life. One who often starred in whatever fantasies I had running through my head, even after all these years. A girl who'd had everything going for her until one mistake had stolen it all. And just like with my dad, I hadn't seen the fall coming in time to stop it. I'd been there at the precipice of Violet's crash, not having any idea what was about to come, and had very likely pushed her to run away instead of fight back.

I may have pushed her to abandon her family the same way my dad had abandoned ours.

CHAPTER FOUR

VIOLET

Four days. That was how long it took for me to grow so bored that the thought of staying inside the house another minute made me want to gouge my eyes out with one of the tourist spoons Grandma had hanging in display cases in the basement. Ones from the Grand Canyon and the Smokey Mountains. Ones I'd dusted three times in two days.

Did I mention I was bored?

I couldn't even bake. Not because I didn't have what I needed—oh no, Grandma kept her kitchen well equipped and stocked for making just about anything basic in my repertoire. I *could* bake—I simply didn't feel like it. For the first time that I could remember, I didn't want to play with butter and sugar and flour, didn't want to try to make the perfect cookie or the tastiest cake. The lack of interest in spending time in the kitchen left me completely unhinged. I *always* baked. Cookies, cakes, pies, treats of all sorts—I ran a virtual patisserie shop out of my home most days. I hadn't baked since I'd crossed into Downriver.

It wasn't as if I was trapped in the house, though. Oh, no. I'd gone to the store for Grandma and ran an errand or two. I wasn't a total recluse. But being out in that town, seeing all the people I recognized from growing up there, made me want to tear off my own skin. Were they talking about me? They were definitely staring…or maybe I was just catching their eye at the wrong time. Or maybe Mary was right, and my shorts were too darn short. I felt monitored. Watched. Exposed.

And that was just the people I didn't quite know, not the ones I'd had some sort of relationship with. When a whole town patronized the same grocery store, you tended to run into people. Every trip, every time I left the house, there was someone calling my name, turning their lips up in their fake smiles, and giving me stiff, insincere hugs. I endured all sorts of *how've you been*s and *it's good to see you home* bullshit. And it was bullshit, because not a single person was actually glad to see me. But that was what this place had taught me—no one said what they really meant until you turned your back.

Except for maybe Jude, who'd at least had the balls—or the stupidity—to call me out to my face. To call me Cowgirl when he knew the connotation behind that word. He remembered that nickname, having never known me, likely having not seen me since the day I'd graduated, when I'd driven out of town for college on the western side of the state. He'd probably seen the Cowgirl Vee video and still believed the lies surrounding it.

Some histories simply refused to die.

I really needed to find my way back to the kitchen and bake something before I went absolutely stir-crazy.

"We should get a watermelon."

Grandma's odd request almost made me shake my head to bring me back to what I was supposed to be doing. Keeping her company. We were sitting in her hematologist's office for her first chemo treatment, which was something I'd been dreading. I knew it would make her sick, but I had no idea how much. Nor did anyone else, it seemed. The nice nurse with the soft smile had warned us Grandma could be tired afterward, or she could feel fine. She could lose her hair, or she could keep it. No one knew anything except for the fact that there was something growing inside her…killing her slowly. And there was no guarantee this treatment would help her at all.

Deadly chemicals streamed into her body from her IV, and all I could do was sit and watch as I prayed that they worked. And tried to figure out why we were suddenly talking about fruit.

"You don't like watermelon."

She shrugged. "I do like watermelon. I don't like how messy it sometimes is, but I think watermelon is a necessity in summer."

"You used to tell me the seeds in the watermelon were dead bugs so I wouldn't eat it."

"Because I didn't want to clean up the mess. You still ate it."

I shrugged. "Of course I did. I like watermelon."

"Dead bugs and all." She sat back, closing her eyes. "But you only ate it when you got older, not when you were little."

"No, when I was little, I thought you'd never lie to me. So I believed you when you told me they were bugs."

"Then you grew up."

"Yeah, and I learned not to take you too seriously."

She smiled, the corner of her mouth wrinkling. "No, you learned that what I'd told you wasn't the truth, which changed your view of the watermelon. You perceived those seeds as dead bugs…until you didn't."

My lips pulled down into what had to be a frown. Was the chemical cocktail already messing with her brain? "Yeah, so?"

"So, perception is reality." She turned to look at me, eyes watery but fierce. "You hate it here because people perceived you as something you weren't. A fact you've never even tried to make them forget."

Her words made my stomach clench, made my heart beat a little faster. Her words made me long to stand up and walk out. But she was still hooked up to an IV, so I couldn't. A fact that had me nearly sweating in my seat. "I don't want to talk about this."

"You never do, but we may be running out of time."

"Grandma—"

"Violet." Her harsh tone shut me up. "People do shitty things, and we all have to deal with the fallout, but that doesn't mean you run and hide. You belong here, with your family. You just refuse to see it."

Before I could answer, the nurse interrupted us to unhook the machines. I avoided Grandma's stare, choosing instead to focus on the nurse. Gentle hands removed tubes from Grandma's port. A soft voice explained possible reactions and stressed how each person was different. How Grandma shouldn't worry, shouldn't think about her chemo as something that could make her sick, and how she should rest instead. "You don't have to fight it all in one day, Ms. Foster. You can retreat for now."

That recommendation from the nurse struck me as familiar, as a reminder of my life since high school. *Don't fight back, don't worry, and don't think about it...just go. Leave everything behind and start over. Start fresh.*

Until the next time it popped up, and the next, and the next, and you finally began to wear out your running shoes.

After a quick vitals check and a plethora of instructions, we were heading home, both of us silent. Me, dealing internally with such a weird day. Watermelon and dead bugs, chemotherapy, my sudden lack of interest in baking, and the endless marathon of my life. All piled high on top of one terrifying thought—this cancer could take my grandma from me long before I was ready to let her go. The ten years I'd stayed away from home suddenly seemed wasted.

"I think I need to go to bed," Grandma said as I helped her into the house, her voice soft and sort of tired. It wasn't bedtime yet, not even five o'clock, but I could practically feel the exhaustion radiating from her. And I understood it. Sometimes, you had to surrender to what your body wanted. She stopped at the entrance to the hall, looking over her shoulder. "You'll be here, right?"

"Yeah, of course. I'm not going anywhere."

"Good. That's good." She turned, heading out of the kitchen but stopping before she made it through the doorway. "You should cook something, Violet. Cooking always seemed to calm you down."

"I am calm." Lies. I was as far from calm as I could be, but the words had come automatically. An almost visceral response to her statement.

And she didn't buy my story for a second. "Sure. You're calm, and I'm running for Miss America next month."

"They may have a senior version."

"Oh, great. Let me just oil up these wrinkles and get right on that."

I chuckled. How could I not? "Love you, Grandma."

"I love you too, you evil child. Now cook something and stop driving me crazy."

If only it were that easy.

I watched her shuffle down the hall to her bedroom, my shoulders slumping and my heart breaking. She'd always appeared so vibrant to me, so large and full of life. Funny and sarcastic and just plain sassy at times. And while her attitude seemed firmly in place, her physical form didn't. Suddenly, with one afternoon of chemo, she looked shrunken. A little old lady, bones brittle and curving, barely able to pick up her feet. Someone who needed looking after, needed protection. Someone I'd have to leave behind again in a matter of weeks.

I needed a distraction before the guilt suffocated me.

The kitchen called to me, the cabinet where Grandma's mixer sat begging me to come. To play. To create something. But looking at the bags of flour and sugar, inspecting the cans of cornstarch and baking powder, didn't alleviate anything. They actually made my anxiety worse. I closed the cabinet doors without taking out a single ingredient. I needed a *different* distraction, apparently.

A blinking message light on the house phone in the corner was my saving grace. I snagged a pen and pressed the buttons to listen to Grandma's voice mails. Time to be useful. The first was from Mary, of course, checking in. The second was Grandma's pastor offering prayers and support. But what truly caught my attention, what made me stop and stare at the flashing red dot, was the sound of Easton's warm voice coming over the line on the third one.

"Hi, Ms. Foster. This is Easton Cole from Second Gear Auto Repair. I wanted to let you know that your car's ready and can be picked up whenever it's convenient for you. Feel free to call the shop if you need anything."

I juggled the phone from one hand to the other after I deleted the message. I shouldn't leave Grandma, but I also didn't want anyone to have to call again because we didn't show up. Hopefully, they could keep the car for the night, and I could deal with it tomorrow. I needed to call them to be sure, though, right? Calling was the responsible thing to do. It wasn't as if I was only calling because of Easton. There were other people who worked there. Maybe Easton wouldn't even answer the phone. Maybe Jude or Colton would.

I hope not.

I paced the length of the living room. I did *not* want to speak with Jude. That left me with either talking to someone who'd make me stutter like a teenager, piss me off, or who I'd never actually met but probably knew everything about my past. Not so great odds.

Readying myself for any scenario, I hit redial and waited through three rings before the one voice I wanted to answer most —and least—came across the line.

"Second Gear Auto Repair, this is Easton."

"Hi, Easton." *Too breathy, too breathy.* "This is Violet...Foster."

"Oh, hi, Violet." No stutters or awkwardness. Hell, he almost sounded happy to hear from me.

"Hi. Again." *Deep breath. You can do this.* "I was just calling because my grandma isn't feeling well today, so we won't be able to pick up her car. As long as she's better, we can come first thing tomorrow, if that's all right."

"Is everything okay?"

"Yeah. Well, no. She sort of, uh…" I pinched my eyes closed and took a deep breath. Her illness wasn't a secret, so I could be honest. But it was something personal and painful, which made me choke up as I fought to find the right words. "She had her first chemo treatment today and needs to rest. I'd rather not leave her alone just yet. Plus, I don't have anyone to bring me there. But if it's a problem, I can probably walk—"

"Don't be ridiculous. Hang on."

I heard the thump of him setting the phone down, then nothing. The silence lasted minutes, way longer than a normal break should have. I was in the middle of a vicious argument with myself over whether to hang up or not when someone fumbled with the phone on his end.

"Violet?" Easton huffed, sounding completely out of breath.

"Yeah?"

"I'm so sorry. Damn Colton decided to be twelve and chase me through the shop with the acetylene torch."

"That…" I grinned, picturing Easton running from a grinning Colton wielding a mini torch like what I used to make crème brûlée. Those boys always had been pranksters. "That actually sounds more like something you would do."

A pause. I bit my lip as silence reigned again, wondering if I'd insulted him somehow. But then he laughed.

"Yeah, that's probably why he did it to me. Payback, you know?"

"I've heard it's a bitch."

"Thanks for the tip." Another laugh, easy and casual, my

stomach flip-flopping at the sound. "Look, I've got a bit of time to kill. I'll drive Beverly's car over and drop it off so you two don't have to deal with it."

I hadn't been expecting that at all. "Are you sure? I don't want to put you out."

"It would be my pleasure." His voice husky, deep, he sounded as if he meant his words.

Relief pulled an invisible weight off my shoulders, and my entire body seemed to slump for a second. I hadn't even realized how tense I'd been until that stress disappeared. "That'd be really nice of you."

"Cool. I'll be there in a few, okay?"

"Perfect." I almost hung up, but there was one more thing I wanted him to know. "Easton?"

"Yeah?"

"Thank you, really." My eyes burned, and my chest felt too full of all the emotions whirling through me, but I held everything together. I had to. "It's been a rough day."

"You're welcome, Violet. I'm on my way."

"Okay." I ended the call and hugged the phone, needing a moment to calm down. My heart slammed against the walls of my chest, though not from fear this time. From excitement. Just talking to Easton over the phone had given me a serious case of the giggles. It was like a first crush all over again. One I needed to shut down…eventually.

Not five minutes later, Easton pulled into the driveway in my grandma's sedan. The car looked freshly washed and maybe even waxed, practically sparkling in the late-afternoon sun. I opened the front door as he stepped out of the driver's seat, both of us smiling.

"Hey." I leaned against the doorframe, trying hard to stay calm. "She looks good."

"Yeah." He studied the car before refocusing on me, that smile still on his handsome face. "She's a well-preserved lady."

"You talking about the car or my grandma?"

He stepped onto the porch, stopping mere inches away from me. "Both…maybe. If that won't get me in trouble."

"None from me, but she might wag a finger at you if she finds out." I wrinkled my nose, looking him over. "I hate to state the obvious here, but you're a sweaty mess." He was, too. His hair appeared darker, dampened with perspiration, and his black T-shirt clung to him like a second skin. Not that I minded.

"Sorry about that." He took a step back as he ran a hand through his hair. "It was hot as hell today, and we don't have air conditioning in the garage."

My reply came naturally, without thought. "Would you like to come in for some lemonade?"

All the dating advice my grandma had ever given me rattled through my head at my unplanned invitation. *Who you see on a first date isn't real. Take your time to get to know a person. Make sure the man has manners and treats his mother and your waitresses kindly. Coffee implies late nights and early mornings—invite the man you'd like to know more about in for lemonade instead.*

I didn't usually drink lemonade, not since I'd moved away, but this was Beverly Foster's house. Grandma believed in the charm of the drink. There was always a pitcher in her refrigerator just in case someone tall, dark, and handsome happened by. Someone exactly like Easton.

"I don't want to cause you any trouble or upset your grandma since she's ill." Easton's words may have meant one thing, but his smile grew, and he rocked forward on the balls of his feet as he said them. Yeah, the man wanted to come inside. Thanks be to Grandma for her lemonade habit, because the idea of him in my space wasn't one to be apprehensive about.

"It's no trouble." I walked inside with him following close behind me. Trying my hardest not to put a little extra sway in my hips. The man was altogether too tempting, though. The sway came whether I wanted it to or not.

"Nice house."

"Thanks." I grabbed two glasses from the cabinet, biting back a smile as I caught Easton checking out more than just the house. The sway never failed. "My grandma's been here forever. Her first husband bought the place but died pretty young. She refused to leave the neighborhood when she got remarried, so Charles—her second husband—begrudgingly moved in."

"He didn't want to live here?"

"Nope." I pulled the pitcher from the refrigerator, hoping the cold didn't tighten my nipples too much. My shirt was thin, and my bra wouldn't help hide a full headlights moment. A little sway was one thing—flashing the high beams was a whole other level of tease. "Charles said he hated feeling as if he were living another man's life. Didn't help that the first husband died in the house."

"Well, I can see how that could be awkward." He took the glass from me, tipping it up for a drink. But as he brought the glass down from his lips, he turned serious. "I'm sorry to hear about the cancer. I didn't know."

My stomach turned, but I did my best to hang on to my composure. "She's strong, so hopefully this won't be too bad."

"Is that why you finally came home?"

Home. To this place. To this house. To my past.

I put the lemonade away, needing a moment to calm my heart. Trying hard to shut down the rising panic inside me. "Yeah, I guess so."

"How long are you staying?"

"A few weeks. Maybe a month." I left off the *at most.*

"Good, good." He nodded and looked away, tapping the toe of one shoe a handful of times. "I'm really sorry Jude was an idiot yesterday."

I shrugged, trying hard to pretend as if it didn't matter. As if it shouldn't. "No biggie. People here remember one thing about me, so being called...*that*... It's going to happen, right?"

Easton watched me, his eyes piercing. Something about his

look felt too personal, too intimate. It made me want to curl up and hide, made my skin feel too tight. "Does it happen—"

"I didn't see anyone following you," I interrupted, fighting back a wave of nausea at the idea of having to answer what I knew he wanted to ask. Of having to think about all the times in the past when someone had recognized me, when someone had mentioned that damn video. Some things I simply couldn't deal with. Heart pounding and skin clammy, I nodded toward the front of the house. "How are you getting back?"

He stared at me for a long moment, his face serious. Inspecting. I looked right back but at his shoulder. I couldn't handle the intensity from him anymore. Couldn't deal with how he made me feel with a look. Didn't need him trying to figure me out. "I was going to walk."

"Give me a minute." I hurried to the phone, dialing from memory the second I had it in my hand.

Thankfully, Mary picked it up on the first ring. "Hello?"

"Hey, Ms. Michelson. I hate to bother you, but I need a favor."

"Is it Beverly? What can I do?"

"Grandma's fine, but she's resting, and I need to drive—" I glanced at Easton, catching his eye as he watched me, stressing my words carefully "—a friend back to work. I'd rather not leave her alone."

"Go. I'll get my shoes on and be in your kitchen in twenty seconds."

"Thanks. I appreciate it. And I'll be back in a few minutes."

"Take your time. I can do my crosswords there just as easily as I can here."

I hung up the phone and set it in the cradle before hurrying toward the hutch where I'd tossed my keys. Taking a few minutes to drive Easton back, to officially end this...whatever it was between us, was worth the guilt of leaving Grandma alone. It would take ten minutes, tops. She'd probably never even know. Besides, Mary would be here to watch over her.

"Let me just take a peek at Grandma, then we can go." I slipped down the hall, breathing deeply while I could. Thankful to be out from under that Easton stare. Grandma's bedroom door sat open just enough for me to see inside. She lay on her side, curled around her pillow as she slept. Perfect. I crept back down the hall to the living room, nodding toward the front door when Easton looked up.

"C'mon, I owe you one."

"Violet, wait." Easton set his now-empty glass on the counter and followed me outside. "You really don't have to drive me back."

"I insist." I dropped into my car and turned the ignition, hiding the way my hands shook. He was too much, too big, too bold, too full of knowledge about stuff I'd rather lock away forever. He was also a strong part of this community, and I...was not. He was everything I shouldn't want to be around. I needed to remind myself of that fact.

Easton huffed and scowled as he slid into the passenger seat, almost slamming the door. "I can't believe I'm in a Toyota."

"You got a problem with my car?" I asked, already knowing how this particular conversation would go. Lots of things in these parts didn't change, including loyalty to an industry that had long been a staple in the region. That fight was familiar, almost calming in a way. That fight, I could deal with.

"You got a problem with American made? With locally made?"

I rolled my eyes as I pulled out of the driveway. "My Toyota was assembled in Indiana, hotshot. Besides, this little lady was cheaper and gets better gas mileage than anything else in its class."

"Yeah, but my old truck's side panels were stamped right here in town."

He still had his truck? That fact shouldn't have excited me the way it did. Not that I could admit that. "Most of that plant is nothing but empty space and sad memories at this point. There's nothing good left there."

"Nothing? No happy memories or fun times?"

"Nothing."

"This coming from the girl who won the watermelon-eating contest three years running at the stamping plant carnival, beating out my friends and me every time. I still remember your smile that last time. You were thrilled with yourself."

I shot him a look, frowning. "That was a long time ago."

"I guess so." Easton went back to staring out the side window, his finger tracing a line across the dash. "Looks like you got a nice, clean break from this place."

I clenched my teeth, memories of my so-called clean break coming back to haunt me. The whispers in college, the guys recognizing me as Cowgirl Vee and assuming things they had no right to assume. The times I'd had to walk out of a party or a restaurant, had to quit a job and look for another. Had to break up with someone or suffer through them breaking up with me when they'd found out. The time I was forced to change majors and later schools when my guidance counselor had found out about the video and had advised working with children would be difficult at best with my history. All because of one mistake...a mistake people seemed to love to share.

"Right," I spat. "Such a clean break."

Easton turned in his seat, watching me again. "Hey, I didn't mean—"

"Yeah, you did." I flew over the train tracks, not even slowing down for the bumps. "You can choose to believe what you want, but there was nothing clean about my break from this place."

When I reached the shop, I pulled right up to the bay doors, spotting Brogan inside. He didn't wave, so neither did I. Let someone else deal with being polite. I was done for the day. Easton didn't move, though, didn't leave. And I'd had enough.

"I need to get back, Easton."

"Sure, of course." Easton pushed open the passenger door and stepped out onto the asphalt. "Thanks for the lemonade and the ride."

"Anytime." I struggled to keep from frowning. I'd wanted him to leave, to stop looking at me the way he was, but…well, I hated to see him go. He was the only person who'd had what seemed like a real conversation with me, the only person who'd made me laugh in days. And I was so sick of being alone.

Easton placed a hand on the roof and leaned in to give me one of those soul-searching looks. "If you or your grandma need anything, don't be afraid to call me. I might stick my foot in it sometimes, but I could still be a friend, Violet."

I had to work to unclench my jaw, doing my best to smile at the man. "Thanks, I appreciate it."

He stared at me for a long moment, looking as if he wanted to say more. But then the moment passed with a yell and a loud laugh from inside the shop.

"You'd better go before Colton goes after Brogan with the torch." I couldn't keep my voice smooth, couldn't get the words out without cracking on one. Easton stared, chewing the inside of his cheek as he refused to look away. But I had a long history of pushing people away. I had the words down pat. "Let me go, Easton," I said, keeping my voice quiet and soft.

His deep frown pulled at a string in my heart, one that was painful. One that I couldn't ignore. Not completely. Still, I sat quietly, watching him, waiting for him to walk away.

Finally, he patted the roof of the car and shut the door, staring long and hard through the open window. "I'll see you around."

I took a deep breath, refusing to let his goodbye affect me. This was what I'd wanted—for him to back off, to stop staring at me, to stop making me feel like some sort of archeological dig. To stop looking for all the things I preferred to keep hidden.

Be careful what you wished for, and all that.

"See ya."

CHAPTER FIVE

VIOLET

I stared at the assortment of processed cheese products and sliced meats in the cooler case, eyeing the pimento cheese with more than a little interest. I hadn't eaten that in ages, not since I'd moved away. I sort of wanted to buy a jar. Grandma would love it, though chemically colored and flavored dairy-free cheese substitute probably wasn't the healthiest thing for her at the moment. And really, wasn't keeping her healthy the point of everything lately?

Pimento cheese craving, denied.

Reluctantly, I moved past the cases and into the fresh fruits and vegetables area, grabbing a few things for the house that caught my eye. Asparagus, cucumbers, a small watermelon—seedless, of course. No bugs for Grandma, not when she was so sick.

The weight of the melon might as well have settled on my shoulders at that thought. Sick didn't begin to describe what she was going through. The chemo was really doing a number on her poor body, something neither of us had been completely prepared for. She could barely get out of bed. Even a small trip to the bathroom was difficult at best for her, which was why I was choosing to grocery shop in the middle of the night while she was sleeping. It was the only time I felt comfortable leaving her alone. Dahlia was due back from her training retreat in a few days, but until then, I was on my own. The responsibility was staggering. So, no matter how exhausted I'd become, I shopped at ungodly hours, pretty confident in the knowledge that Grandma would sleep soundly while I was gone, and that she had a phone next to her bed to call Mary if she needed help.

I yawned as I made another loop past the apple stand. A very slow loop. Even my mind was too tired to truly focus on what I was doing. On the plus side, the store was practically empty so late at night. The only people I saw as I wandered past the closed bakery section were a couple of employees stocking shelves and an older lady in her housecoat and curlers turning her cart down the frozen foods aisle. Typical goings-on at the all-night grocery store. Unless you watched horror movies, then you might expect more zombies. Though, by the way I was walking, I could have been mistaken for a zombie. My motions were slow, sluggish almost, my body tired. It was well past midnight, and I'd been up since before dawn taking care of Grandma. If there *were* zombies in the grocery store, I'd be one of the first eaten by—

"Can't sleep?"

I jumped, spinning, and without thought, tossed the zucchini I'd been holding at the man who'd spoken. It hit him in the shoulder with a thud and fell to the floor, doing no damage whatsoever. It wasn't until the squash went rolling across the overly polished tiles that I realized who I'd just attacked with produce. "Oh, gosh, Easton. I'm so sorry."

Easton dove for the errant vegetable. "I didn't mean to scare you."

"You didn't." I huffed a laugh at his raised eyebrows as he held out the zucchini. "Okay, you did. But only because the place is so empty, I was imagining zombie scenarios."

"And you figured a vegetable was the go-to weapon against the undead?"

I shrugged. "It's not organic."

He tilted his head, considering the zucchini. "Second death by residual pesticides. I can see that."

I laughed as I grabbed the zucchini and tossed it back into my cart. Bruises be damned, that squash was a solid weapon in my arsenal and would be honored for its service by being part of some ratatouille.

Easton seemed a bit uncertain, nervously running a hand through his messy hair. Though I guessed that was my fault...I hadn't exactly treated him fairly the last time we'd been together. In fact, I'd probably been more than a little rude.

"Look," I said, pulling my shoulders back. "I apologize for the way I left things the last time I saw you."

"It wasn't anything." He waved me off, shaking his head. "Water under the bridge and all that."

"But I was wrong. I know you—"

"Hey, Violet?" He grinned a little, making me pull up short.

"What?"

"It's good to see you. Mind if I shop with you for a while?"

I stared, unable to think. Unable to blink, really. I'd like to have said I'd grown too jaded for that sort of line to work on me, but I'd be lying. It worked. It worked perfectly.

Though I wasn't about to tell him that.

"Sure, I guess."

"Pretty sure that's the same answer I got back in eighth grade. Not really a resounding yes."

Eighth grade. When we'd danced together. "I still danced with you."

"You did, which is why I'm taking that halfhearted response

seriously." He grabbed an empty cart that sat next to the salad greens display and pulled up next to me. "Let's shop."

Grocery shopping with Easton Cole. Middle-school me swooned. Adult me…well, I swooned, too. Some things were evergreen.

"So," I started as we began walking toward the aisles. "What are you doing here so late?"

"I just got off work." He blew out a breath, almost seeming to be bolstering himself. "What about you? Can't sleep?"

I led us down the snack aisle, our two carts hogging all the space. "No, I could sleep for days right now if I didn't have things to do. I hate leaving Grandma alone when she's awake and might need me, so I wait until I know she's asleep to get things done. Tonight was a late one for her."

He hummed, investigating the shelves stocked with bags of chips. "You sure that's the only reason?"

I reached for a box of crackers on the other side of the aisle, focusing on the label as if it held some sort of secret to world domination. Or peace. Whatever, so long as I didn't have to watch Easton. "Yeah, why else would I come here so late?"

He didn't answer, so I darted a look his way. He was standing stock-still, frowning, still staring at the rows of brightly colored bags of chips. I inched closer, putting the crackers back on the shelf and grabbing another brand instead. The seconds stretched painfully, the tension between us growing. It was like a cloak, weighty and pulling me backward. I couldn't take it.

"Why don't these things ever say what's really in them?" I asked, needing to fill the silence. "Like, instead of calling these cheese and peanut butter sandwiches, they should be called bright-orange-nothing-like-cheese-squares-of-death-with-chemicals-between-them-that-taste-nothing-like-peanut-butter. Catchy, no?"

Thankfully, Easton chuckled, but then he grew serious again.

My stomach knotted. I knew that expression. Had seen it on other faces a hundred times. Here came the talk.

"Why don't you ever come home, Violet?"

My sigh was unavoidable, and so was the burn in my chest over having been asked this question. We both knew why I didn't come home. As much as I wanted to lie or laugh it off, to complain about how small this place seemed and how much more there was to do in Chicago, I couldn't. I was too tired to lie, too worn out to line up my defenses. I set the crackers back on the shelf, and I faced my inquisition. "I can't be *me* in this town. People here don't let you grow. They judge me because of a choice I made in high school, but they refuse to acknowledge that maybe—just maybe—dealing with the fallout from that changed me. That years of school and work and life have shaped me into someone else. I'm stuck being looked at as the same girl from high school whenever I come back."

Easton was quiet for a moment. When he did speak, it wasn't accusatory or to defend the people he dealt with every day. No, it was to defend...me. "There's nothing wrong with the girl from high school."

My ears burned, and I couldn't look into those eyes of his. They were too honest, too filled with something close to understanding. I fingered the car keys in my pocket before heading down the aisle, ready to leave crackers and conversation behind. "Maybe you don't see anything wrong with her, but I do. I made the wrong choice on a lot of levels, and I own that. But I'm not her anymore, and the people here won't accept it. They keep trying to shove me into that little box."

He followed me into the breakfast foods aisle. I grabbed a couple of boxes of oatmeal and a canister of grits. Instant, but they'd do. Grandma needed bland foods, and grits had always been a favorite on Sunday mornings. Dahlia hated them, but she was out of luck. She could make all the food choices when it was her turn to run the house. Which reminded me. I grabbed a box of honey-nut-cluster cereal on the way back to the cart. Dahlia hated them even more. She'd gag just seeing them on the shelf, which was a good enough reason for me to buy them. That was what she'd get for working in Puerto Rico with her hot-as-fuck Pilates mentor while I was cleaning up vomit.

When I returned to my cart, I did a double take. It certainly didn't seem like mine at first. "Uh, Easton?"

"Yeah?"

I held up the errant box. "Did you put this in the wrong cart?"

He didn't look my way, staring instead at a box of some kind of sugary cereal I hadn't had since I was a kid. "Put what in the wrong cart?"

"The chocolate puff cereal."

"Nope, not in the wrong cart."

I looked down at the box, then at his almost-empty cart. "But I don't eat this."

"I do."

"Are you suggesting I should make you breakfast?"

He opened his mouth to respond, then stopped, his lips turning up in a sexy almost-smile. "I was sort of hoping for marshmallow bars, but I'm up for whatever you're willing to give me."

"Marshmallow bars?"

"Yeah. You know, like the ones with the rice cereal? You used to make the chocolate puff ones for the cheerleader bake sale thing every spring." He shrugged, suddenly refusing to meet my eyes. Looking almost shy. "I loved them."

I glanced at the cereal again. "You want chocolate marshmallow bars?"

He shrugged, all casual and calm. "Yours, yeah."

And oh, that boyish look grew. Bad boy, cranky Easton was hot, but this? This Easton was a life-ruiner. Charming, shy Easton wouldn't just make me want to let him into my bed. He'd make me want to let him into my heart. He'd worm his way into my life with that smile and those eyes. He'd destroy my entire world. But damn, by the way he moved, I had a feeling he'd be worth it.

"You want *my* marshmallow bars?"

With two easy, loose-hipped steps, he practically surrounded me. His body, his scent, his whole aura. This man was too big, too overwhelming. This man would swallow me up and make me disappear, a not-so-unappealing proposition. He reached out all slow and methodical, his eyes pinning me in place. With the slightest caress of his fingers on mine, he took the box of cereal from my hand and held it over my cart. Questioning. Practically asking without a word if he could put it back in there.

"I used to wait until you weren't paying attention, then I'd buy all the bars just because you made them. It pissed off Jace every time."

My lips turned up into a grin. I took the box from his hand and placed it in my cart. "That might be the best reason to make those chocolate marshmallow bars I've ever heard. I'll need more than this cereal to make them for you, though."

He inched closer, his shoulder brushing mine. "Yeah? You'll really make them for me?"

"Sure," I said, a little more breathless than I'd planned.

"I'd owe you one," he said, leaning over me. His eyes were so bright, so captivating. He stayed in my space, watching me, almost caging me in against the cart. The heat between us flared brightly as he stood there, close enough to touch but not. Not *yet*, though I wanted to. And if the way he looked me over as he finally backed away was any indication, he wanted to as well.

Definitely a life-ruiner.

"You wouldn't owe me a thing."

"I don't like owing people," he said, his eyes growing serious. "If you make me treats, I'll pay you back. You can have me at your beck and call."

There was no resisting that one. "I've always wanted a beck-and-call boy."

Easton's laugh boomed through the store. "I walked right into that one, though I'm serious. You make me treats, and I'll owe you. That's a promise, and I never break a promise."

Of that, I had no doubt. "You've got yourself a deal."

"Excellent. C'mon, treat maker," Easton said with a nod toward the end of the aisle. "Let's finish up our shopping."

I sighed dramatically and rolled my eyes toward the ceiling. "So demanding."

He gave me a wicked smirk. "You ain't seen nothing yet."

We continued meandering through the aisles, my cart filling up much faster than his. When it was about halfway to the top, Easton added his stuff to the kid's seat area and started pushing it, leaving his behind.

"Taking over my cart, Cole?"

"Just trying to be a gentleman, Foster."

I stayed by his side as he made little comments while strolling down the cleaning supplies aisle. "Look, if someone needs to use fifteen types of air fresheners in one house to control odors, maybe they should just clean more." And around the back of the pet department. He frowned at a tank full of little orange fish. "My cat would go aquarium-diving for these."

That pulled me up short. "You have a cat?"

"Yeah. Dolly. I rescued her when I moved out of my mom's place. My trailer was awfully quiet with just me there."

Trailer. Huh. He still lived in the park, then. "I never pictured you as a cat guy."

His lips twitched, a smile trying to break through. "Well, as Colton always says when someone comments on Dolly, every guy likes a little pussy in their life."

I snorted a laugh, the two of us getting louder as we headed toward the front of the store. It wasn't until we reached the liquor department that we moved to opposite sides of the aisle.

"Beer drinker?" I asked, heading for the wine as he approached the cooler case with the craft six-packs.

"Sometimes." He glanced at me over his shoulder, eyebrow up. "Wine drinker?"

I shrugged. "Sometimes."

"Hmm." He chuckled as he checked out the beer, while I moved on to reading labels. I occasionally liked wine, but usually that was when someone else was choosing it. I'd worked in enough restaurants in Chicago to have narrowed down my options to white and not red, but I didn't recognize any of the bottles on the shelf.

"Having trouble picking?" Easton stepped behind me, his body so close I could feel the warmth at my back.

"Yes. I mean, I drink wine, but I don't know what kind I normally like. Plus, I just realized I don't even know if Grandma has a wine opener at the house. She's a gin drinker."

"So, if you don't know what kind you like and you don't know if you can open it, why not grab something else? I seem to remember you liked coconut rum and pineapple juice back in the day."

Jesus, the man had a long memory. He was right—rum and pineapple was my drink of choice back in my underage years. But we hadn't hung out in school, and our friends hadn't been friends. How did he learn that?

And why did the fact that he knew that make me want to jump his bones right there in the grocery store?

EASTON

Shit. I had to step away from her, but my God, the girl was so irresistible. A simple evening of grocery shopping was making me want to toss her ass on the floor so I could crawl between her legs and hear her moan in the middle of the store. What woman had the ability to do that? I wasn't some teenage boy with a libido bigger than his brain. I had control over my dick…or at least I'd thought I did. But then Violet Foster had walked in and started talking about zombies and pesticides and marshmallow bars, and all bets were off.

Strolling to the shelves with the hard liquor, I did my best to stop thinking about getting Violet naked. If I could just concentrate on food and not her, I'd be fine. But I could still smell her perfume, still feel her eyes on me. There was no way to avoid her, no way to hide from her while I dealt with my…problem. Not that attraction should be a problem, but I had a feeling she wouldn't be thrilled if she were aware of how hard she made me without even trying.

I took a deep breath and searched out a bottle I knew she'd appreciated once upon a time. Stalling, really. We both needed a minute or two. Me, to calm the fuck down, and her, to find the courage to stick around. Giving in to what I really wanted, I glanced at Violet out of the corner of my eye. She was staring at me, her teeth visible on that pink bottom lip of hers. Biting it. Looking like she wanted to bite me. Shit. I was going to have to jack off when I got home.

"You still like sweet drinks?" I asked, trying my damnedest to concentrate on the bottles on the shelf instead of the image of her hand wrapped around my dick in place of my own.

She shrugged. "Sometimes."

"Sometimes. Like you like wine sometimes." I chuckled, taking a bottle of coconut rum from the shelf. Drinks, I could do. Drinks were easy and a good distraction. "So you like rum still?"

"I think so."

"You're not sure?"

She frowned, her nose wrinkling in the most adorable way. "It's been a while. Everyone I know drinks wine, so I haven't had hard stuff in years."

I nodded, creeping closer, trying hard to keep my body in check. But her eyes were bright and watchful, her skin slightly flushed. And good goddamn, she was looking at me like…like how I was looking at her. "If you don't always like wine, why drink it?"

She shrugged. "Everyone I know—"

"Everyone you know drinks it. I got that. But why do *you*?"

Her head jerked back as if no one had ever asked her about herself. And maybe no one had. Or maybe she never gave them the chance. Because as much as this was Violet, the popular girl from high school, this was also Vee, the girl living with the ramifications of having been filmed having sex, of that video having been leaked all over the damn world. There had to be a few trust issues there.

Slowly, Violet dropped her eyes to the bottle in my hand. Then she reached for it, every inch almost like a battle fought. A battle for her truth, maybe. Or a battle against her attraction to me, which was perhaps a little wishful thinking on my part.

When she finally grabbed the bottle, when her little hand wrapped around the outside of mine, she shivered. "Are we friends, Easton?" she whispered, suddenly appearing shy.

"Sure. Of course."

"Friends hang out together, right?"

"Some do."

She took a deep breath as if preparing for something. "Would you like to have a drink with me? As my friend? I could use a break from…things."

As if there were any possible way I'd say no. "I was just about to ask you the same thing."

She nodded, smiling. Looking relieved. Looking as if she'd just bested some sort of beast or completed some sort of feat. And maybe she had. The girl was running on pure will, it seemed. Maybe asking me out had been a little beyond her comfort zone for the night. I was glad she had, though.

"I should grab some pineapple juice." She took the bottle of rum from my hand, smiling up at me. I liked it…too much. Brogan was going to be in full mother-hen mode when he found out about this, but I wasn't about to put on the brakes when she was looking at me like I was something she yearned for. Something she craved. Trying for anything more than friendship with Violet Foster—again, so many years after I'd crashed and burned while asking for a date—was quite possibly the best worst idea I'd ever had, but I was going to follow it through. By starting out as friends.

"We can go to my place," I offered without thinking.

My mistake was clear in the way Violet reacted. Back straight, muscles clenched, she turned her head to look over her shoulder, not quite meeting my eyes. Every single inch of her locked down and on the defensive. "I asked you if you wanted a drink. That wasn't an invitation for anything else."

Shit. Cold voice and harsh words—she thought I was trying to get in her pants. Not that I'd be against it, but she wasn't ready. I could tell that from a mile away.

"I'm not asking or expecting anything, Violet." I stepped closer, moving around her so I could look her in the eye. Her expression stayed closed and guarded, the pain and fear in her eyes screaming that those scars of hers ran deeper than I'd been prepared for. I hadn't meant my offer the way she'd taken it, but I could see why she saw it as a come-on. "Your grandma is sleeping, and my house is empty except for Dolly. That's the only reason I offered. If that makes you uncomfortable, we can go someplace more public."

She kept her eyes locked on mine, her face giving nothing away. But I felt it. I knew it. She was ready to run. Just offering what she thought was a proposition for more than friendship had been enough to set off those fight-or-flight instincts, and she was a woman who chose flight. Too bad for her, I always chose fight.

"Violet, I swear to you, this is just a couple of old high school friends catching up. I've got no other intentions."

The look on her face gutted me, the distrust there warring

with something akin to fear and making me want to destroy everyone who'd ever hurt her. "Honest?"

"Honest." I shrugged and offered up a smile. "At least nct yet."

She chuckled, her shoulders relaxing. "Friends sounds good. I don't have friends here anymore, and getting ground up in the rumor mill isn't really what I'm looking for this summer."

"Understood. So how about we pay for these groceries and get rolling? I'll drive us someplace public for a drink, and then bring you back here to grab your car."

If her sunny smile was any indication, she liked that idea. "Sounds perfect."

And it would be, once I figured out how to be just friends with the woman I'd dreamed about being mine for most of my life.

CHAPTER SIX

VIOLET

"You are *not* taking me here."

"Why?" Easton asked, glancing at me as he turned his truck into the driveway of what was essentially our town's lover's lane. "It's a public spot but sort of private in the back. No one will bother us."

"Right, because they'll all be too busy making out."

"What?" He looked around the lot. "It's the parking lot of the ice arena."

"Yeah, in the back. Where all the kids used to go to get a little *privacy*. Or were you not one of the many who fooled around back here?" I grinned as his eyes went wide, wondering what sort of memories that question brought up.

"Shit. I forgot about all that." He pulled to a stop, probably considering his options. "It seemed like a good idea when we left the grocery store. I promise I didn't bring you here to make out with you."

"It's fine," I said, my voice a little sharper than I'd intended. I was with someone I wanted to be a friend, but that last comment of his sucker-punched me. Was he just not attracted to me? Had he seen the video and—

Anger and humiliation shut off that thought quick. Of course, he'd seen the video. The whole town had watched it, even those without internet. He probably felt the same as all the others I'd run into over the years who'd seen it—either expecting more from me than I was ready to give simply because I'd given it before in a public way, or disgusted by my actions. Sometimes even a little of both.

But Easton didn't seem like one of those guys. He didn't seem pushy or overbearing, and he certainly didn't seem disgusted. Maybe, just maybe, he really was someone I could be friends with. If I could just keep those memories of the video locked away for an hour or so.

"I haven't been here in years," Easton said as he pulled to a back spot facing the woods. There were only a handful of cars in the lot, probably high school kids who'd snagged some late-night ice time. In a town so close to Detroit, rentable hours in a rink were hard to come by. At least in my day. I had many a memory of steaming up the car windows with Jace in the wee hours of the morning after he'd finished an early-morning time slot for hockey practice.

I shrugged, pushing thoughts of Jace out of my mind. "Yeah, though it hasn't changed much."

Easton pulled out the cups and rum we'd brought with us, balancing the pineapple juice on his thigh. When he finished making my drink, he handed me the red plastic cup, pulled out a beer, and turned off the headlights. Darkness immediately blanketed us, making the cab of his truck feel much smaller. More intimate.

"Did they take out the lights?" I asked, trying to keep my voice steady.

Easton laughed and unscrewed the cap of his beer. "Probably.

Brogan's cousin Tyler runs this place now. His grandpa retired and handed it down to him."

"Well, no wonder. Tyler was practically the make-out king, if I remember correctly."

"Pretty sure Colton would argue that the title was his."

I shook my head and swallowed a sip, nearly humming at the sweet-tart taste of my drink. "Colton was the make-out god."

"I didn't know you and Colton—"

"Oh, no. I was with Jace through most of high school." *Until the video,* I thought but didn't admit. "I just know the stories."

"There are plenty of those."

"He still wild?"

"Not as much as before." Easton took a swig from his bottle before settling back against the seat. "He's no wallflower, but he's not going through women like Kleenex anymore."

"He left many a broken heart at old Downriver High."

"As did you, Miss Congeniality."

I rolled my eyes. "Oh, please."

"You always were so blind to how you drove the boys crazy. Pretty sure Brogan walked right into the doorframe in E hall every day for a month because you'd smile at him as you left chemistry class."

"Liar."

"Girl, you have no idea. You turned my head for years."

My heart skipped a beat. "Now you're just sweet-talking me."

He leaned forward, taking up so much room in the cab of his truck that I felt surrounded by him. "Not sweet-talking. Not exaggerating either. Just telling the truth."

"Liar," I whispered again, staring into those bright blue eyes of his. Getting lost in his closeness.

"Nope. Not lying." He dropped his gaze to my lips, and my breath caught. Oh God, how I wanted him to kiss me. I knew it was a bad idea, knew it would cause problems I really wasn't in the mood to deal with, but none of that mattered in that moment.

It was dark, we were alone, he was close and so fucking handsome…and I wanted to feel his lips on mine.

But he didn't kiss me. He blinked then leaned back, giving me room to breathe instead. Room I no longer really wanted. Room I actually sort of hated.

I took another drink of my cocktail, hoping my hands weren't shaking. "This is good. I haven't had it in forever. At least not since college."

"You went from Western straight to Chicago, right?"

"Yeah." I took another drink, the alcohol warming me from the inside out. Making the rough edges of my thoughts smooth once more. "Left WMU to go to the Culinary Institute, then got an offer to start at a restaurant downtown, so I stayed. My grandma warned me, but I totally didn't think about things like starting salary and cost of living when I made my move."

"It's expensive there?"

"Expensive doesn't begin to describe it." I lolled my head to the side, smiling. "But I'm not without skills. Three restaurants later, and I'm in the kitchen every day making treats for a living and earning a decent salary."

"Do you like that kind of work?"

"I do. I enjoy baking…probably more than anything else I've ever even thought about doing." I slouched in the seat, kicking off my shoes and bringing my feet up on the dashboard. "Food doesn't require me to be smiling and calm when I'm in front of it. I'm allowed to have a bad day in the kitchen, to curse and throw things and slam my hands into dough. I beat the shit out of bread twice a week and love it."

"Yeah, you might get in trouble for beating up a coworker," Easton said, completely straight-faced. But then he grinned. "Though I'd sort of love to see you all mad and raging."

"I bet, so long as it wasn't you I was mad at."

"Truth." He held up his bottle in a mock salute. I smiled back, suddenly completely intrigued by his lips again. They looked so soft. So kissable. Positively bitable.

Stop thinking about Easton's lips. "So. I make desserts, and you're a mechanic."

His hand brushed against mine, making me shiver. Instead of pulling away, he kept it there. The lightest of touches. The simplest of gestures. That move made me swoon hard.

"Automotive Technician," he said, his voice a little softer than before.

"What's the difference?"

"Fuck if I know."

I coughed a laugh, nearly choking on my drink. "God, you're such a smartass."

"Yeah, but it's part of my charm." He tugged on my hand. "C'mere, pretty girl. It's too dark to see you all the way over there."

His words wrapped around me like a blanket, the feel of his hand pulling me closer, warming me from the inside. From everywhere. "I thought we were being friends."

"We are, but I like to actually see my friends' faces when I talk to them."

I smiled and answered him with a shift closer. He tugged again, so I crept across the seat a little more. Two times, three. Four. Until we were close enough to touch. Close enough to do things other than hold hands. And I wanted those things. I'd drunk just enough to feel a little sleepy instead of buzzed. Just enough to truly relax. And Easton was looking at me as if he liked me being this close.

"Why didn't you become a teacher?" he asked, his breath ruffling my hair.

"How do you remember that I wanted to be a teacher?"

"Junior year career fair. You said you wanted to teach. Plus, you used to talk about the teaching program at WMU. I assumed that was why you were going there."

"You have a great memory." I leaned against his chest with my head back, staring at the ceiling. Avoiding his eyes again. "I like your truck. It's the same one from high school, right?"

"Same one. It was my dad's before it was mine, though."

"I think I remember that. He left town at some point, right?"

"Yeah," Easton said, his voice growing a little rougher. "Packed up and took off without a word senior year."

"I'm so sorry. I can't even imagine." And I couldn't. I'd lost my mom when I was too young to have strong memories of her, but the idea of losing Dahlia? Losing my grandma? Of one of them walking away from me? Just the thought killed me inside.

"Most people can't," Easton said, sounding a bit stronger. "It was a rough time, but we made it through. Family pulls together in times like that, you know? Me, my mom, my little sister…we became an unstoppable team." He took a deep breath, shifting me even closer. "The only thing my dad left behind was his cars. We all picked one, and then my mom sold the rest. My mom still drives his old Cadillac, my sister Gracie drives my dad's Chevelle, and I got his truck."

"So it had good memories for you?"

"Fuck no. My dad leaving town was the worst thing that ever happened to us, but I refuse to try to pretend it didn't happen. Besides, it's a good reminder that people aren't always what they seem."

"Seems really brave, to face your past like that."

Easton hummed his approval. "That's a definite truth. Now quit trying to avoid my question. Tell me why you're not a teacher right now."

I'd never told anyone but Dahlia about the situation with my guidance counselor freshman year. Not even my grandma knew exactly why I'd dropped out of one school and rushed off to another. And I hadn't ever expected to tell someone I barely knew, like Easton, but my guard was down, and my lips were loose because of the alcohol. Or maybe that was just an excuse and I wanted to tell someone, anyone, the truth. "The guidance counselor at Western made it very clear that parents wouldn't want their kids taught by someone who'd starred in porn."

Easton's body went stiff, and his hand clenched the steering wheel tight. "You didn't *star in porn*."

My harsh laugh probably wasn't the reaction he expected. "Try to make people see that distinction and let me know how you get on, because I've been failing at that for years." I waved my hand, not wanting to continue down that conversational path. "What are you still doing here, Easton Cole?"

"Chatting with you," he replied, his voice deep and soft.

"Not the literal here. Downriver here. Why didn't you leave?"

"I never wanted to."

"Liar." I turned and pointed at him, my eyes crossing a bit as I tried to focus. "You told me once that you hated it here."

He was silent for a long time, staring at me. I couldn't look away, couldn't have put an inch between us if I'd tried. And by the way he kept his hand locked with mine, I'd guess he felt the same way.

"I did then. That night...picking you up in the rain and talking...I've thought about it a million times since," he finally whispered.

He remembered. Something unknotted inside me, something warm and comforting. Something that felt an awful lot like being safe. I smiled up at him, almost ready to cry. "You saved me."

"Sometimes, I think I made you run." His words were soft and low, more confession than anything else. But he didn't need to confess to me.

"I didn't think you even remembered."

"How could I forget? It was the first time I'd really spoken to you since you'd shot me down for a date."

"I didn't shoot you down."

"You said no."

"Yes, but—"

"That's shooting me down. But that night in the rain, I got to spend a little more time with you, even if it wasn't under the best circumstances."

Or just plain under the worst. "You said nothing mattered as much as being happy and safe did. You gave me permission to look for my future outside this place."

"I remember that." He nodded, looking down at his beer bottle like it held the answers to all the secrets in the world. "And are you? Happy and safe out there?"

I finished my drink before twisting in the seat again and leaning my head against his shoulder. "I think so. Getting away from everything was what I was looking for. I wanted to disappear for a while. Everything here is so in-your-face—too many families intertwined, too many people knowing your every move. Chicago is busy and noisy and crowded and way too expensive, and there are days when I hate it, but I'm truly me out there. There's no hiding or stressing about what other people are saying behind my back there. I get to live my life without the judgment I got here."

He nodded, leaning into me to drop his empty bottle in the bag at my feet, grabbing my cup to do the same. "Yeah, I guess I can see that."

But his words didn't register. I was entranced by him, staring hard at his arms. The way the muscles flexed and stretched, the strength they exuded while doing something as simple as dropping items into a paper sack. He was no longer the boy I remembered. The one who'd made me get in this very truck all those years ago. He was a grown man, one I found ridiculously attractive.

As he wrapped an arm around my shoulders and pulled me even closer, I sighed. And then the alcohol completely took over as I opened my mouth.

"Jesus, when did you get so big?"

CHAPTER SEVEN

EASTON

Violet was so close, leaning in, staring at my mouth. My mind went blank, too lost in images of her to know what to do or say. I'd pictured her this way a hundred times, thought about what it would be like to have her all to myself even though I'd never told anyone. But that had been back in school, back when I'd had a broken family that needed me to be their caretaker and Violet had had a boyfriend who'd treated her... Well, he'd treated her well until he hadn't. Even before that night at the pizza place, I'd noticed her. Had harbored a secret crush on her. And through all the years she'd been gone, I'd never lost that little bit of attraction. Had never fully let go of her as someone I wished I'd had a chance to know better.

But I'd never been as close to finding out the secrets of Violet Foster as I was in that moment. I knew this was a bad idea—like stopping on the tracks and playing chicken with that oncoming train. I could practically see the freight train heading for me from miles away, but I couldn't make myself jump clear of the tracks. I was going to risk it all on this girl, this woman, because I'd always been willing to. I'd just never had the opportunity before.

Violet leaned closer, her eyes on mine, giving me enough of a signal to say fuck it all. I *wanted* to kiss her. I wanted to grab her and hold her as that train crashed into us and destroyed our worlds. I'd wanted her in some way, shape, or form for years, and I was finally giving in and having her.

I inched forward, one arm on the back of the seat to hold myself up as I herded her backward. She dropped her knee to the side as her shoulders hit the passenger door, leaning back, practically spread before me. Giving me room to crawl up her body and almost pin her in place. I wanted to shift closer, to press my body against hers. To feel every inch of her. I ached for it even as I resisted. Even as the pressure of my cock, restrained as it was, made my hands tremble with need.

Jesus, she seemed so small as I hovered over her. Tiny, almost. It had to be an illusion, the shadows playing tricks on my mind. Violet wasn't a tiny girl, wasn't petite or waif-like. Yet there in the dark in the cab of my truck, she seemed small and almost innocent. An odd thought, considering what I'd seen her do in a grainy security video a lifetime ago.

And fuck, didn't that thought make me feel like an ass.

Refocusing on the girl right in front of me, I leaned in. Not wanting to push, but definitely making my move. She matched me, her body mimicking mine to bring us closer together. I kept my weight on my arm, but there was no way around covering her with the way she was leading me down the seat. Not if I was going to reach her lips. And I would…I had to. At that point, only a refusal from her would get me to stop.

"Easton," she whispered, bringing her hands to my shoulders.

"Yeah?" I paused just before her lips brushed mine, making her wait for it. And she did—she waited. My arm shook and my heart raced as the reality settled over me—I was about to kiss Violet Foster.

"I never got to say thanks for the pizza all those years ago," she whispered, her breath sweet as it blew across my lips.

"Your smile that night was thanks enough."

She squeezed my arms once and smiled up at me in that same way she had so many years before. Something about the darkness, the warmth of the truck cab, the quiet of the night outside. It spoke to me. Pulled a thread inside of me until I was wound too tight to do anything other than snap.

As that thread broke, I pressed my lips to hers without a second thought to the consequences. Soft and warm, she kissed me back, moving her lips with mine. Letting me taste her, letting me submerge myself in the scent of vanilla that was simply Violet. Letting me bite down on that soft flesh just enough to make her jump.

She gasped and pulled me closer, nearly wrapping herself around me, her soft skin fire against my own. And, oh God, did I like the feel of her...everywhere. This was no gentle first kiss. This was strong and wild, a kiss filled with attraction and chemistry. Violet's lips on mine felt right, and the way she immediately opened for me—how she stroked her tongue against mine without waiting for me to lead—was the hottest thing I'd ever experienced. In the cab of my truck, behind the ice arena, I was living my teenage fantasy, and it was better than I'd ever imagined.

Violet became more aggressive as I deepened the kiss. Matching my moves and letting me know she wanted more. Greedy in the best possible way. She tugged on my arms, her little nails scraping over my flesh. Trying to move us closer, something I willingly gave in to. The vinyl seat creaked beneath me, but I didn't care. It only added to the sound of her breathing, to the little gasps and sighs she uttered as I made sure she remembered our first kiss.

She hitched her knee over my hip to keep me where she wanted, and I moaned. She was just so damn warm all over. I wrapped my arm underneath her, my hand moving to grip her hair, to clutch the softness of it so I could control her movements that much more. And she let me…which was almost my undoing. That and the throaty groan she gave when I tugged just a little.

Needing more, I slid my other hand down to her hip, inching over her ribcage and waist along the way. Fuck, her skin was so hot and smooth, so much the opposite of mine. I hoped she didn't mind the roughness of my hand, because I couldn't stand the thought of letting her go. And still, I kissed her deeper. Ran my tongue along her lips, tasting the sugary-sweet flavor of her drink. Another pass, a tiny bite, both of which earned me a little gasp of pleasure. Just as I'd hoped.

Her hand dropped to the back my thigh, grabbing my flesh, kneading it. I groaned and yanked her closer, wrapping myself around her in a possessive sort of way that made my cock practically weep. She was so strong, so tempting. So addictive. There was no denying her anything. No pulling away from the scent of her, the sounds. The taste. I let my weight rest against her, just enough to truly feel her body all along mine. Enough to tease both of us into heavy breaths and whispered curses without pushing her into the door too hard. And fuck, it was good—warm and soft and perfect—yet I wanted more.

Cautiously, slowly, I slid my hand under her shirt and up her stomach. Stopping only once my fingers rested at the bottom of her breast. Daring yet restrained. Violet groaned and hissed a curse, arching her back into my touch. Giving me the green light for more. I pressed forward, my fingers running back and forth over the thin fabric of her bra. Pulling it down enough so I could get to her skin. Somewhere in the back of my mind was a high school boy screaming about getting to second base with Violet Foster, but I ignored him. I wasn't a high schooler anymore. Second base wasn't going to be enough. Not with her. No way.

But just as I wrapped my hand around her breast, as my thumb flicked her nipple and elicited the most amazing groan from her, as my hips jerked forward to press my cock against where I so wanted to explore, a horn sounded outside the truck. I jumped up in time to see a carload of kids race off across the lot, probably a group of teenagers out past curfew to take advantage of open ice at the rink. Probably not having seen a single thing through the tinted windows of my truck. Probably just having really bad timing. Interrupting bastards.

"Shit." I groaned, hanging my head so my forehead rested against Violet's. My hips were still pressed in between her legs, my aching cock nestled snugly where he really wanted to be. Almost.

"That's what I was going to say." Violet placed a single, soft kiss against my lips before she wriggled out from under me. "I can't believe that just happened."

"Me neither." I sat back and licked my bottom lip, trying to get enough blood back up to my brain to think clearly. "I'm not sorry about it, though. Well, maybe."

Those bright eyes narrowed. "Maybe?"

"Not about kissing you," I said, reaching to weave our fingers together. "I'm only sorry I haven't at least taken you out on a date before I went and slid my hand up your shirt."

"You want to take me on a date?"

"Of course, I do."

Her silence wasn't quite the reaction I'd been hoping for, nor were her words. "We're just friends, remember?"

Shit. I'd forgotten about that. "Then it's a friend date. Dinner with someone you like talking to."

"And who you like kissing?"

"Friends kiss."

"Really?" Her eyebrow raise was nearly as perfect as my sister's. "You kiss Colton lately?"

Aw hell, but I could play this game as strong as she could. I leaned over her again, pressing her back into the door. Crowding her. "What happens in the garage stays in the garage."

Her laugh was more beautiful than anything I'd ever heard. Add in the fact that she had her hands on my arms and was pulling me closer as she laughed at something I'd said, and that moment would be one I'd probably never forget.

When she quieted again, meeting my eyes in a tense sort of stare that did nothing to relieve the ache in my jeans for her, I pressed my lips to hers in one more kiss. A small one. A fucking perfect, intimate one. And when I pulled away from her again, when I had her relaxed and smiling and looking up at me like I was someone she felt something for, I went for it. "Say yes, Violet. Tomorrow…dinner."

She shrugged, but there was a smile tugging at her mouth. "Maybe."

"Just maybe?" I inched closer, pulling her against me once more. Ready to charm her any way I could. "I never take time off work, but I'll do it for you. Don't make your friend beg."

She laughed and kissed me, yanking on my hair to hold us together before finally whispering a quiet "Probably" against my lips. I grinned and kissed her back, dragging my tongue against hers and my hands up and down her back. Fuck, this woman was more than I'd ever dreamed. More than I could probably handle.

But I was ready to try, even if being friends might kill me. "I'll take probably for an answer."

CHAPTER EIGHT

EASTON

"You're insane."

I brushed past Brogan, shouldering him a little harder than he probably deserved. "It's doable."

"With three guys here to pick up the slack while you play Sherlock Holmes on Rick's engine, sure. When you said we needed to move some things around, I didn't realize it was going to take a time turner. There's no way you can meet that deadline." He leaned against the side of the ancient Land Rover that had become my nemesis. It had also become my priority, as the owner had just cut my time to complete the job by three days.

I was so screwed.

"I can deal with the engine while you and Jude—"

"Jude's out for two days," Brogan interrupted. "He's heading out to Lollapalooza, remember?"

And suddenly, I felt like a chump. An overscheduled, forgetful chump. "Fuck, that's right. And Charity's coming into town, which means we lose Colton for the weekend." I shook my head, facts and figures and hours and schedules racing through my mind. Not only would we lose him in the shop, we'd lose all contact. Colton was the king of disconnection. "When's Colton leaving for up north again?"

"Tomorrow, motherfucker. What'd you do now? Agree to fix the unfixable in some sort of superhuman time frame again?" Colton swaggered into the bay with Gracie, my younger sister and the best damn bookkeeper I could afford, at his side. Both looking far too pleased with themselves for my liking.

"It's not unfixable. Besides, if we didn't take the job, the guy would just go to someone who would." I didn't need to tell them that everyone else had already turned Rick down. No sense digging my own grave any deeper.

Gracie hopped up on the workbench. "Yeah, but that *someone else* would have given the guy a realistic time frame."

I waved her off. "It's fine. I got the time to get this thing running."

"What about your new girl? Weren't you talking about that mythical event you called a date?" Colton asked.

I wilted on the spot, closing my eyes and clenching my hands into fists. *Fuck and me.* Violet. I'd just asked her out on a date for tonight, had promised I'd call her today to set it up after one hell of a goodnight kiss on the hood of her crappy car. I was going to have to break those plans. If this engine were going to be rebuilt in time, there'd be no dates for me this weekend. I couldn't afford to take an entire evening off with Jude and Colton gone. "I'll text her and let her know work is a little crazy right now. Maybe we can get together next week or something." Even I heard the uncertainty in my voice, but the guys didn't call me on it. Missing my date with Violet, not fulfilling my promise to her, didn't sit well with me. None of this sat well with me. All because of that my stupid mouth.

"Good luck with that, big brother." Gracie swung her legs and zeroed in on Colton. "So, Charity's coming to town, huh? You and your little friend got any big plans?"

His expression turned serious. "Sex. That's what Charity and I do—we have sex."

"Well, aren't you just boyfriend of the year."

"She's not my girlfriend—we have an arrangement regarding her visiting and us having sex." He shrugged and crept closer to Gracie, who'd slid off the bench and stood glaring at him. "C'mon, beloved Gracelyn. Don't tell me you're the old ball-and-chain type. We both know you go through the men in this town fast enough to give *me* a run for my money."

The garage went still, the silence heavy. My feet stayed rooted to the floor as I tried to control the instinct to stomp that asshole into the ground. My mind attempting to balance the need to beat the ever-loving shit out of one of my best friends for talking trash about my sister and the desire to whack Gracie upside the head and tell her to keep her damn pants on. Or at least keep her mouth shut.

Brogan ended up responding faster than I did.

"What the fuck did you just say to her?" he said, his voice cold and even. Too even. The calmest, most reliable member of our crew didn't get mad often, but when he did…well, that was something you wanted to avoid. And everyone in that room knew it.

"It's fine, Brogan. I'm not insulted," Gracie said, waving him off. "Colton's just jealous because, unlike him, I can actually convince a date to stick around for more than a single night."

Colton's lips turned up in a sickeningly sweet sort of smile. "Oh, Gracie. One night's all I need."

"Keep telling yourself that, sweetheart."

"Enough. Both of you. We're supposed to be working." Brogan flung a wrench onto the workbench before heading for the door at the back of the shop. The guy was obviously upset, not that I could blame him. Brogan had always been overprotective when it came to my little sister.

The door leading outside slammed closed behind Brogan

before Colton could utter a single response. "Guess we pissed him off."

I smacked him upside the head, unable to resist the urge. "Show the girl some fucking respect, Colton."

"Maybe we should go after him." Gracie looked toward the door, something almost like guilt on her face.

Colton tossed a wrench in the air to catch, the picture of ease. "Nah, he'll be fine. Guy's been getting his panties in a bunch for months. I think *he's* the one who needs to get laid. Though it sounds more like Easton's up for the next round on the mattress carousel."

"Fuck off, Colton."

"Aye-aye, Captain." He flipped me off in some sort of perverse mock salute before heading over to an old Ford LTD and pressing the button to put it in the air. As he got to work, I caught Gracie's eye and inclined my head. She understood the gesture and strolled toward the office with me following her like a guard dog. Typical, really, seeing as that was what Brogan and I had been doing since she'd gotten out of diapers.

"What gives?" she asked once we had the door closed behind us.

"You tell me. Anything I need to know?"

"Not unless you want me to get really personal with you about my sex life."

"Not particularly."

"Then nope, I'm all good."

Her attitude made me want to rip my hair out. "Gracie, you know Colton's not a bad guy—"

She laughed, head thrown back, hand on her chest, guffawing to the ceiling. "Are you kidding me?" she asked once her little laugh fest ended. "You think I care what Colton thinks? The man's been a mattress-hopper almost since puberty. Trust me, that's one person who shouldn't be throwing stones at anyone."

"His mouth gets the best of him sometimes is all."

"That's one way to put it." She sighed and headed toward the desk. "Mrs. Jeffers called me."

That caught my attention. "About what?"

"She needed help cleaning up one of her flower beds. Said some of those darn kids trashed it, even though 'those darn kids' usually means me, and I certainly didn't mess with her flowers. I don't need that sort of drama in my life."

"You should have called me. I'd have—"

"Jumped in to save the flowery day?" That single eyebrow winging trick was one only Gracie and my mom could pull off, and it frustrated me to no end. "Other people can fix things, you know."

"I know that."

"Do you? Because it seems to me you're a controlling jackass who refuses to sit back and let anyone else prove they can handle shit."

"Wow, Gracie. Why don't you say what you really mean?"

"Sorry, it's just…you work enough. Let someone else take care of things at the park. And at the shop. And…everywhere. Not everything in life needs the Easton Cole stamp of approval."

If I hadn't known my sister as well as I did, I might have missed the sadness in her voice. The pain she seemed to be trying to hide. "Something going on you need to talk about?"

She scoffed at that. "And have you try to swoop in to fix things for me? No thanks. I'd rather handle this one on my own."

"Okay, but I'm here if you need me."

Her eyes met mine, so wide and clear. Honest eyes. "I know that. Everyone knows that. Who's there if you need someone?"

My brow tightened. "I've got Brogan and Colton—"

"Not like that. Who takes care of you? Who gives you comfort?"

"Gracie, I'm not sure—"

"Never mind." She waved a hand around as if shooing some

errant fly. "Just something that's been on my mind lately. What else is going on? Why'd you pull me back here?"

I paced the length of the room, thinking about Violet and wondering what she was doing. Which reminded me… "Jude called Violet Foster 'Cowgirl' the other day."

"Violet…as in *the* Violet Foster? My old math tutor and the girl whose life imploded in high school, Violet Foster?"

"One and the same."

"And that's who you asked out. The date."

"Yeah. I did."

"Wow. You've been harboring that crush for over a decade. Acting on it took balls. I'm proud of you."

"Not really where I was going with this."

"Right. Jude called her the old nickname people used in high school to shame the poor girl for daring to have sex. The bastard," Gracie spat, not missing a beat. "How she'd take that?"

"Quiet, sort of." I shrugged. "She looked ready to claw her way out of my car, though. Whether to escape or to attack Jude, I have no idea."

"If that were me, I'd have bitten off my tongue and used it to choke that Jace guy years ago."

"That might be the grossest visual you've ever used."

"Thank you." She gave me a sarcastic sort of curtsy before settling at my desk. "What really happened with Jace and Violet, anyway?"

"You don't remember?"

"I do. I mean, let's face it, that legend is pretty epic. But I never figured out what was truth and what was pop culture, you know?"

"Yeah, I do." I sat across from her and kicked my feet up on the filing cabinet. "Though now that you mention it, I'm not even sure what was real. I know there was a video of them having sex, and they broke up over it. The rest…"

"Could be Kardashian-esque spin."

"Exactly."

Gracie was quiet for a moment, her eyes unfocused and her brow furrowed. "Why'd they break up?"

"Huh?"

"Well, I mean, I've seen the clips. She had sex with Jace, but it looked consensual, so it wasn't a rape issue."

I nearly choked. "Damn, Gracie."

"Blunt is my thing. You know this. Keep up." She sat back, raising her high-heeled shoes to rest against my desktop. "So why the split if it was just them on an average Saturday night?"

I ran a hand through my hair, remembering. "The night before the rumors started, I saw her walking down the side of the road in the rain. I picked her up."

"You never told me that."

"I never really had the chance to. You, Mom, me, we were all…"

Her eyes met mine, both of us probably feeling the sting that never really went away.

"Dealing with Dad's leaving," she murmured.

"Yeah. He took off right around the time the tape came out, and I was dealing with…that." I rubbed a hand over my face, chasing away the anger thinking about that man brought up. "Those last couple of months of school are sort of a blur."

I sighed and dropped my head on the back of the chair. Dad… His taking off on us had thrown our already small family into a tailspin. I'd been forced to pick up a lot of slack because I'd been the only male in the house, had been forced to take on a lot of roles I hadn't been ready for. But I hadn't been alone through all that. Gracie had needed to grow up way too quick, and my mom had lost her husband. We'd all been so deep in our own heads, helping each other out had become next to impossible. But we'd done it. In ragged jerks and starts, we'd made it through that darkest year together. But none of us would ever be the same.

Gracie took a deep breath and shook her head, probably

pushing away the same memories dragging my mood right down with hers. "We were all just trying to hold it together."

But her acknowledgment didn't relieve my guilt. "Violet was a shell of a person those last couple of weeks. I should have stepped in to help her, but I wasn't paying attention. She had no one, did she?"

"Sure didn't seem like it."

"No wonder she ran as soon as she graduated."

"I'd have run too. Hell, I'd still be running if that happened to me. Even if it was just so I didn't kill the bastard."

My office suddenly felt like a prison, like a cage. I jumped to my feet and paced the short length a few times. I could see the back of the bowling alley through the window, the scene of the so-called crime. Jesus, how hard had it been for Violet to come back over here just to drop off her grandma's car? To be that close to the building where her world had imploded? For a runner, the girl had nerves of steel.

I turned over memories and rumors in my head, looking for something tangible to hold on to. I couldn't put my finger on why, but the entire situation seemed darker somehow. More intentional. I'd always assumed the video had somehow been leaked and Violet had simply taken the brunt of the judgment because she seemed to be the star of the show. I'd never thought about why the two had been at that spot in the bowling alley or how the film had gotten out. I'd never given Jace's reactions to the events a second thought.

I was now. Second thoughts. Thirds. Every one only made me rage inside a little harder. I'd hated that Jace fucker in high school for dating the girl I'd crushed on, and I hated him even more now for destroying her life.

"You really think Jace shared the video?" I asked, my hands in fists as I fought for some sort of control. "That he purposely set her up somehow?"

"Does it matter? If he did, he's a disgusting jackass who needs a good, swift kick in the balls. But if he didn't, then he's worse."

"How is he worse?"

Gracie appeared at my side and stared out the same window, probably seeing the back of the bowling alley, too. "Because during those last few months of school—as guys patted him on the back and Violet slunk through the halls with red-rimmed eyes—he never once defended her. He let his friends, his sister, and all the rest of the student body kick her when she was down, and he never said one word to help her." Gracie curled into my side, snuggling under my arm as soon as I raised it for her. "Jace let her hang as the town whore, while he became a hero. I would have run, too. And, Easton? I know you don't want to hear this…but I'd never have come back. Her being here isn't a sign or a new start—it's a fluke."

I knew that. I didn't want to focus on it, but I knew it. And I hated it.

My sister sighed and smacked me on the chest. "You'd better text her that you can't make your date. Give her some time to make other plans."

I knew that too. But I just had to ask the question I didn't want to know the answer to. "What are the odds of her sticking around, you think?"

Gracie took her time answering, still staring out the window at the back of the bowling alley. "You care for her."

I grunted, unable to answer her. Knowing the answer didn't matter—she already knew.

"She's not a project, Easton."

"I know that."

"Do you? Because right now, it sure seems like you're looking to fix something here." She sighed. "You can stop taking care of everyone else, you know. Dad's been gone a long time, and we're all fine without him. We figured it out."

Wrong. She was so very wrong. "Drop it, Gracie."

"Fine. But I know you, Easton. You've been trying to control everything since Dad left, to fix things and make everyone else's life easier, while you took on all the stress. You can't control Violet Foster, and you're not the one responsible for fixing anything in her life."

"I know that."

"Then you shouldn't be asking what the odds are for her sticking around. You already know they're slim to none. I hope I'm wrong for your sake, but that's the truth. And there's nothing you can do to stop her from running again."

I knew that too.

CHAPTER NINE

VIOLET

"Hey, all. I'm home. And look—I smuggled in Puerto Rican limes!" Dahlia strode through the door, clothes as bright as ever, light-red hair smoothed back in her ever-present bun and holding up a bag of bright green fruit.

I'd never been happier to see her.

"Keep it down, woman. Grandma's sleeping." I gave one final glance to my phone before getting up. I'd been obsessing over the silent device for at least the last hour, hoping like some kind of love-sick kid that I had the guts to call or text Easton. I'd also secretly been wishing he'd call or text me instead and arguing with myself over whether or not I should even go on a date with him, considering the situation. Hence the staring at the phone instead of actually dialing or texting or...anything.

"Sleeping already? Sorry. I didn't know," Dahlia whisper-yelled. I was pretty sure she was the only person on earth who could pull that off. Everyone else ended up sounding hoarse or as if they were choking on something. Instead, my cousin sounded all happy and young and...perfect. As usual.

Dahlia set her bag down with a *mea culpa* sort of expression on her face then took three exaggerated, silent steps in my direction. She looked like a cartoon villain sneaking into the bank in the middle of the night. An image that made me chuckle.

"God, I've missed you." I greeted Dahlia with a hug, the two of us clinging to one another for more seconds than was probably considered normal. "It's been too long since you've come to visit me in Chicago."

"Tell me about it." She huffed and blew her wispy bangs out of her eyes before turning her bright stare my way. "I'll make us some tea." And off she went. Dahlia tended to blow in like a whirlwind, all full of life and happiness. Ever the optimist, the woman shone in a way not many did. People were attracted to her for many reasons, but it was her obvious love of life that drew most in. And she did love it—she loved it hard and rough and loud, like two people caught up in a passionate affair.

"I have to tell you about the resort we stayed at. Yoga on the beach at dawn followed by mimosas? That was a thing." Dahlia moved about the kitchen, chattering to me in her bubbly way. The sound was soothing in its normalcy, the energy calming. Something I always forgot about until I was back in the same room with her once more.

As she set a kettle on the stove, my phone pinged. I tried not to rush for it, edging my way around the chair to the table with slow steps that tested every ounce of my control. I wanted to dive for the device, but I also wanted to wait and delay any sort of disappointment. What if it was an email? What if it was from one of my bosses or a friend from Chicago? It might not be Easton. I wouldn't know until I looked, though.

When I finally reached the phone, I picked it up and held on to it for a good minute before swiping the screen to life. New text message...from Easton Cole. My heart flipped. Actually seemed to flip right over in my chest. I was in so much trouble.

"What's going on over there?" Dahlia glanced at my phone then back at my face, her eyes curious.

"Nothing." I clutched the phone a little tighter. "Just a text."

"Looks like more than just a text."

"No, it's really just a text." One I'd been both hoping for and dreading all day. And if there was anyone who could understand that feeling, it was my cousin. Might as well admit why this text felt different from the rest. "It is from a guy, though."

Dahlia waited, her smile growing. "A guy in Chicago?"

"No, here. A friend. Easton Cole."

"You mean Easton Cole from high school? Of the trailer park trio?" She did *not* look happy anymore. "Best friend of Colton Bearn?"

I shrugged, knowing her feelings for Colton ranged from simple dislike to pure hatred depending on the day. "One in the same."

"Hmph." She began opening cabinets, obviously searching for something. "Why's he texting you?"

"We sort of went out."

"Like on a date?"

"Kind of. As friends."

Dahlia stopped banging around and stared at me. "How do you *kind of* go on a date?"

"We bumped into each other at the grocery store and went for a drink."

She nodded once, solid in her opinion as she stated, "Sounds like a date."

"We're just friends." I swiped my screen again, this time clicking through to the messaging app. "He was supposed to get in touch with me today about meeting up, though."

"As friends?"

I shrugged, avoiding that question. Easton and I weren't really friends. Not in the strictest sense of the word. But whatever we were, whatever was happening, felt good. Felt right.

My stomach knotted as I read the screen.

Hey. Just so you know, I've had some stuff come up at work and am super busy. I'm not going to be able to go out tonight. I'll text you, though. Maybe we can get together again in a few days.

Aaaannnnddddd…there went that thought.

"Not even friends, it seems." I bit my lip, typing in a quick, *Sure. Whatever works,* before pocketing my phone again. "I think he just blew me off."

Dahlia held a tea bag in her hand as she frowned in my direction. "Oh, well that sucks."

It did suck. It sucked hard. I'd actually gotten my hopes up and been excited about seeing him again. Stupid me. Shaking off my disappointment, I painted on a smile. "Forget him. Tell me more about your trip to Puerto Rico."

As expected, Dahlia's eyes lit up. "You know how we were there for leadership training and to film a promotional video for the franchises? Well, at the last minute, my boss—"

"The arrogant dickhead," I interrupted, having heard far too many stories about her boss not to.

"Exactly. So, the arrogant dickhead decides, as we're packing the van to take the videographer and team to the waterfall where we had arranged to film the video, that he'd rather shoot in some ancient, dilapidated building in Old San Juan. Without site prep or a permit. Without knowing *which* dilapidated building. So here I am, in my Pilates Bar gear, walking up and down dirty, tourist-ridden streets trying to find something suitable for his new vision and trying to appease the rest of the instructors by buying them rum drinks at a bar. I swear, if I had a flux capacitor, I'd go back to the day I met the arrogant dickhead and tell him to take his job offer and stuff it."

"And yet, you still work for Pilates Bar."

She shrugged. "I love Pilates and teaching students how to

achieve better body balance. I just hate the corporate crap I have to deal with—and my boss. The rest of my team is amazing, the instructors are all phenomenal, and the equipment I get to work out on every day is the best available. Even the marketing and recruiting stuff I do is a challenge I enjoy."

"When arrogant dickhead isn't involved."

"Precisely. It would be the perfect job if I didn't have to deal with him." She held up two mugs, nodding toward the family room. "Come. Let's have some tea."

We ended up sitting across from each other, both trying not to make too much noise as Grandma slept on. Dahlia set the mugs on the table along with a full teapot and settled into the cushions. I didn't really like to drink most teas, but I had to admit the cup felt good in my hands. Warm and solid, reassuring in a way. A reminder of my past. Dahlia had always made a pot of tea and given me a cup when we talked, ever since we were children. That had been her thing. When she'd admitted her first kiss had been with Wyatt Bearn, it had been over a cup of white tea. When I'd told her Jace and I were dating, there'd been green tea. And when I'd admitted to her what had happened with the video, I'd cried into a cup of Lady Grey. Tea and Dahlia went together. Always.

"How is she?" Dahlia leaned forward, teacup in hand and bright eyes locked on mine. Completely focused on me.

"Good. She's—" I cut myself off. That automatic response wasn't what I needed to say. Dahlia deserved more truth. "Well, as good as we could hope. She sleeps a lot and can't do too much right now because of the nausea, but Mary's gotten her out to a few events, and we go for daily walks together. It could be so much worse."

Dahlia nodded and took a sip of her tea before sighing, giving me a serious look that had my back stiffening. "And how is it being home?"

I really hated that word. "This isn't home to me anymore."

"Sure it is. This place is home to both of us, and you know it.

You can run as far as you want, but the family roots grow deep in this area." She pointed a finger my way. "Your roots."

"My roots must have been severed in a storm or something." I sat back, clutching my teacup. "I never feel comfortable here."

"That's because you refuse to claim your place and demand people accept you."

"No one's going to accept me. Not after what I did."

Dahlia sighed. "Why don't you go see Jace already? I'll even help you beat his ass so you can get some closure on that whole debacle."

As if that was an option. "What's done is done. There's no sense digging up something that's buried in the past."

"Is it buried, though? Because that particular zombie seems to keep running amok in your life. Maybe it's time to break out a shovel and cut its head off once and for all."

"Like you're such an expert at ending things and moving on, right? Who's Wyatt playing hockey for now?"

Dahlia flinched and turned away. Obviously hurt, which hadn't been my intention. Her history with Wyatt Bearn—and his twin Colton, by proxy—was long and complicated, something not easy to move on from. Something impossible to forget. Considering my own past, I had no right to throw even the hint of that in her face.

"I'm sorry," I murmured. "It's been really stressful here, and I'm on edge. I shouldn't have said that."

"No, I get it. And you're right, I'm not the poster child for perfect relationships. I've also never done what you have, so I can't speak to how I'd handle it all. But that doesn't mean I'm not right about you needing closure. God knows I keep searching for it."

I swallowed back the sick feeling her words brought out of me. This was where Dahlia and I always differed. She'd never done the things I'd done, never would. I was the perpetrator, and she was the victim, which set us up for clashes on too many things. But ten years of arguing hadn't given us any answers, and neither would one more round.

"Maybe someday we'll both find it."

"If we're lucky, I guess." She stood, looking exhausted all of a sudden. "Traveling today wore me out. I think I'm going to unpack. Maybe take a nap while Grandma's sleeping."

"I need to run to the pharmacy to pick up a few things. You'll listen for her?"

"Yeah, of course. Two's better than one, right?" She hugged me, clinging tight. "It really is good to see you, cuz. I'll never stop fighting for you to come home because I miss you so much when you're gone."

"I know. And I've missed you too." I squeezed my eyes shut tight and held on to her, wishing there was some other way for us. Wishing for a rewind button or a chance at a do-over.

Wishing for things I could never have.

"I *am* sorry for everything," I whispered. "I never doubted for a second that what I did to Jace was wrong."

Dahlia held me tighter. "I know, and you need to stop beating yourself up about it. We all make mistakes."

Not her, though. Wyatt had, Colton definitely had, but Dahlia had stayed strong and true. Had never faltered. And had gotten nothing but heartbreak for her loyalty. I slumped against the counter as she walked away, my head hanging and my chest tight. We all made mistakes...but the cost of mine seemed so much steeper than others around me.

My phone dinged with another text. One that didn't make me run this time. One that didn't make my heart flip even when I saw it was from Easton.

Well, not flip nearly as hard as before, at least.

My sister says that text sounded like a blow-off. That's not the case at all, okay? My workload is insane right now. Otherwise,

I'd be there. I'm looking forward to the next time you assault me with non-organic produce.

My smile was unstoppable, the way my heart sped up unavoidable.

You're on—just don't wait too long.

Is this like that Cinderella story? You have a midnight curfew?

Not tonight, I don't.

It took a minute for him to respond, but the wait was worth it.

If I had more than five minutes to myself, I'd make sure you used that time well. Sadly, I don't. In fact, I need to get back to it. Text me later?

I grabbed my keys and headed for the door, silly grin firmly in place.

Absolutely.

CHAPTER TEN

VIOLET

One text led to twelve, twelve led to fifty, and the next thing I knew, we'd chatted all day every day, back and forth for three solid days. Normal chats about our days and what was happening. Deeper chats about our feelings on politics and world events. Books and movies were covered the second day, while music took center stage the evening of the first. Our texting was get-to-know-you time in the form of written words instead of spoken ones. And it was amazing.

All those texts led me to an understanding of how busy Easton was at the shop, how determined he was to make his mark as a businessman. Admirable traits for sure, if only he weren't working so hard for it all. I had a feeling the way his dad had left the family without a safety net had a lot to do with his ambition, but that would be just a guess. One I wouldn't want to pry and ask about.

Still, the conversation was good, the pings and vibrations distracting me from the worries and stress of Grandma's care.

And when Easton sent a note asking if we could finally have our dinner date, I was more than happy to say yes.

Time for some in-person communicating once more.

I spent the afternoon running errands for Grandma. Ones that certainly didn't seem necessary but that she asked me to do. All the while, I questioned her motives. It was if she was purposely trying to force me back into the neighborhood. Butcher shop, produce stand, dry cleaner—I saw more people I knew in two hours than I had in the two weeks I'd been back. Plus, I had to run to the mall to buy a pair of sandals for my date. All the peopling exhausted me and made me want to become a hermit once more.

By the time Easton knocked on the front door to pick me up, I was feeling particularly antisocial. The running around town had taken its toll, and I'd reverted to my introvert self. If I were back in Chicago, I'd have canceled my date and holed up in my living room wearing yoga pants and eating ice cream. No good could come from unassing a couch when you felt the way I did. But this wasn't Chicago, and my date wasn't with some random guy. This was Easton Cole, who'd once picked me up and taken me for pizza as my world had crashed down around me. Who had a smile and a sense of humor that made me feel truly happy for the first time in years. Who I didn't want to disappoint. So, I donned a sundress with bright flowers, painted my lips red, and made sure my dark hair hung in shiny waves.

But I missed the hell out of my yoga pants.

When I opened the front door, my jaw almost dropped. All thoughts of yoga pants and ice cream flew right out the window. Easton stood on the front porch in dark dress pants and a long-sleeved, button-up shirt. His hair was brushed back, his dark waves contained in a way I'd never seen. And he smelled so darn good. The man on the porch was decidedly not my friend. Not even close. He wasn't even trying to tone down his hotness. The bastard.

"Hi," he said, eyeing me with a small smile. "You look amazing."

I fingered the hem of my sundress, my heart practically fluttering. The look on his face was worth unassing my couch for. "I don't look nearly as good as you."

"I'll argue that to my last breath."

"Smooth talker." I grinned. This man and his charm were going to be the death of me. "C'mon in. I need to say goodnight to Grandma, if you don't mind."

"Of course." He stepped inside, bending to kiss my cheek as he passed. The moment his lips touched my skin, I swear my heart swooned. He was such a contradiction. So strong but sweet, so masculine and yet so soft when he handled me. An attractive mix for sure.

I led him into the family room, excitement making me want to skip or jump or…do naughty things to the man behind me. But all that would have to wait. "I'm going, Grandma."

"Okay, baby," she said, looking up from her crossword. "You two have fun now."

"I'll have my phone if you need me, and Mary said she'd stop by after bingo to check on you. Dahlia should be home by ten from the gym."

She rolled her eyes. "Do you believe this, Easton? My granddaughter thinks she can't leave me alone for a few hours."

"We're just worried about you, Ms. Foster," Easton said, smiling and being just as charming as I'd learned he could be.

Grandma snorted, not buying his brand of attention for a second. "A real Romeo, this one. Go on now, kids. Get out of here and leave this old woman in peace."

"Yes, ma'am." Easton grabbed my hand but didn't pull. Waiting for me to make the move to leave.

"Okay," I whispered.

"Oh, Ms. Foster?" he called before we made it to the living room. "Colton's going to come by to check on the car tonight."

"Why? Is something wrong with my Betsy again?" Because every car she'd ever driven had been named Betsy.

Easton met my eyes, a knowing look in his. "No, ma'am. He just wants to check on the radiator we installed. Make sure none of the hoses have come loose with any driving you've been doing. He'll probably come to the door when he gets here, just to let you know he'll be outside. Smack him upside the head if he's not as polite as he should be."

"Well, that's something to look forward to."

Easton winked at me then led me back through the house and out the door. As soon as we were outside, I stopped him with a hand to his chest. I rose onto the balls of my feet, peering up at him, stretching to press my lips to the corner of his mouth.

"Thank you."

Easton squeezed my hip, brushing his lips against mine before pulling away. "I figured you'd be worried."

"I would have been." I grabbed his hand, letting him lead me down the driveway once more. "You're very thoughtful."

"Nah, I just want your undivided attention for the night," he said with a smile. The charmer back again, totally making me fall for him. Easton helped me up and into his beast of a truck, then hurried around to the other side. "I'm sorry I brought the truck. I grabbed the wrong keys and didn't think about it until I was already on the road over."

I ran a finger along the dash. The old-style bench seat seemed massive, and the open floorboard with nothing between us left a lot of options should the time ever come. I used to dream about this truck, about Easton kneeling on that floorboard and pressing his upper body against mine. About being on my knees in front of him and teasing him with my tongue. The basics of the interior design of the old beast had led to a ton of teenage fantasies.

"I love this truck," I murmured, stretching a hand across the edge of the bench seat.

Easton seemed surprised. "You do?"

"Yeah. It fits you. Way more than some fast car." I looked him over, from the top of his head to where his shoes rested on the pedals. "You don't seem like a sports car kind of guy."

He grinned and shook his head. "I am, but for daily driving, I prefer this old thing."

"So do I."

"Noted." He started the engine with ease and backed out of the driveway, heading north once he reached the main road. *Time to go on our not-so-much-friends-anymore date.*

EASTON

"And there were strawberries and chocolate everywhere. It took me hours to get it all out of my hair."

I held my hand up, trying my damnedest not to roll out of my chair from laughing. Violet's stories from the different restaurants she'd worked at were hilarious, and she'd been telling me a doozy about a broken food processor and an angry pastry chef for the past ten minutes. Eyes bright, hands flying, she was animated and alive and present. Completely with me in the moment. It was an amazing sight.

"Sounds like you love what you do even when things go wrong."

She smiled, a sweet, pure expression I wanted to see more of. "I do. I'm comfortable in a restaurant or bakery. It feels right. I assume you feel the same way in your shop."

"Yeah, I do. It's where I belong." I grabbed my wine and took a sip, trying to ignore the way my cell phone buzzed in my pocket. A distraction I refused to give in to.

"I think it's awesome that you built a business with your friends. That has to be such a benefit, knowing those two have your back."

I stared into my glass, swirling the dark liquid slowly. "I never really thought of it like that, but yeah. They'd never let me down."

"You're lucky."

"I am." Another buzz. There was no ignoring the darn thing any longer. Not with Colton scheduled to meet Violet's grandmother and with Brogan dealing with a few things at the shop for me. Either one could need me.

Before I could say more, the waiter approached. "Anything else I can get for you?"

Violet sat back, smiling up at the man. "Not for me. But that custard tart was amazing, and the texture was absolutely perfect. Please give my compliments to your pastry chef."

The waiter smiled in a way I'd seen before when people interacted with Violet—true and vibrant. He saw how genuine she was, how kind. And he liked it. As did I. "I certainly will, miss. Thank you for the warm compliment."

He handed me a black folio and walked away, leaving Violet and me alone once more. Alone with my phone going off over and over again.

Violet glanced at the folio. "I can—"

"Don't," I interrupted, shaking my head. "I invited you out tonight, so I've got this."

"Friends can split checks."

"Friends can treat each other to dinner now and again, too."

She sat back and smiled. "Seems like you're always buying me food."

"You can make me those cereal bars, and we'll call it even."

Her eyes narrowed, but her lips were caught trying to rise into a smile. Finally, she huffed as if it was such a hardship. "We'll see."

"I'm actually surprised you haven't made them yet. I figured you'd be baking up a storm with all the time on your hands."

Her smile dimmed, and she tangled her fingers in her napkin. "I haven't really felt much like baking lately. But I will...soon."

"I'm sure you will." I leaned across the table and pressed a soft kiss to her lips, unable to resist a moment more. "Thank you for coming out with me."

"Thank you for asking me."

There were so many things I wanted to say, but the incessant vibration of my phone in my pocket distracted me from just about everything. I needed to check it. Otherwise, I'd never be able to relax.

"While he swipes this, I'm going to run to the restroom." I slid my card into the slot and motioned to the waiter when he caught my eye. Two minutes, and I'd know if we needed to go back.

As soon as I was out of sight, I pulled my phone from my pocket.

Ten text messages, all Colton.

The Eagle has landed.

The Owl is well, no signs of mice in the nest.

She's making me lemonade!

Damn, man, this stuff is out of this world. I may never leave.

The Owl wants to play something called Rummikub. I see myself being here awhile.

She smoked my ass at the game.

I refuse to admit how badly I lost the second game.

Shit shit shit...Dahlia just pulled up. This is about to get interesting.

Pretty sure that girl has my balls tucked inside her purse. Think you can get Violet to convince her to give them back?

*The Owl is safe and warm in her nest with her owlet, and my
balls are still missing. This Eagle is out.*

I chuckled and hit the call button. Colton answered on the
first ring, already in smartass mode. "If you're phoning *me* from
your night with Violet, you're doing dating wrong."

"Fucker. You had me panicking at the table with all those
messages."

"Just keeping you in the loop, boss man."

The things I owed him and Brogan for watching out for me
were endless. "Thank you. I mean that."

In a rare moment of seriousness, Colton simply replied,
"You're welcome. It was a surprisingly fun night."

"Okay. We've got a shit-ton of work at the shop tomorrow, so
make sure you're ready for a long day."

"You know, maybe you should think about taking a few days
off. Take your girl on a little up-north adventure. You can use my
cabin."

As good as that idea sounded, I knew it wouldn't work. Not
with the backlog of work at the shop and Violet needing to take
care of her grandma. Still, it was something I had to remember. A
weekend in the woods and on the water with Violet sounded a bit
like heaven. "She's not my girl, not really. Besides, she's here for
her grandma. I doubt she'd be willing to leave for a weekend."

"Ask her. Whisk her away for a few days of debauchery, and
then convince her to move home. I may need her to run
interference with Dahlia for the rest of my life."

"That bad?"

"No balls, man. Gone. Missing." Colton chuckled. "Pretty sure
she snagged them with her claws at some point during the verbal
beatdown."

I grimaced. "Ouch. Your brother owes you big-time."

"Yeah, tell me about it. So I sort of need Miss Violet to help me out here. Maybe if she moved home, she could talk her cousin into not trying to kill me every time we see each other."

"Right, like she'll just leave her life behind and come back here with all the shit people put her through."

"She's got family here, East. Everyone needs family around them, even if it's the kind you pick instead of the one you're born into." When Colton got serious and started spouting off, his words were the kind that hit you right in the gut and warmed you with truth. But that never lasted long. "Too bad you picked me and Brogan. We're sort of the family you never wanted but got stuck with after other people got married. We're your weird Uncle Eddies."

"Shitter's full, Clark." I shook my head as he laughed. "I need to get back to Violet, but thank you again. I really appreciate you taking time to help me out."

"Anytime. You know that. I'm just glad you finally took some time off work. I'm pretty sure you haven't done anything for yourself in a few years."

A few. Maybe. "Yeah, well…we've been building the business."

"I know, but there's more to life than work. Like that hot piece of tail you're chasing. Take care of her, man."

"I will. Now, go have fun."

"You too, boss." He hung up without a salutation, not that I needed more words from him. The man was right. I needed to forget about work for a few hours and focus on Violet.

I pocketed my phone, took a quick trip to the restroom, and then strode back to the table. Violet caught my eye from halfway across the restaurant, lifting her chin and smiling. That look, that peaceful, happy expression, made my entire world seem to tilt. It was at that moment, as I weaved my way through the tables, that I knew.

She wasn't my girl yet, but she would be. I'd move heaven and earth to make sure of it. But first, I wanted to get her alone.

CHAPTER ELEVEN

VIOLET

When a man who looked like Easton Cole, who was as thoughtful and charming as him, asked you to go home with him for a drink and a movie, you didn't say no. Which was how we ended up heading to his side of town instead of mine after dinner.

"It's been years since I've been here, but it still looks the same." I stared out the window as he turned into his neighborhood. The trailer park looked exactly as I remembered it. Wide streets, lush, green lawns, and mobile homes spaced out along each road in a perfect angled pattern. And the flowers! I'd forgotten all the flower gardens decorating the park. So many patches of bright colors dancing in the breeze. The place might as well have been a work of art.

"Things don't change too much on this side of Van Horn, though I had no idea you'd ever been here."

"The soccer team came through every year for those fundraising tag sales. People here were always so nice."

"I forgot about those sales. I bet you came to my door a time or two."

Teenage me would have fumbled my speech if Easton had answered the door. Adult me wouldn't have done much better. "Could be."

"She'd probably remember." Easton waved at a curvy woman in a flowered halter top and jean shorts who stood in what I had to assume was her driveway. The lady smiled wide and bright, waving back.

"Friend of yours?"

"My mom." He laughed at my wide eyes. "You can meet her another day. She's probably hanging out with Mrs. Jeffers tonight. The two like to play poker."

"Your mom still lives in the park?"

Easton nodded, keeping his eyes on the road. "My sister too. Pretty sure most of the people in this park are original residents. Everyone sticks around and stays close to one another—we're all family. Well, other than Brogan and Colton. They're just burrs on my ass."

I laughed, distracted by the colorful patches outside the window. Each trailer had bright flowers in front of it, and whole gardens of annuals lined the sidewalks. Some trailers had toys in the yard, some had porches with rocking chairs or padded swings, but all of them looked cheerful and tidy. There was no sign of neglect, no trash or damaged homes. The place was as neat as a pin.

As we turned another corner, I caught sight of a couple dogs running around a fenced-in side yard. The two brown hounds raced the length of the chain link, practically smiling. A man stood at the gate, a bucket of some kind on his arm. He waved at Easton as we drove past, and Easton waved back.

"That's Colton's uncle, Dalton. He manages a scrapyard in the city. Finds me parts for some of the older models we get in now and again. He's also my ex-cousin by a marriage that ended a few years back."

"So…not really related."

"Exactly. But I liked him, so I kept him in the divorce and gave up seeing my actual cousin."

That was something you didn't hear every day. "Really?"

"Yeah. My cousin cheated on him, so we sort of took his side."

"Oh." The truck suddenly seemed too small, too warm. My gut twisted and burned, but as we drove farther into the park, the charm of the place distracted me from the dread slowly building around my heart. I watched the bright hues pass by, loving the way the reds, yellows, and oranges seemed to intermingle into a vibrant patchwork quilt. The walkways looked as if they were surrounded by rivers of fire, and the overall effect practically stunned me. How could I have forgotten those flowers? "I've never seen a neighborhood with so many flowers."

"That's old Mrs. Jeffers, the poker queen. She plants them along every street each year. Well, she used to. Now she sits in her wheelchair and tells us where to plant them. We had about fifteen guys planting pansies a few months back."

Be still my heart. "That's really considerate. Has anyone ever told you you're sweet, Easton Cole?"

"I do try, Miss Violet. I do try."

Easton swung his truck into a parking spot in front of a single-wide trailer with a screened-in front porch. My eyes took in every detail, devouring it in mere seconds. The trailer itself appeared unassuming—a simple deep-beige color with white trim and green shutters. Just like the others, it looked neat and tidy with pots of flowers lining the front and more along the sidewalks. And yet, that small, metal building practically terrified me for all the assumptions that would be made if I walked into it.

I took a deep breath and tried to keep my voice steady as I said, "I can't believe you still live here."

"Never saw any point in moving. I could have rented an apartment, but then I'd have to deal with sharing walls with strangers. At least out here, I have my own space. Plus, my mom and sister needed me. Old Mrs. Jeffers needed me. There was work to be done here, so I stayed."

He didn't move, didn't reach for the door. Instead, he waited as I stared out the window and tried to find my breath. This was a big step, coming home with Easton. There were implications and possibilities, even if we just sat on his couch chatting. Anyone who saw me get out of his truck would be talking about us tomorrow. Everyone here knew him, and most of them probably knew *of* me. They'd think the worst of what was about to happen…and they might just be right.

"Hey," he said, all quiet and soft. "There's no pressure here. We're just a couple of friends hanging out."

"I know that," I whispered.

His brow furrowed. "Then why are you sitting there staring at my trailer like it's the seventeenth level of hell and I'm about to toss your ass to the bees and stinging insects?"

"The stinging insects were in the vestibule, not one of the levels." I smiled as best I could, reaching for the door handle. "I read Dante in Humanities class, too, you know."

He grabbed my hand, stopping me from opening the door. "We can go somewhere else. I just thought it might be nice to get out of the crowds."

I shook my head and pushed open the door, refusing to let my nerves ruin our night. "This is fine. I'm just being silly."

"You sure?"

"Absolutely." I hopped out of the truck, careful not to hit Easton's black sports car in the neighboring spot.

Easton met me at the front of the truck and grabbed my hand. "It's not silly if it upsets you."

"I'm not upset."

"You sure? Because it didn't seem that way for a second there," he said as he opened the screen door for me.

"I'm sorry—I swear I'm okay with being here. I'd like to see where you live. I'm just worried about talk."

Easton hummed softly, an almost disgruntled sound. "Talk."

"Yeah, like the talk that'll happen when people see us together. When they realize who I am and remember…stuff about me." My mouth twisted into what had to be a grimace as I considered how bad that could be for him. "I'd hate for my reputation to mar your business. I know it's still relatively new."

Easton shook his head and opened the inside door for me, keeping his eyes on mine the whole time. "There's not a whole lot that can mar my reputation more than my own actions already have. Add in Colton's shenanigans, and I'm amazed anyone trusts us to *wash* their cars, let alone fix them. Yet they do, and that shouldn't be affected by who I choose to hang around with. Besides, people will talk no matter what. I, for one, refuse to let them make my choices for me."

"If you're sure."

He grabbed me around the waist, pulling me into a kiss that set my heart racing. Deep and searching, right there on his porch for all the world to see, he kissed me like he'd been waiting to kiss me for days. Months. Years. He kissed me like a man starving for a kiss. He kissed me like every woman deserved to be kissed. I melted, need and desire and blatant lust ablaze inside me. My entire body surrendering itself to his kiss.

"I'm sure about wanting to spend time with you," he murmured when he finally pulled his lips from mine.

"Not fair," I grumbled, licking my top lip. "That kiss was… totally not fair."

"Gotta play to my strengths." He placed a soft peck on my nose, then turned me around and patted my ass, encouraging me. I stepped inside his trailer but stopped dead in my tracks. It was so not what I expected. The floors were wood with what looked like a wool rug creating a separation between the walkway and the conversation area. And it was a conversation area—the couches faced each other, a chair the only piece of furniture turned toward the flat-screen television mounted over the bookcases along the wall. The furniture was definitely somewhat new, the lines clean and the colors tasteful. Very manly without being a bachelor pad. Almost elegant, in a modern sort of way.

"This is…" I started, not knowing how to finish. Holy cow, he even had art on the walls. Bright, colorful paintings that reminded me of his shop windows. Honest-to-God pictures of the not-dogs-playing-poker variety.

Easton chuckled. "Not what you expected?"

I shrugged, feeling somewhat like an idiot for being surprised. "Yeah. It's really nice. Surprisingly so."

"Just because I live in a trailer doesn't mean I'm trash."

The tone of his voice, the harshness there, had me spinning around to face him. "That's not at all what I meant. I was thinking more bachelor-pad-ugly than any kind of trashy. I swear."

Easton sighed, fighting to lift his lips into a smile. "I know, but that's what a lot of people assume, especially after my dad left and we had to go on state assistance until my mom and I were able to work enough to get our feet under us. People always remember that time, but they forget that we were like everyone else before he left. Plus, outsiders see mobile homes and think cheap, trashy, and crime-ridden."

They did. I remembered a lot of friends refusing to visit the park for the tag sales and talking about the people who lived there as if they were somehow less than the rest of us. "That's totally not what I thought. And there's no way anyone could look at your home and think cheap."

"I always did like to break convention." He walked into the open kitchen, turning on strategically placed lights as he went. "Can I get you something to drink? I don't have any pineapple juice, but I can make you something sweet if you like."

I grinned as I slid onto the barstool at the island, my fingers running across the stone top. "No thanks. I think I had enough wine at the restaurant."

Easton grabbed a beer from the refrigerator, then leaned

against the island directly across from me. "I hope you had a nice time."

"I did. The restaurant was beautiful, and my dinner was amazing."

"It's a bit of a drive, but that place has been a favorite of mine for years."

"I can see why."

Just then, an orange cat came running into the room with its tail in the air. Easton positively lit up as he bent to pick her up. "There's my girl."

"Oh, she's gorgeous."

He snuggled the kitty close, the two rubbing their faces together. "This is my Dolly. Dolly, meet Violet."

The cat eyed me from under her owner's chin, her cute little face almost hidden.

"Hey, Dolly." I was rewarded with a single tail flick. "Yup. She's a looker, all right."

"Yeah, she's a pretty one." He set the cat down, making short shushing sounds as she purred and wrapped herself around his legs. "She's also loud and likes to wake me up in the middle of the night by head-butting me."

"Sounds like a perfectly functional cat-human relationship."

He chuckled, watching as Dolly ran off for the other end of the trailer. "That's what people tell me." Easton took a drink of his beer, then came around the island and offered me a hand. "Come on. Let's go get comfortable."

And didn't that sentence sound so dirty as heard through my wine-and-kiss-addled mind? With only the slightest hesitation, I took his hand and followed him to one of the couches. My heart raced the whole time, my body almost overly warm. Easton was charming me right out of my anxiety this evening. From the way he'd opened doors and kept his hand on my back as we'd walked into the restaurant, to how he made sure everything with the meal was to my liking, he'd gone all out on the charming scale this evening. He'd been a true gentleman, and that fact made me want to rip off his clothes and see how ungentlemanly he could be.

"So," he said as he sat down and turned to face me. "We've done drinks—"

"And making out behind the ice rink."

Easton laughed all warm and deep. "Yes, completely unplanned but definitely not unwelcome."

I bit my lip as he inched closer. "Agreed."

His eyebrows rose just a bit. "Good to know. So, drinks and make-out time, and now dinner. Does that make this our first official date, our second, or maybe even our third?"

I pursed my lips, pretending to give his question some serious thought. "Second. Definitely."

"Perfect." He inched closer, setting his beer down as he leaned in.

"Why perfect?"

"Because there's no way I would do this on a first date, but a second seems okay." Easton leaned farther over me, practically pushing me back against the couch. My mouth went dry. He was going to kiss me. Right there on his couch with no one around to interrupt us. Did I want this? Did I dare throw caution to the wind and just do what my body wanted me to? There would be repercussions. There were always repercussions. I'd never had sex with someone who knew about my fallout, who I *knew* had seen the tape and been there to witness my crash and burn. Fuck, what if that was the reason he was hanging out with me? What if he just wanted a shot at Cowgirl Vee? What if—

Easton grabbed something from the table behind me and sat back. The space he left gave me room to breathe, gave me time to think.

"What are you doing?" I asked, nearly breathless.

He smiled and held up the remote. "You mentioned zombies the other night at the grocery store. I looked it up, and there're four movies streaming this month. Thought you might like to watch one."

Zombies. He remembered me talking about zombies after I'd hit him with non-organic produce. The man was lethal to my control.

My lips were on his before I could think, before I could tell myself to hold back. This man—this ridiculously handsome and generous man—had just surprised me in the best way. It wasn't often people remembered such inconsequential details, and even less likely that they'd take the time to make sure there were zombie movies available to watch before going on a date with me. We hadn't made plans to come back to his place. It had been a spur-of-the-moment decision. Or maybe it hadn't. Maybe Easton had hoped the night would end this way. Maybe he'd planned it.

Thank God he'd planned it.

Easton slid his hands right to my hips and pulled me close, manhandling me in a way that was both forceful and easy. A way that made my heart beat a little harder, a little faster. I moaned and deepened the kiss, needing more of him. Wanting so much. When the contact simply wasn't enough, I threw caution to the wind and my leg over his lap. Straddling him. Pressing myself against where he was already hard. Shivering at how needy I felt already.

His kiss became rougher, more urgent, even as his hands skated along my sides and up to my breasts in the gentlest way. The juxtaposition, the sweetness under the desire, had me desperate for more. Every roll of my hips brought another sigh, every time he nipped my bottom lip or sucked it between his teeth another groan. Soaking wet and practically panting, I arched into his touch, wishing for more, hoping he'd take the hint and—

"Yes, more," I said as he grabbed my breasts over my clothes. Heat and need exploded within me, my nipples tingling as he teased them with his thumb. I hadn't had a dry-hump session in years, hadn't remembered how good they could be. Easton hadn't even gotten his hands in my pants, and I was already so close. So wet for him. So ready to let go and just come.

I dropped my head onto his shoulder and rocked my hips, craving so much more. Desperate to just give in and get what I needed. Ready to give him things I probably shouldn't. Chasing that high I knew we both needed. Both craved.

With a sudden groan, Easton thrust up harder, lifting me with the strength behind the move. There was no denying how good that felt, how the move made goose bumps appear on my arms. Our bodies were completely connected, nothing but fabric in our way. He was hard and hot, pressing into where I was already so wet, so wanting. A shiver made its way up my spine as he rubbed against me in one long, slow press. So good, so much, so fucking wet. I dropped my head back and pressed my breasts into his hands, wanting more. Needing the feel of his hands on me, the sensation of his skin on mine, the pinch of his thumbs teasing my nipples again. He didn't disappoint. Easton took my position as an invitation and nuzzled into my neck, biting softly, still rocking his hips and making me want to scream. Want to cry. Want to tell him not to stop.

But when Dolly brushed against my leg and let out a loud meow, my brain and my body stopped working in tandem.

"Shit," Easton said, growling slightly, breaking his rhythm and looking over the edge of the couch toward the orange fluff ball. "Sorry—she can be a pest."

That pest sauntered to the couch across from us and hopped up, making herself comfortable. Watching me. Bringing the reality of the moment back into crystal-clear focus.

"Easton." I dropped my head to his shoulder, something dark and heavy forming in my gut. Something almost fear-like, but not quite. He didn't push me, though, didn't try to keep going. Instead, he edged back against the couch and slid his hands to my ribs.

"We can stop. I didn't bring you here for this."

His whispers made me shiver. His voice so deep, so rough on

my ears. I shook my head because my body didn't want him to stop, but my thoughts had already scattered, and my brain would win this one. "I know. And it's not that I don't want you, because I do. So badly. I'm just not quite ready for—"

His lips found mine again, a soft kiss that made me sigh and sink into him.

"No explanation needed," he whispered, letting his hands wander along my sides and over my chest. He teased me through the fabric, rubbing gently over my nipples on each pass. Seemingly unable to stop, not that I tried to pull away or anything. "Though you're going to have to climb off my lap if you want me to actually be able to think."

I laughed, my face warm as I kissed him one more time. "Understood."

But we didn't untangle from one another. Instead, I stayed in his lap, kissing him with soft presses of my lips to his. He continued to tease and torment my breasts, rubbing and squeezing and pinching in a way that made me need once more. That brought about a slower heat this time, a campfire as compared to an inferno.

"I thought we were stopping," I finally said, giving his bottom lip a nip for good measure.

He made a sound like a growl and pulled his hands from my breasts, the move slow. Almost reluctant. "We are. I promise."

I giggled and rolled across his lap one more time. "Okay. Done."

"Tease." He grinned as he sat back against the couch, working his way into the corner with a remote in hand. "Come here."

I crawled in between his legs, leaning into his chest when I fell along him. With little more than a couple of wiggles, I found the perfect nook to snuggle against, the perfect spot along his muscled chest to lay my head and relax. Even Dolly seemed to agree as she hurried over to join us on the couch.

"Thanks," I whispered to him as I stroked the orange fur of his cat.

He leaned down and kissed the top of my head before clicking through the different menus on the screen. "For what?"

"For being you." I pointed to a picture as it came up on the TV. "I've heard good things about that one but haven't had the time to watch it. Have you ever seen it?"

"Nope. But tonight seems like a good night to give it a shot."

"A first for both of us." I curled deeper into his embrace as the movie began to play, Dolly a warm, soft weight against me.

Easton wrapped his arms around me, reaching down to rub Dolly's head. "Sounds perfect."

VIOLET

"Get out, Violet." Grandma heaved again, her entire body tensing with the strain of trying to empty her stomach when there was nothing left.

"Not happening. You held my hair back a time or two when I was sick. It's my turn." I pressed the wet washcloth to the back of her neck and bit back my instinctual response to empty my own stomach.

Grandma's entire body sagged. Again. "Violet, please."

"No," I snapped, rubbing her back to soothe my harsh tone. "I'm not leaving you alone right now, so you just concentrate on trying to feel better."

"This isn't how I wanted to spend my Thursday night."

"I know, but this is what we have to deal with. It'll pass." I handed her a glass of water, praying like hell she could keep the liquid down. She took it without argument, sipping delicately until the water was halfway gone. Four ounces, maybe. Not great, but better than nothing. I had to keep her hydrated. That was what the nurse had said when this bout of vomiting had gotten so much worse than all the days before.

Grandma moaned as she handed me back the glass. "You shouldn't have to take care of me."

"You'd do it for me."

She turned her head, watery green eyes meeting mine. "Yeah, I would."

And she had. Numerous times. This was nothing in return. "Then we're even."

A knock at the door made my own stomach plummet, and a look to my phone screen to check the time had me cursing. Dahlia had booked a private lesson over an hour away, so it was just Grandma and me. I'd planned to go out with Easton tonight anyway since my grandma seemed to be doing okay, but then she'd gotten sick. And she'd stayed sick all evening, which pretty much killed any plans I'd had for leaving. Too bad I'd forgotten to tell the person I had plans *with*.

The doorbell rang a second time before I could even figure out how to handle the mess.

"Just go, Violet." Grandma waved her hand as she started taking deep breaths, obviously still feeling sick.

"And leave you here to puke all alone? Never."

She chuckled, sounding almost exhausted. "Masochist!"

"Totally," I whispered as I headed for the front door, wondering how much Easton was going to be mad at me for canceling our date so late. I should have called or texted, but I'd been hoping since the first moment Grandma had started throwing up that she'd magically feel better. Now he was here, on my porch, and there was no way we were going out. I couldn't leave her alone like this.

Easton smiled when I opened the door, but his brow furrowed as he looked me over. "Interesting outfit choice."

I rolled my eyes and stepped back to let him in, tugging at the torn, ten-year-old concert tank I wore over my yoga capris. "What? You mean dinner wasn't someplace casual?"

He raised his eyebrows, not needing to say a word. And I... Well, I felt worse than I probably looked. *He* looked good. Better than good. Dressed up, cleaned up, still a little dirty in all the right ways good. Way better than just friends should be. My libido was going to kick my butt when I told him he had to go home alone.

But Grandma dumped cold water right over any thought of how good Easton looked. "Violet? I'm tired."

I moved without thought, forgetting Easton and hurrying toward the weak voice coming from the hallway.

"Let me help you." I grabbed Grandma's arm, holding her up. Shit, she felt so small, so cold.

"I'm sure Dahlia will be back soon. Why don't you—"

I groaned as her eyes became unfocused, as her face went pale, then green. Holding her up, I tried to hurry her back into the bathroom, but it was too late. The water she'd drunk ended up all over the wood floor, splattering the walls and her housecoat. I hopped back a step to miss being hit, not that it did much good.

"I'm sorry," she said as she coughed. "I'm so sorry."

"Don't be sorry. I just want you to feel better." I pulled her toward the bathroom, doing my best not to step in the sick. Even managing to holler over my shoulder, "Easton, I can't go out tonight. I'm sorry. I'll call you tomorrow."

I shut the bathroom door behind us and helped Grandma back to the floor.

"No," she said, her voice weak. "You should go."

"Not happening."

"Vi—"

"Not happening. Next subject."

She sighed. "God, you're stubborn."

I smiled, remembering all the times she'd called me that over the years. Remembering how Easton had called me the same.

"Yeah, because you taught me how to be. So, buck up, lady. We're in this together tonight."

Fifteen minutes and two bouts of dry heaving later, I finally walked out of the bathroom with my arm firmly wrapped around her waist.

Easton stepped into the hallway from the opposite end. "Everything okay, ladies?"

If my face didn't let him know how shocked I was to see him, I was sure my words did. "What are you doing here?"

He shrugged. "I thought I could help."

I gaped at him. I hadn't expected him to stay, especially after he'd watched Grandma throw up all over the floor. But he had, which left me with a conundrum—I had no idea what to say to him. I simply stood there and stared until Grandma squeezed my arm.

"Violet, honey, help me to bed. I'm really tired."

"Of course." I jumped and turned her toward her door.

Before I could walk her to her room, Easton stepped in, holding my gaze as he reached slowly for Grandma's arm. "I can help you, Ms. Foster."

"That'd be nice, Easton." Grandma patted his arm, her head bowed and her voice quiet. "I'm a little too tired tonight to do much more than shuffle."

I let Easton lead her down the hall. A handful of steps in, Grandma slumped, her knees buckling. Like some sort of superhero, Easton swooped in and picked her up, carrying her the rest of the way with ease.

"Which room?" he asked when he came to the three doors at the end of the hall.

"On the right."

He walked purposefully into Grandma's room and waited by the side of the bed. I rushed behind him, turning down the covers as quickly as I could. There was such care in his hold on her, such concern on his face. If I hadn't been so worried about her not feeling well, I probably would have had a serious case of the swoons. But vomit and fear really didn't make for a romantic moment.

Once we had Grandma situated, Easton followed me back down the hallway toward the living room. "Think she'll be okay?"

"I hope so."

"Is it the chemo, or something else?"

"Chemo. It's…horrible."

Easton stopped me, tugged on my elbow until I turned his way, and then kept tugging. "I'm sorry, Violet. That can't be easy to watch."

I curled into his arms, needing him more than I was ready to admit. Relishing the comfort his embrace offered. I'd felt so alone dealing with Grandma being sick. He'd saved me from that. Without being asked. "I can't believe you stayed."

"You looked like you needed some help." He pulled me closer, surrounding me with his warmth and his scent, giving me my first chance to relax in hours.

As he rocked me slightly from side to side, I caught a glimpse of the spot where, not long before, Grandma had gotten sick in the hall. My heart swelled and my eyes burned with tears I wouldn't let fall. I had to pull out of his hold, to move away from him, before I lost control and sobbed.

"You cleaned up."

"Seemed like the right thing to do," he said, reaching to run a hand over his neck. Making me realize he was no longer wearing the nice dress shirt he'd arrived in, just a white T-shirt he must have had underneath it. Still gorgeous, still looking like my hero for the night. Maybe even more so.

"Thank you." I rose onto the balls of my feet to place a kiss on his cheek.

His hand landed on my hip, soft, not holding me in place. Just touching. "You're welcome."

We stood that way for a few long, comforting minutes. Not

speaking, simply existing in the same space. And it was exactly what I needed to settle down from the anxious hours I'd spent taking care of my grandma. I didn't want flowery declarations or promises thrown my way. Easton had supported me with his actions, not his words. Something that I'd never realized was so special and rare until that moment.

But all good things had to come to an end...especially when you smelled like vomit. "I should probably grab a bucket or something for her, just in case."

"Yeah, sounds good." He frowned. "I can throw the towels I cleaned with in the wash."

"That'd probably be best. C'mon, everything's in the basement."

Easton helped me collect buckets, toss the towels into the washer, and get a glass of water for Grandma, then followed me back to her room.

"I'm sorry I ruined your night," she mumbled as I set everything around her so she wouldn't have to get out of bed.

"Stop apologizing. You didn't ruin anything. Right, Easton?"

"No, ma'am. Not a thing."

"Nice boy," Grandma mumbled. "Much better choice than that asshole Jace."

I chanced a glance at the man himself, fighting back a smile. Easton was very focused on the floor, refusing to look my way. At some point, we were going to have to talk about my past. The very thought made my stomach flip, though. I'd have to tell him about...everything. Jace, the video, college, the jobs, the men. No way did I want to have to do that. Easton would never look at me the same. He *was* a nice boy, and I...

I was Cowgirl Vee. And unfortunately, I always would be. But tonight wasn't the time, and this wasn't the place.

"So," Easton said once we were back in the living room, leaning against the wall in some sort of super sexy and yet casually cool pose. How did he pull that off?

"So." I rocked on my heels, likely looking less cool and definitely not sexy. "I really need to take a shower."

His eyes darted down. Taking me in. I couldn't even imagine what he saw. Raggedy tank top, no bra, black yoga tights, vomit on my feet. I was most certainly a mess.

"Yeah, uh. I can see that." But then he smiled. "Though if you wanted to put that shirt back on, I wouldn't object."

I glanced down, surprised. This old shirt was so thin, so threadbare. But it was a favorite. "Why do you—" And then I saw the way my nipples were silhouetted under the fabric, the hard peaks trying to poke through, surrounded by the shadow of the darker skin around them. I crossed my arms and gave him the closest thing to a glare I could imagine. "Are you trying to sneak a peek at my breasts? That's not very friend-like."

"There's no sneaking, really. They're right—" he pointed and circled his finger "—there for all the world to see."

I faked a solid glower. "Bastard."

"I can't help but stare. You're the most beautiful woman I've ever seen."

My breath caught. Who talked like that? Especially to someone with vomit on their feet? Easton did, of course. And I was helpless against his charm. A fact that was becoming more and more apparent with every second we spent together. This was dangerous territory—an introduction into a space of feeling and emotion. And though my head was screaming at me to back up, to run away, the rest of me wasn't so sure if that was the best idea.

And for once, I told my mind to shut up for a few hours. "Would you like to stay for a while?"

He grinned all slow and sly. "Really?"

"Yeah. I mean, I'm not inviting you into the shower with me, but we could hang out once I'm done. If you'd like." I wanted him to stay, wanted to spend more time with him. That thought was scary and made my stomach drop as if I were on a roller coaster, but it was honest. Terrifying, but honest.

"I'd like very much." Easton pulled me into his arms, wrapping me in a hug and pressing his lips to my forehead. "Go wash up and put some clothes on. I'll order us a pizza."

"Okay. Thanks." I stayed still, though. Stayed close to him. I wasn't ready to let go just yet. "I'm sorry I ruined—"

He placed a finger over my lips, the warmth of his skin sending a single shiver up my back. "You ruined nothing. Family comes first. Now, go. I want you cleaned and…at least partially dressed in ten minutes."

"Yes, sir," I said with a laugh. "I'll put on my best yoga pants."

As I hurried down the hall, I was pretty sure I heard him mutter a "sinful ass" comment. Not that I minded.

EASTON

I was on the couch, television remote in hand, when Violet walked into the family room. My heart fucking skipped, and my breath tried to freeze right there in my throat. How did that girl do this to me? Make me feel like a kid again, like the luckiest bastard just to be allowed to be near her? There was no denying it. I was a goner.

"Hey," she said quietly, her voice soft. Awkward, almost. That wouldn't do.

"Hey yourself. I ordered the pizza. Pepperoni and olive, right?"

She stared, eyes locked on mine. Good God, my heart and my dick were both far too responsive to her every expression, her every breath. Her every look. I had to get myself under control, but she was even more beautiful like this. Hair wet and hanging down, no makeup on her face, looking young and perfect. So much more *her*. That hate gurgling within me for what Jace and his stupid fucking video had done to her burned hotter, brighter. He'd hurt her, had sat back and watched her crumble. But I'd help her put herself back together...if she let me.

"How do you remember that?" she asked, all soft and breathy.

And wasn't that the question of the hour? How did I remember so much about that night? How could I not? Seeing her shadow through the pouring rain as she'd trudged home, the way her hair had lain soaking wet and dripping just like now, how I hadn't been able to stand the thought of letting her out of my sight when she'd seemed so broken, so hopeless. So the opposite of what I'd always known her to be. We hadn't even spoken through high school, had never really had a reason to, but that night, I'd taken her for pizza and had given her a chance to dry off before dropping her at this very house. And it was one of the most vivid memories I had outside of the ones of my family.

"I remember everything about that night, Violet," I whispered, giving her my full truth. I stood, approaching her slowly, afraid of scaring her off. My mind kept circling around the past, which meant I needed to take that step. Needed to know. "But I don't *know* everything about it. What happened with that video?"

Her hands shook as she pulled a lock of hair away from her face, her eyes not meeting mine. "What you expect happened. I had sex in a place with cameras. It was filmed, and the video got out."

Blunt. On the offensive. Hiding. That wouldn't do. "You forget that I picked you up from the side of the road in the pouring rain."

Her eyes met mine, glaring, pain-filled. "I forget nothing."

I nearly took a step back. That expression, the anger and the hurt, it wrecked me inside. Jesus fuck, what had Jace done to her? "Then explain it to me. You had sex, no big deal. But something else happened to make you attempt to walk home in a downpour. Something that hurt you. The idea that I didn't do more to help you has haunted me for years."

She huffed a disbelieving breath and shook her head. "You've seen the video, I assume?"

Fucking Colton. I wouldn't have seen the infamous video, had refused to watch it after that night, but he'd brought it over. He'd played it, and I'd sat rapt by every frame. By her. She'd been so fucking gorgeous, I'd barely been able to blink. "Yeah. Once."

A sarcastic laugh escaped her lips. "Once. Wouldn't it be nice if everyone had only seen it once?"

The look on her face as she implied I'd watched that clip more than I admitted was one I knew would haunt me forever. She didn't believe me, whether it was because she didn't trust *me* or she just didn't trust, I couldn't tell.

"Violet—"

The doorbell rang before I could finish my sentence. I breathed a curse, but Violet relaxed, almost seeming to welcome the interruption.

"Must be the pizza," she said. Her voice was calm, no longer angry. Relieved, really. As much as I hated giving in, perhaps bypassing the conversation for the moment was best. I'd come at her too hard, obviously. If I wanted her to tell me anything about that time, I was going to have to change my tactics.

"I'll get it, and then we can ignore the fact that I started this conversation and get back to talking about which vegetables would make the best weapons during a zombie apocalypse."

She nodded, but her eyes were trained on the floor.

I lifted her chin with one finger and angled my head to finally meet her gaze. "I'm sorry I brought it up. They're your secrets, and I shouldn't have tried to make you tell me them. I just…I want to know you, Violet Foster. Everything."

After a quick kiss to the cheek, I hurried to the door. She needed a moment to collect herself, and I needed one to get my head on straight. The topic of Jace and the video were off-limits. For now, at least. Hopefully we'd be able to talk about it eventually, but I had my doubts. Violet wasn't the face-your-demons type. She'd run from her past, just like she mentally ran from our conversation about it. And the last thing I wanted was to make her run.

Once I'd paid for the two pies, I met Violet in the kitchen.

She'd laid out paper plates, napkins, and a couple of jars of spices and Parmesan cheese. I eyed her hard, searching for signs of distress and nearly sighing when I didn't see any. She looked calm, which both eased my mind and sent my stomach plummeting. She wasn't dealing…she was hiding. Again.

"Two?" she asked, her brow drawn down as she took in the boxes in my hands.

I pushed aside my worries, wanting to enjoy my evening with her. Even if it was borrowed time. "One for me, one for you."

"I won't eat a whole pizza."

I shrugged. "Leftovers. Besides, I can't eat green olives on my pizza."

"You could have just bought one. I don't need my own just because I like a particular thing."

I leaned down, pressing my lips against hers for the briefest of kisses. "You're worth an extra pizza."

Her cheeks darkened, her blush spreading in a way that made my dick sit up and take notice. Damn, this girl was something else. Innocence and pure sexual energy combined with a fragility that made my inner caveman exclaim *mine.* I wanted to fuck her and protect her, an odd sort of combination at times. But it was time to eat, not to throw her up on the counter and crawl between her legs, no matter how much that was what I would rather do.

Plates and drinks in hand, I followed her into the family room where we set up a mini picnic on the coffee table. Those tights she wore pulled across her firm ass as she bent to set napkins next to our plates. I almost got caught staring, but I focused on the pizzas when she turned around.

"Movie or TV?" I asked, refusing to even glance at her. *Don't look at her ass. Don't look at her ass.*

Thankfully, she sat down on the floor, removing the temptation. "Whatever."

"I didn't see any zombie shows or movies on, so hopefully nostalgia will win out." I turned on an older movie, one of those teen flicks from the eighties. All I remembered was some guy and a duck, I think. Or maybe he was named Duck. Wait, wasn't there something about a name and a major appliance? Shit, I had no clue, but the main actress was a redhead. Violet had once been a redhead, though her hair hadn't been as bright. Still...the look appealed.

After a dinner filled with mocking comments about the movie, we moved to the couch. For the longest time, we sat stiffly beside one another, not talking, simply staring at the screen before us. Awkward and totally not right. Not enough. I had to change the vibe between us.

Feeling just like I had on some of my first dates as a kid, just as nervous and afraid of failure, I stretched and dropped my arm around her shoulders. Thankful when she didn't shrug me off. Once I had a hold of her, Violet snuggled into my side and sighed. *Jackpot.*

But then she looked up at me with a mischievous expression. "While I haven't dealt with the old stretch-and-grab since I was a teenager, I have to admit that was utterly smooth."

Busted. Not that I minded. "I try, though that move only has a seventy-five percent success rate. It was a risk."

"It paid off."

And just like that, the awkward tension dissipated, leaving behind something warmer and subtler. I ran my fingers up her arm as she leaned into me, liking the way her skin felt. Liking the way *she* felt. She shifted closer, head on my shoulder, dropping her hand to my knee. Killing me with one simple touch. Setting me on fire when that hand moved up my thigh. Way up.

I was in so much trouble.

CHAPTER FOURTEEN

I was in so much trouble.

Easton was never supposed to get under my skin like he had. I wasn't supposed to start falling for him. Wasn't supposed to want to touch him the way I did. But that innate sweetness about him—that kindness buried under his rough-around-the-edges exterior—was irresistible. It drove me crazy. I wanted him, and I wasn't willing to back off.

Testing the waters, so to speak, I moved my hand back and forth. A simple, subtle rub. Barely anything, at least not to me. But Easton's thigh tensed, the muscles bunching beneath my fingertips. Jesus, the man was just so solid. My touch obviously meant something to him.

Emboldened by his responsiveness, I rubbed more, but with wider, longer strokes, pressing harder on each pass. Easton coughed, slipping down in his seat a bit, his knees spreading. Giving me more room, it seemed. I bit back a smile and pretended to watch the TV as I really concentrated on him. Every stuttered breath, every twitch in his leg. Every clench of his fist when I moved my hand higher. Every single response feeding my own desires, making my breath come quicker. My skin warm at the thought of what my touch was doing to him.

Daring, bold, wanting him for more than a simple make-out session, I inched my hand over the top of his thigh, letting my fingertips trail along the inner seam of his pants. Imagining what it would feel like to have his hand on me. Squeezing as a quiet moan escaped my lips.

"Shit," Easton said, his voice quiet but forceful. I glanced up, ready to make a joke, but he cut me off. Using one arm to yank me toward him, he crashed his lips to mine, kissing me with a strength I hadn't expected. Stealing my breath and making my heart jump. I pushed up, hands on his thighs, responding to his kiss in kind. Needing more. Wanting so much.

We were all lips and tongue, moving in a hot, wet, sliding sort of kiss. A kiss that was just as intense as he could be. A perfect kiss that sent heat blazing through my body, making me moan. Making me clench. His lips felt good, but his hands grabbing at me—owning my flesh with their hold—nearly made my world explode right there.

Easton pulled me with him as he lay back then rolled me underneath him. His weight on me was like a drug, one that set my heart racing and lit my body on fire. One that made me mewl like a cat. I tried to move, to writhe or thrust or do something to ease the ache his touch set off, but Easton wanted to be in control. He pinned me down, notching his hips between my thighs, pressing against me in a way that made me gasp.

And all things good and sweet, wasn't *that* just the best feeling in the world?

"We're on your grandma's couch," he whispered just before he kissed and bit his way down my neck.

I threw my head back, eyes closed. "I know."

He chuckled, one huge hand cupping my breast and pushing it up to meet his mouth. Even through my clothes, I could feel the heat and the dampness of his breath. The pressure of his lips on me. I didn't think I'd ever wanted to be naked more than right then. "Should we go to your room?"

Good idea in theory, but there were memories in that room. Good and bad, many tinged with Jace. I didn't want to mar this moment with all that. Didn't want to taint what we were about to do. "Please. Here. Now."

I gripped his shoulders as he nodded once, letting my body wrap itself around him. Squeezing him closer with my thighs around his hips. Rubbing against where he was already so hard.

"Fuck," he said with an intensity that made the word sound almost like a prayer, rocking his hips into mine and pressing on just the right spot. "This feels like high school."

When he rubbed over my clit in a way that made me see stars, I yanked his head to bring his face back to mine and bit his lip. "High school sucked. Make this better."

There was no hesitation from Easton, no verbal response to my challenge either. He was a man of action, not words, so he acted. He pressed me into the couch, kissing me harder, longer. Demanding deeper kisses and more contact. His entire body shifted with every roll of his hips, muscles bulging in his legs and arms. His chest and abs. Good God, his abs felt like steel against me. I needed to explore him, to feel every inch of his body, but our current location didn't lend itself to too many maneuvers. We were pretty much locked in one hell of a good position, and I wasn't going to ruin that by trying to be creative. I'd take my time another day.

Impatient, I reached between us. Easton pulled back, staring down at my hands as I worked the fly of his pants. A button, a zipper, a slide of fabric on skin, and Easton's breath speeding as my hands did the work. As I moved the needle on this night.

"You sure about this?" he asked, finally bringing his eyes back to mine. They were so dark, the pupils wide, a look of wildness in them. Face flushed, breathing hard, holding himself above me on one arm, he was the epitome of sexy in that moment. Of carnal desire and a need that would have to be slaked. And I wanted him more than I'd ever wanted anything.

"Still friends, right?" I pulled him, needing his weight. Craving his closeness.

He nodded slowly, his brow pulled down. A lie, but one I was willing to look past. I wasn't even sure which side of friendship we were on anymore. I wasn't even sure it mattered. His warmth had become my favorite drug, the roughness of his hands a high all on its own. God help me, but I was ready for this sweet addiction. Ready and wanting it.

Easton rolled his hips against mine, meeting my lips for a soft, sweet kiss, his breath warm on my face. And then his hands were everywhere. Pulling up my shirt, fingers sliding under the waist of my pants and panties to yank them both down. Back up to tease my breasts. Down again to push what he could over my hips and thighs. But he kept coming back to my mouth, kept kissing me as if those kisses were like air. Kept breathing me in with every pass. I was strung tight, needing so much more, tired of waiting for it. An ache that needed to be eased had settled between my legs, one that grew with every pass of his rough hands on my skin. One that craved more of his soft lips on my body. My flesh burned for more, and it was time to take it. I was certainly able to undress myself, even lying underneath a man the size of Easton.

I kicked the fabric off one leg, too hurried to bother taking them off completely. Needy and desperate and wanting. And wet. So damned wet. Easton grabbed my bare thigh, fingers pressing deep into my flesh while he pulled my leg over his hip. His skin was so warm, his muscles hard under my hands. Strong. The rich scent of him—that deep, natural manly essence that told me he wasn't the kind of guy to wear cologne—blanketed me. Making it hard to breathe anything but him. Making it hard to find where he ended and I began. His erection sat nestled where I wanted it, sliding over me in a most obscene way. His hips driving into mine as I spread my legs wider for him. But he didn't push inside. Not yet. He teased. Rolling his body, using his flesh to drive me farther up that hill toward a crash. A good crash...the kind that would leave me breathless and shaking. The kind that would take away all the memories and fear, the worries and stress.

"Damn, Violet. You're so fucking soft and wet," he whispered, his voice gritty with desperation.

I nodded into his neck, too turned on to care about words. I was a needful thing, all nerve endings and desire. Set on one goal, one thought, one want. And Easton was what I wanted. "Please."

He chuckled, edging down my body. His mouth leaving a path of fire as he trailed kisses along my sternum and to my breasts. Every inch of me responded, growing warmer, itching for his touch. I arched my back, wanting more. Offering myself to him without words.

He answered me by grabbing my breasts, his hands rough against my skin, his touch firmer than I'd ever been prepared for. He pushed my breasts together—sucking, licking, biting my nipples. A constant stream of pleasure tinged with pain at the heart of me. My whole body shook, tremors rocking me from head to toe as he teased me past the point of surrender with the sheer desperation in his touch. He didn't try to be gentle or soft, to treat me as if I was a delicate flower. No, he manhandled me, and I loved it.

"Easton," I gasped as the emptiness inside created a deep yearning, as my body clenched once, twice at the nothingness. "Please."

He gave my nipple one last, long lick before he jumped back to his knees, reaching behind him as he did. "Gotta get a condom."

I nodded, running my fingers up those abs I'd felt earlier and lifting his shirt. Damn, he was gorgeous. Not body-builder hard, but muscled and toned. Fit. He grabbed my wrist and brought my hand to his mouth, kissing the palm before setting it on my thigh.

And then he moved, and there was nothing else in the world to focus on but that.

His fingers wrapped around his cock, his hand stroking three times up and down his length, teasing himself in an almost unconscious way. Getting ready for what I knew was about to happen. Working toward it. Every inch on display, every touch for me to watch. And I did—I was helpless to look away.

He stared at me while I watched his hand, his eyes a physical force against my skin. "You're so fucking gorgeous like this," he murmured, his voice soft and deep. Hot.

"God, so are you." I ran my teeth along my bottom lip as I slid a hand down my stomach. As I let my fingers drag along the flesh made wet by Easton's actions. As I watched his eyes grow wilder because of what I was doing.

With a single nod, he tore open the foil square. He kept his eyes between my legs while his fingers rolled latex down his length, as his hand gripped the base tight and held it steady. His cock was much like him, solid and wide. Substantial. The thickness of it made me clench for him, made my fingers slip inside myself for one brief moment as I imagined him there. But then I didn't have to imagine anymore.

Once the condom was on, Easton pushed my knees wider, bringing his fingers between my legs and moving with mine. "You sure about this?"

I nodded, unable to speak. Needing to feel him so much. His fingers ran softly along my flesh, teasing, sliding over my clit and circling me but never edging inside. Leaving me empty and wanting. Brushing mine aside to take over.

"Easton." My voice was a cry, a mewl, a plea, and a prayer all in one. And Easton knew it. He had to.

"Wait, baby, just let me take care of you."

My mouth fell open when he slid two fingers inside. Slow... dragging them along my flesh. I gasped and groaned, shaking all over, my hands clenching at his shoulders as he worked himself deeper. But while my body sang for him, he didn't make a sound. Didn't ask if I liked it or if it felt good. He knew. He was confident and sure kneeling between my thighs, teasing me harder. Bringing me closer. The man knew exactly what he was doing to me, and that might have been the biggest turn-on of all.

I reached for him, unable to stop my hips from rocking into his hand, wanting more than his fingers. Craving all of him. "Please."

"You've gotta stop begging me, baby," he said, twisting his hand and working me faster. Keeping his thumb on my clit and driving me absolutely mad with the need to come.

"Want more," I whispered, meeting his eyes.

He growled and shifted forward, licking his lips as he practically hovered over top of me. "I've been hard for you since the moment you walked into my shop in those fucking tiny shorts. Do you have any idea how much I want you right now? I'm going to come so hard and fast when I get inside you. I already know, and I can't wait. But I want this to be good for you too. Let me take my time. Let me get you off so I don't feel like a chump."

And wasn't that just the hottest thing he could have said to me? I nodded. Accepting. Letting him do what he wanted to my body. Giving myself over to the sensations he caused.

Easton moved back to his knees, staring hard where his hand was driving me toward a release I desperately needed. Why was it so hot to watch him watch me? To see that level of intensity and concentration on his face? I had no idea, but I loved it. Loved knowing he was right there with me, doing everything for *my* pleasure and holding back his own.

He plunged his fingers in deep, pressed hard on my clit in the process. I gasped and arched my back, a full-body shiver rocking me.

"I'm gonna—"

But I never finished my thought. Easton surprised me by shaking his hand up and down at a speed that stole my breath.

The sensation was something I'd never experienced before. Rougher than I would have thought I'd like, the action brought every nerve ending to the party in the matter of a second. I couldn't hold back, gasping and lifting my hips off the couch to seek out just that little bit more. Easton held firm, pumping his fingers deep as he shook. As he held my hip with his other hand to stop me from pulling away. Five seconds, ten…he didn't let go or let up. My entire body rocked as I pumped against his hand, my legs shaking with the strain of holding my hips in the air. Of opening wide for him. Easton kept up with me, working me toward my ending. Rubbing, pushing, squeezing, thrusting—and yes, shaking—until I broke. With a gasp, lights exploded behind my eyes and my body locked down, every muscle clenching in time with my orgasm.

Before I could catch my breath, Easton was on top of me, pushing my hips back into the couch with the sheer bulk of his own. The head of him slid its way inside, nudging deeper with every quiver and shake. The sound of my own wetness interrupted our heavy breaths, something that probably should have embarrassed me but didn't. Easton had done that to me, had made me come so hard and long. He'd made me practically drip with desire for him.

"Love how wet you are," he mumbled, his lips brushing against mine. "Wanna taste it next time."

I groaned and gripped his shoulders, needing his body on mine, craving his weight again. And he gave it to me. Pressed me into the couch as he pushed forward. As he finally slid inside where I needed him most. Stretching my swollen flesh in a way that made me clench around him.

"Oh hell, Violet." He shifted his hips, his arms shaking and his breathing harsh. "How can you be so hot? You're burning me up here."

I bit down on the muscles of his neck, too far gone for words. Easton grabbed my thigh and pulled it up and over his hips, opening my legs wider for him. Spreading me in the only way possible. I let my other leg fall over the edge of the couch, giving him as much room as I could. Giving him everything. And Easton took it all, not holding back. He thrust hard and deep, never faltering, pushing me up that hill with every press, every breath. Every touch of his flesh on mine.

He clenched my thigh then let go so he could slide it down, grabbing my ass. Kneading the cheek and pulling me tighter to him. Changing the angle and sliding deeper. So much deeper.

"God, yes," I gasped as he hit something inside me that made me shake. He did it again, watching me, still so intent on me and my pleasure instead of his own.

As I closed my eyes to chase the tingles running up and down my spine, he bit my lip. The shot of pain centered me back on him, gave me something to focus on as he slid his tongue along it.

"You feel so good wrapped around me like this." He grunted and thrust again, pressing deep and holding, rocking himself against my clit in a way that made me want to scream. "Can I make you come again? I want to feel you come. Need to feel it."

I clawed at his shoulders, pulling him closer. "So close. More."

He leaned down, letting his weight push me deeper, keeping his hips jerking into mine. "I'll give you more, baby. Shit, I'll give you everything. All of me...I'm yours. Take what you need."

A tiny flash of not-just-friends flashed through my mind, but I was too far gone to care. Shaky, sweaty, completely over the edge, I slid a hand between us to rub my fingers against my clit. To push myself toward that release. Easton groaned and thrust harder, whispering words of encouragement like *that's it* and *get it, baby*. Like *so fucking hot* and *come on my cock*. Dirty words that made me shiver. Made me inch closer to that place of complete abandon right before the crash.

Made me come.

I clenched around him, clinging to his shoulders as a second orgasm rolled through me. As the pleasure-pain of it destroyed me once more. Easton grunted and thrust even harder, shaking the whole couch. Lifting my hips off the cushion as he strained toward his own ending. Making my orgasm stutter and drag on, keeping me riding that knife-edge between enough and too much. And it was good, so good. And then it was perfect.

He stiffened above me, grunting as he held himself deep inside, cords of muscle along his neck flexing as he arched back. Beautiful as he let go. As he jerked and pressed and bit his bottom lip. As he groaned in the sexiest way imaginable and gave himself over to his own release.

When he was finished, he placed his forehead on mine, breathing hard, his body finally relaxing. "Not a chump."

I laughed, holding him closer and running a hand down his cheek. "Never a chump."

"It was a close call."

"Doubtful." I huffed a laugh, settling into the couch, basking in his weight and his warmth surrounding me. "I've thought about this for so long."

His head jerked back. "Really?"

I nodded, almost shy as I made my admission. "I had a bit of a crush on you back in the day. Of course, just about every girl did."

"Liar."

"It's true. You were that perfect blend of bad boy, funny guy, and sweet charmer. Plus, you've always been hot as hell." I ran my hands over the muscles of his arms. "It's even more now."

"You're doing very good things for my ego." He laughed, ducking his head in my neck. "I thought about you too. In ways far too inappropriate to bring up."

"Good thing my grandma needed her car fixed."

"Thank God for a leaky radiator and improper backing up." He chuckled, then ran a hand over my hair. "You need to come home more often."

Easton kissed my nose before reaching between us. As he dealt with cleaning up, I turned on my side and tried to ignore the empty feeling of the truth settling over me. While I was happy to be back, I couldn't stay. I had jobs, an apartment, and a life. I had some semblance of privacy and anonymity in Chicago. If I came back here, I'd never know if someone was looking at me because they wanted to say hello or if they were trying to match me to the video. I'd never find a place to just be me.

But as Easton settled himself on top of me, rolling us to the side to snuggle in a way that was decidedly uncomfortable but totally worth it, I pushed aside the worry and took full advantage of the moment. When I was wrapped in his arms, reality could wait to attack. He'd keep me safe…

For now.

CHAPTER FIFTEEN

VIOLET

Four in the morning. Not a so-called normal wake-up time for most people, but something I'd grown used to over the years. Baking—making doughs and layers of cake and frostings—took time. That time tended to be in the early-morning hours.

I rolled out of bed, deliciously sore in so many places. Easton had definitely not been a chump the night before. He'd lived up to every teenage fantasy and then some. I'd be feeling him all day, and I wasn't the least bit sorry about that.

Once the coffee started brewing, I headed straight for the refrigerator. I needed my butter and eggs to come to room temperature or close to it. Once I'd collected those items and set them out on the counter, I snagged the grocery bag that had been sitting in the pantry for days. The one from the night Easton had run into me at the store. The one with the chocolate puff cereal and corn syrup in it. Grandma would have cream of tartar for sure, and sugar and vanilla were staples. No worries there.

I lined up all my ingredients, pulled out the stand mixer from the cabinet, and poured a cup of coffee. Easton wanted me to make him chocolate marshmallow bars. I had another hour before I could do that because I didn't want to attempt to whip cold eggs, but maybe there was something else I could start with. Something to play with that might entice Grandma to eat something with a bit more fat and calories than her bland diet had offered lately. Something yummy but not too sweet.

I puttered around the kitchen, looking for something to get my rusty wheels spinning. I hadn't baked in weeks, hadn't even thought much about it. My options were relatively restricted by what I had on hand, but otherwise, I had free rein. No rules or menus to follow. I could make anything so long as the ingredients were on hand.

It was when I opened the refrigerator and saw the bag of limes Dahlia had brought home in the crisper that the idea hit me. It was a recipe I'd seen on a competitive baking show I loved—Yorkshire gingernuts with lime. The ginger would be good for Grandma's digestion, and the lime would cut the sweetness enough to hopefully not make her sick.

"Brilliant," I whispered, pulling out the limes and grabbing more of what I knew I'd need. Powdered sugar, cream cheese, flour, spices. I dug through drawers until I found the microplane and manual juicer, ducked into cabinets to locate the right baking pans and piping supplies.

My heart beat a little faster as I filled the countertops, and I started humming somewhere along the way. This. This was what I loved. This was where my heart truly lived. Baking and cooking and making delicious treats for people to enjoy. I loved it—always had. Grandma had taught me to bake from the time I was old enough to stand on a chair at the counter with her. Making a treat for her would be something like paying her back. And the marshmallow bars for Easton? That was something else. Something I didn't want to think too much about.

I had the gingernuts in the oven, the lime filling made, and was working on the homemade marshmallows for Easton's treats when Dahlia exploded into the room.

"What's all this?" She peeked into the mixing bowl. Her hair was tied up into a strict bun, and she wore brightly patterned yoga pants with a slouchy sweatshirt over her colorful sports bra. Typical wardrobe for my fitness-obsessed cousin.

"I woke up inspired. Heading into the office?"

She hummed, stealing a fingerful of the lime filling and moaning at the taste. "This is amazing. And yes, I'm off to teach a class full of middle-aged women how to keep from peeing themselves."

That...what? "Try me again."

"It's true. You gotta work your core, or when you get older?" She raised her eyebrows, moving both her hands in a dropping motion in front of her hips. "Gravity takes over. You should take a class with me."

Been there, done that, hated every second of it. "Yeah, I'll take a pass. I get enough of a workout in the kitchen."

"There's no such thing as enough." She popped a kiss on my cheek. "I'll be back this evening. You're good here?"

Good? Good was an understatement. "I can handle things today."

My phone pinged, Easton's name popping up on the screen. Something Dahlia definitely noticed.

"Early-morning texts? I had no idea you two had moved your relationship forward."

Forward. Backward. Sideways. On top of one another. Whatever. "Yeah, well...we're friends."

"Liar." Dahlia turned and skipped toward the back door. "Make sure to hang a sock on the doorknob so I don't interrupt anything interesting."

If my face grew any hotter, it might set the cabinets on fire. "No socks necessary."

Lies.

But I would stick to that story until the day I died.

I waited until Dahlia left to even reach for my phone, delaying that satisfaction of seeing Easton's words. I couldn't wait for long, though.

You awake yet?

I glanced around the kitchen, taking in the mess I'd made. Breathing the scent of the gingernuts. Taking in the soft green color of the lime filling and the stiff peaks of the beaten egg whites for the marshmallows. I was more than just awake. I was busy and excited and making things I hadn't thought about in a number of years.

Things that would likely never sell in any of the restaurants I made pastries for in Chicago.

My mood deflated a little, reality hitting me over the head. Nothing about this feeling, this excitement that had been building inside of me since I'd woken up, could last. I was baking again, which only reminded me of work. Of my commitments in Chicago. Of the need to return to my lonely little life there. To leave Downriver and disappear into the crowded city streets once more.

To walk away from Easton—from his rough hands and smooth words, from his body, his smile, and his kindness—and get back to my reality.

Soon, but not yet. I still had some time. And I still had Easton to reply to.

A good distraction made every day a little brighter, and Easton Cole was the best sort of distraction.

CHAPTER SIXTEEN

EASTON

I walked into the shop with a smile on my face and my phone in my hand. Talking to Violet would be a great way to start my day, even though I'd had to go home alone the night before. I didn't want to wake her up, though. It had been a long night. A fucking fabulously long night. One I wanted to have again. Maybe not a call—maybe just a message. If I couldn't wish her good morning in person, I'd do it over text.

You awake yet?

"Morning," Brogan hollered as I headed for the office. I nodded in his direction, too distracted by my phone pinging to start a conversation.

Yeah. I was up early today.

Well, good morning, then.

Good morning to you. Working hard?

Soon. Got a brake job to do this morning, then a transmission to look at. Busy, busy.

I grabbed a cup of coffee from the machine in the office before heading to the garage. I wasn't two steps out the door when the next text came in.

Are you going to be getting dirty?

I huffed a laugh, typing one-handed as I made my way across the concrete.

Absolutely. Why, you coming by?

Maybe. I need to take Grandma to an appointment this afternoon, but I'm free until then.

Stop by if you can. If not, meet me in my shower after? I may need some help getting all the grease off.

I set my coffee on a workbench just as another ping sounded.

Tell me a time, and you've got yourself a date.

I'll get back to you once I get some work under my belt.

You do that, and maybe I'll give you something other than work under your belt later. :)

I love the way you think. Text me later.

I grinned and unlocked my toolbox, ready to get to work now

that I knew I was going to see Violet later. I'd worried when I'd woken up, wondering if she'd freak about last night and go running. Apparently, she was hanging right in with me. Brave girl.

"You're in a good mood this morning." Brogan brushed by me as I tucked my phone in my pocket.

"Had a date last night."

"With the no-longer-Vee-just-Violet?" Colton asked.

I pointed the wrench his way. "Call her that again, and I'll be shoving this right up your ass."

"Ooh, kinky." Colton grinned. "Does that imply you got your dick stroked by someone other than Rosy Palm last night?"

Brogan snorted a laugh. "Man, he is going to tear you up if you keep being…you."

"What?" Colton rolled his eyes. "You two are jackasses. Maybe if you both got a little more ass, you'd be in better moods."

"You are pure class, man," Brogan said as he grabbed the air wrench.

"Pure class getting all that ass," Colton said with a grin.

I laughed. There was no stopping it. We always picked on Colton and his revolving door of female company, but he had a sense of humor about it. The man was pure bravado. "Anybody pull the outstanding orders yet? I'm waiting on a gasket for this beast before I rip the transmission apart."

Colton wiped his hands and headed toward the office. "Not yet, but I can call Dalton."

Before he could make it halfway across the floor, the man himself appeared in the open bay door.

"Speak, and the boss shall appear." Dalton grinned and tossed his hands in the air.

I shook my head, chuckling. "Pretty sure that's 'the devil appears,' Dalt."

"Me and the devil. My ex-wife would say we're one and the same." He dropped a box on a rolling chair before looking over the truck on the hoist in front of me. "That's just a damn shame."

"What is?"

"That those poor people paid so much money for such a piece of shit."

I shook my head and stepped underneath the truck in question. "Tell me how you really feel, man."

"Yo!" Colton yelled. "Where's our shit, man?"

Dalton may have been the manager at the scrapyard and a supplier of ours, but he was also Colton's family. And he never let us forget it. "That's Uncle Man to you, kid."

"I'm eight years younger than you." Colton tossed his rag on the bench. "I'll give you 'kid.'"

The two roughhoused in between the lifts, both laughing and egging each other on. Typical shit around here. Me? I kept working. Still thinking about Violet. Still in a damn good mood. Wondering when I could get her naked again. And how. And where. The possibilities were making me want to say *screw this* and walk out, but I couldn't. Being the owner of a business and supposedly a responsible adult sometimes sucked.

"Hey, Easton," Dalton called when he and Colton had stopped playing Gladiators or whatever they called that. "I noticed you had some company the other night."

I didn't bother looking his way, knowing he'd be smirking. "Nosy fucking neighbors."

"Your mom and sister noticed it too. As did the rest of the park. You're the talk of the town right now."

That got my attention. Violet wouldn't like people gossiping about her. "Everyone needs to mind their business."

Brogan laughed. "The Terrace Neighborhood Watch strikes again."

I grunted and went back to work. Having grown up in the Terrace Trailer Park, I knew exactly how tight all the neighbors were. We couldn't get away with shit in the park, not with all the eyes on us. I stuck around because I loved the feel of the place and the closeness of everyone, but sometimes that closeness could bite you in the ass. Like today.

Dalton grinned. "You gonna tell me who that brunette with the great ass was?"

I pointed my wrench at him. "Keep your eyes off her ass."

Colton chuckled. "You'd better watch out. He's got a massive hard-on for that one."

"Really?" Dalton looked me over, his pale eyes almost proud. "It's about time."

"What's that supposed to mean?"

"It means you've been practically acting like a monk for years. Good to see you making a few moves. Pretty sure even Brogan's gotten laid more than you lately."

I glanced at my best friend, my eyebrows up. "Something you want to share with the class?"

He tossed a rag over his shoulder and grabbed an oil wrench. "Nope."

Dalton laughed, a deep sound that nearly echoed through the shop. "You boys will never change. Especially you, Easton."

"Yeah? And why's that?"

"Because you're all so damn stubborn."

I yanked on the wrench, trying like hell to release a frozen nut. "I'm not stubborn."

Colton snorted. "Says the man working on a decrepit Land Rover all because he simply couldn't say no."

Dalton just had to add his two cents. "And the man out at five in the morning today running the street sweeper around the park."

"Someone has to do it."

"Yeah, someone." Dalton popped under the Rover, eyeing me hard. "Not you, though. You've got enough on your plate."

He wasn't wrong, and yet I'd made a promise to look after things at some point. I never broke my word.

"That's not him being stubborn," Brogan said, finally setting his phone down. "That's his need to be in control at all times."

"That's enough," I said, having heard this particular argument a thousand times. "I don't need to control everything, but no one else is stepping up at the park to handle shit. You want the job?"

Brogan shut up then, as did Colton. Dalton just grinned.

"You really need to stop trying to do it all, kid. You don't need to make up for anyone else's mistakes." Dalton gave me a smack on the shoulder before heading toward the doors. "All right. That's enough cracking around. I need to get my tired ass back to work."

"You're not tired, Unc." Colton flashed a grin. "You're just old."

Brogan and I laughed as Dalton gave chase, the two Bearns running after one another through the bay doors and out into the parking lot. Dalton was a good guy—one of my favorites in the park—but he'd gone through a nasty divorce two years ago that had sent him spiraling. One caused by my cheating cousin. Luckily, he'd never held her bullshit against my family or me. Not that Colton would have let him. Still, it was good to see Dalton back on his feet and sober once more. Plus, it was nice having someone who ran a salvage yard as family. He was always able to scrounge up parts when we needed something oddball.

But he was wrong this time. I did need to make up for my dad's mistakes. I needed to make sure everyone saw how we'd pulled ourselves out of being destitute and found success. No one would ever be able to say the Coles weren't hard workers.

"UPS pulled up as I was saying goodbye to Dalton," Colton said as he jogged back into the shop. "I'll sign for it."

"Cool, thanks." I raised the lift a little more to put the car higher in the air and stepped underneath it, losing myself in plugs and filters and combustion. Fixing shit had always been a passion of mine. From the time I was a kid, I'd liked playing with tools and taking things apart. I wasn't always so good at putting them back together, but I tried. And I enjoyed the challenge.

But today, it was a bit too hard to concentrate. My mind was stuck on Violet-mode, plus the incessant beeping of Brogan's phone kept pulling me from my job. Every time I glanced up, he was staring at the screen or typing into it. My own phone sat silent, but I recognized that obsession.

"You got a girl on the other end of that thing?" Which would be amazing. Brogan barely dated, and he never seemed to have relationships.

"Why'd you think that?" he asked as he slipped his phone into his pocket.

"Uh, because you're staring at that screen like it's a lifeline. What's up?"

Brogan sighed and shook his head. "Nothing, man. Just...old stuff resurfacing."

My good mood faded a little. Brogan was usually pretty steady, calmer than Colton or me for sure. The look on his face, the worry there, put me on alert. "Need anything?"

"Nah." He shrugged, refusing to meet my eyes. "But thanks for the offer."

"Okay, but I'm here if you need me." I gripped his shoulder as I walked past, wishing there were more I could do but knowing he'd have to come to me in his own time. "I'm going to check on Colton. I can't do shit without that part, and he's taking his sweet time out front."

"Yeah, he tends to do that." Brogan met my eyes as his phone pinged again, though he didn't reach for it.

"You sure you're okay?"

"I'm great. No worries, man." The smile he gave me was too fake, too forced, but I respected the effort.

"If you say so." I frowned and headed for the office. Brogan would ask for help if he needed it, that I was sure of. I just worried he'd try to handle shit on his own for too long. We had always worked as a team, ever since elementary school. If he needed Colton or me, we'd be there. Hell, Colton's twin brother, Wyatt, would come running if any one of us needed anything, and he was off playing professional hockey and living the life of a star. That's how tight our crew was.

A bell tolling from the front was the only warning I had before Violet herself breezed into the office, some sort of boxy metal thing in her hands, and all thoughts of Colton and Brogan and the Land Rover of Doom disappeared. Short skirt, legs on display, tank top…the woman was pure sex, innocent and sultry all at the same time. Looking good enough to eat. And she was mine. Every inch of her. Every expression. Especially that look on her face before she came—that was definitely mine. I wanted it. Wanted to be the only man to put it there. Ever.

Filled with emotions I couldn't yet identify, I let my thoughts shut down and focused on the one thing I could…the one thing I wanted… Her.

"Hey, Easton. I made you a treat."

I stalked toward her without a word, loving the way her eyes tracked me. The way her breath caught. How she almost seemed to know what was coming.

"You're the only treat I want."

"Eas—"

My lips were on hers before she could finish my name. She responded to my kiss, returning that intensity. Feeding my desire. Dropping whatever she'd been holding and wrapping her arms around my neck as I devoured her.

"Need you." I picked her up and wrapped her legs around my hips. "Need to make you mine."

She didn't argue. "The guys?"

I grunted and carried her as I walked to both doors, locking out any unwanted intruders with a flick of the latches. "Taken care of."

She didn't kiss me again, though. "No cameras?"

I wasn't like that bastard, Jace. "None. I swear."

"Thank God."

"Yeah?" I asked, breathless, so fucking wired, I thought I might rip the fucking clothes off her body in a second. Thankfully, I didn't have to. She tugged at my work shirt, untucking it and working the buttons open one by one. I laid her on the edge of my desk, unwinding her legs from my hips so I could drag her panties down the length of them. Giving her ankle a little lick for good measure.

"You're so worked up," she whispered, running her heel over my thigh and up along my ass.

My hips jerked, and I grabbed her thighs harder. Almost too hard. "I'm sorry."

"Don't be. Until later. You can be sorry for the ruined chocolate marshmallow bars I made you later."

That stopped me. "You baked?"

She huffed a laugh. "Marshmallow bars are not baking. But yeah, I might have dabbled in the kitchen a bit."

I ran my hand up her thigh, torn between wanting to slow down so we could talk about this and wanting to say fuck this conversation and attack her. Luckily, I had solid control. "That's great. What else did you make?"

"Do you really want to talk about croissants and macarons right now, or do you want to get under my skirt?"

Easy answer. "Right. Chocolate marshmallow bars can wait."

She tugged me closer, bringing her knees higher on my waist and spreading her legs for me. I leaned in and stole a kiss, groaning at the taste of her on my tongue. She upped the ante, reaching to unfasten my belt. I was practically shaking with my need for her, ready to dive inside that sweet spot she'd graced me with less than twelve hours ago. But twelve hours was too long. Hell, two hours was too long. I needed her all the time. Every day. Every hour. Right then.

I opened my fly and pushed my pants over my hips, too impatient to wait any longer. Thankfully, she lay back and wrapped her legs around my hips again. Reeling me in. Pulling me right against her. Seemingly just as anxious as me. And just as needy.

"Easton, please." Another tug, a wiggle, and…

Oh God, right there. I was *right there*.

"Violet—"

"Don't stop. I'm covered, so don't stop."

I slid inside her without prep, without making sure she got hers first. Without anything between us. But I'd learned her tells last night. I knew she was already ramped up. Knew I could get her off before I came. I slid in and out slowly, working my way deeper, loving every sigh and groan and gasp. Every wet smack of the two of us together. Every second I spent inside her heat. There was nothing like the feeling of her surrounding me—of me bare inside her. Nothing at all. It was heaven and hell, the greatest pleasure and the most exquisite torture as I fought to keep a shred of control. To not simply fuck her hard against my desk and get mine without taking care of her needs.

Soon, though. Real fucking soon if the way her entire body had started to quiver was any indication.

Standing straighter, needing to tease her more, I pulled her legs up and set her feet on my shoulders. Sliding deeper inside my new favorite place on earth. When Violet moaned all loud and long, I moved one hand to caress her breasts while the other zeroed in on her clit. Keeping her on edge. Working every part of her I could reach. My fingers rubbing, tweaking, massaging that little pearl the best I could. Violet arched her back, her legs shaking as I kept thrusting, kept teasing, kept focusing on her clit. On her pleasure. As I gave her everything I had to give.

From this position, I could see everything. Could watch myself slipping inside her over and over again. Another slide, almost all the way out this time before pushing back inside. And damn, she looked so good taking all of me. So, so good, it made my cock ache even more. Made a tingle start in my spine and tickle its way up my back. I wanted to dive inside her, to drop to my knees and taste every inch of her. It was a need, deep and dark and full of some kind of ownership claim. I knew that. Still, it was hard to resist. I'd get my face in that pussy soon, taste her pleasure, learn her with my tongue and lips. Soon. But not yet. Right now, I needed her just like this. Splayed before me with my cock buried inside her. Needed it more than I needed to breathe.

"Easton," Violet said as I pushed her forward, testing her flexibility. Damn, she was beautiful laid out for me like this. Beautiful and sexy, almost too much to be real. But she was real, all right. I could feel her heat wrapped around me. Could smell her perfume and sex. Could hear every breathy sigh and little gasp, every moan and grunt as I fucked her right there on my desk. She was definitely real...and mine.

"Come on, baby. You're so close." As was I, so I changed my angle, moving both her legs to the same shoulder and twisting her hips a bit. Twisting to plunge deeper. Violet clawed at the desk as my body shook. Completely lost to the sensations I was giving her. Just me. Only us. And fuck, she was even tighter this way. Constricted in a way other positions didn't offer. I was going to lose it, but not yet. I had to get her there first. Had to take care of what she needed.

"Gonna make you come," I said, keeping my thumb on her clit. Keeping a rhythm as she rocked back against me. Hell, she'd swallowed me up, helped me go deeper than before with every wiggle of her hips, and I loved every fucking second of it. "Gonna make you come on my cock, pretty girl. Want to feel you squeeze me just like this. You're so beautiful when you come, did you know that? All wild and out of control. Give me that, Violet. Give me you."

I thrust harder, grunting on every stroke, waiting and watching and feeling as my girl writhed underneath me. And then she gasped, head flying back, breasts thrust up in the air as her back arched off the desk. And I felt her. Felt that pussy squeezing me, felt the muscles in her legs tighten as her orgasm crashed over her.

Thank fuck.

I couldn't hold on a moment longer. I thrust deep, bending over her and forcing her legs back as I came inside her. All warm flesh and girl and the smell of sex around me. And I loved it. Loved everything about that moment.

Hell, if I let myself admit it, I was beginning to love her.

"Fuck being just friends," I said, unable to hold back in my sex-addled state. Unable to let her go, no matter how much I knew hanging on would push her away. If I'd taken the time to think about my words, I wouldn't have said them. But in that moment, with my bare cock still inside her and every inch of me screaming that she was the one I wanted more than any other, I couldn't hold anything back. "Be with me, Violet. Be mine."

The stillness broke through my haze, crushing my hope. Reminding me of the start of a race, where the contestants were locked and ready but waiting for the gun to go off to tell them to run. Violet was a runner, and my words could very well be the starting pistol.

Fuck.

Violet didn't jump up and run, though. No, her start was slower. More of a creeping toward the finish. More painful. She pushed me off her, avoiding my eyes. Slowly taking her body away from me and shuttering every inch of herself behind the barricades she'd obviously built over the years. I tucked myself away as I watched her, as I stared at those walls I'd torn down going right back up. Her movements were meticulous and calm—the way she straightened her skirt, how she retrieved her panties from the floor, the slide of her hands over her hair. Choreographed, well-practiced, and a total distraction. She was giving herself time to think, time to work out her answer. And I could already sense that I wouldn't like whatever it was.

Finally, she stopped moving. "I don't want to hurt you, Easton."

"Then don't."

Her eyes finally met mine, the expression in them killing me. "I can't move back here."

"There's *can't* and there's *don't want to*. You're using the first as your excuse when, really, your reason for not coming home is the second. I'll make you want to."

She froze, practically rooted to the floor. Staring at me for a long, drawn-out moment. And then she sighed. "You'll make me do a lot of things that aren't good for me, won't you?" Her smile was barely visible as she bent to pick up the foil-covered pan she'd dropped. The chocolate marshmallow bars she'd promised me. The ones she'd let go of when I'd attacked her like a starving man. With slow steps, she came to me, rose onto the balls of her feet and kissed my cheek as she pushed the tray onto my desk. "This was a lot of fun and not at all what I was expecting when I came to drop off these off, but I have to go."

"For now or…for always?"

"For now. Today, I have to go for now. Grandma has a doctor's appointment, and I need to drive here there."

I grabbed her fingers as she tried to walk away, hanging on for one extra moment. Needing more time with us connected. Clinging to the only part of her I could. "Thanks for coming by and for the treats."

That smile was better. More real. "Thanks for not being a chump again. Sorry about dropping the marshmallow bars."

"I'm sure they'll be fine. And if not, I'll eat them anyway."

"Give the really messed-up ones to Colton."

"They're mine. All mine—I'm not sharing." I licked my lips, finally letting go of her. Fighting back the pressure in my heart as she moved away from me. "Come see me later?"

A shrug. She gave me a shrug and a halfhearted sort of smile. "Maybe."

There was no telling what hurt more—that bullshit answer or watching her walk away and not knowing if she'd ever be back.

CHAPTER SEVENTEEN

Driving was a good thing. A moment of freedom when I felt trapped. It let my mind wander, let my body relax as I followed roads and signs. Driving was my escape, and I'd missed it since I rarely drove in the city. Public transportation was too easy, and traffic was too thick to enjoy being behind the wheel. But in the suburbs around Detroit? Out farther west where neighborhoods turned to small farms? Driving became a true pleasure.

I should have been driving across the state, could have been home by then with how much I'd driven after Grandma's appointment, but instead, I'd literally driven in circles most of the afternoon. Circles that led me right back to where I apparently wanted to be.

The sun hung low in the western sky when I parked in front of Easton's trailer. His dark, obviously empty trailer. I chewed my lip and tried my hardest not to drive off as I sat there looking toward that metal box. I could have driven over to the shop, but I really wanted to get him alone. I'd messed up horribly that morning. I hadn't meant to—I'd been in such a state after having sex on his desk. Emotionally raw and almost needy. I wasn't used to feeling that way, wasn't used to fighting a connection like the one I felt for Easton. So when he'd told me to stay, when he'd offered himself to me if I could only come back, I hadn't known how to answer. I'd known what I wanted to say, but there was no way that could happen. I couldn't come back. He knew that, and still, he'd pushed.

And my God, had I wanted to give in and take him up on his offer, which was why I'd left. And yet, I found myself in front of his trailer. Wishing he were home. Needing to…fix things? I didn't even know for sure. I just knew I needed to talk to him. Needed to see him.

Unfortunately, Easton's truck wasn't in his spot, and I was too set on my plan to talk to him in private to make the drive to the shop. I sat in my car for a good ten minutes wondering what I should do. Stuck in the quagmire of the mess I'd created. Had it really been over ten hours since I'd run out of the shop? Where had the day gone? And why hadn't I just had the guts to go back and face him? He'd wanted to talk to me, but I'd run from him and then ignored his calls and texts. I was an asshole.

"You okay, dear?"

I startled, tearing my eyes away from the trailer. A woman stood on the sidewalk watching me. Her wavy, dark hair hung past her shoulders, her face so familiar, it threw me off-balance. I felt as if I knew her, but I didn't know how. "I…yeah. Just… waiting for someone."

She glanced to the trailer and back, cocking her head at me. "You looking for Easton?"

"Yeah. I guess I am."

"You must be Violet, then. I'm Constance, Easton's mom." She smiled, probably at the surprise I knew had to be showing on my face. She wasn't old enough to be Easton's mom, or at least, she didn't look old enough. But I remembered her from the first day

Easton had brought me over here. I hadn't met her, but I'd seen her from a distance. No wonder she looked so familiar.

I hopped out of the car, my mouth suddenly dry and butterflies dancing in my stomach. "It's nice to meet you."

She looked me up and down, her smile growing. "You're adorable. No wonder my son is so smitten."

If I'd have still been a teenager, I might have blushed at her words. I definitely swooned a little bit, assuming Easton had told his mom about us. What little *us* there was.

Constance nodded toward the end of the block, still smiling. "Why don't you come on over to my place and get out of this sun? He'll be home soon enough."

"Oh, that's okay," I said with a shake of my head. "I can just head home and call him later or something."

Her eyebrow winged up. Just one. A trick I wanted to learn. "You head home, and you won't come back. It took some guts to come out here. Stick around. Entertain an old lady."

That was probably the last descriptor I'd use for her. "Old?"

She grinned. "I'm not, but I like to spout that off to Easton's friends. It gets him all riled up for some reason."

"I can see why. I definitely wouldn't call you an old lady," I joked as I leaned into the car to grab my keys. I hadn't intended on meeting Easton's mom, especially not without him there to act as a buffer. But I couldn't exactly tell her no.

Besides, her crooked smirk was too much like Easton's. "Flattery will get you everywhere."

I followed her to the front porch of a trailer around the corner. Like the others, it was neat and clean, not extravagant but definitely in good shape. Hers had sage-green shutters and a beautiful cedar front porch with screening all around it to keep the bugs away. A perfect outside oasis.

"This is gorgeous." I headed for one of the plush couches as Constance slipped through the door.

"Thank you," she hollered from inside. "Easton and the boys built this porch for me when they were in high school."

I looked around the space with new eyes. Easton, Brogan, and Colton—maybe even Wyatt—had built this with their own hands. There were windows and trim pieces, even a ceiling fan spinning up above. I was amazed. "That was really nice of them to build this for you."

Within seconds, Constance was back, carrying a tray with a pitcher and glasses. And with a sarcastic sort of smile on her face. "Nice, my ass. They nearly got expelled for hanging a sign from the roof of the school, and this porch was their punishment."

"Thank you," I said as she handed me a glass of icy lemonade. "I remember that sign. It was a condom ad slogan for the game against the Trenton Trojans, right? I think I have a picture under it still."

"And a funny slogan, at that," she said with a smile. "But his father and I didn't work as hard as we did to keep him in the district just for him to throw it away his junior year. I practically had to hump Principal Hardy's leg to convince him to let Easton come back to school."

Lemonade burned when you choked on it, especially when it backed up into your nose. Constance chuckled and handed me a towel, waiting out my choking fit.

"Sorry," I said once I finally caught my breath again. "That took me by surprise."

"Understandable, and I can relate. Finding out my son was hanging out with Violet Foster was certainly a surprise to me."

I stared, my stomach slowly knotting. "Excuse me?"

"What, you think I don't know who you are?" The question was innocent enough, spoken in the soft, friendly voice of Easton's mom while she peered at me from across the porch, but the meaning behind it—the truth there—that was harder. Brutal and humiliating, really. I scrambled for something to say, for something to offer as an explanation. In the end, I had nothing, but Constance did, apparently. "I don't care about what you did or didn't do all those years ago. That's not where I'm going with this conversation."

"You're not?" My face burned. Easton's *mother* knew about my sex tape. That reality tore right through my mind. Every inch of me burned, every possible blade of embarrassment laid bare over me. This was a nightmare.

"No. Everyone makes mistakes. Lord knows me and my kids have made more than our share." She sat back and gave me an appraising look. "No, I'm more worried about what you're doing now."

Words didn't make sense anymore. "Now?"

"Yes, now. You haven't been home in years. What have you been up to?"

I glanced at the wooden planks and shrugged, unable to hold her gaze. Still fighting the sting of being recognized by her. "Working. Life. The usual boring sort of stuff, I guess."

"I have a feeling that's not true."

Something in her tone, in the way she said the words, gave me the courage to look up. This woman was actually interested in what I did and who I was, not just who I'd once been. My voice was soft when I spoke, barely more than a whisper, but it was more than silent. "I bake. I...work in restaurants making desserts. I'm a pastry chef."

"Baking is an art form and a science. Hell, cooking in general is a much harder job than people give credit for. Why are you embarrassed by that?"

I shrugged again, to which Constance chuckled.

"I'm not an inquisition squad. I'm just curious about the girl my son chooses to spend his time with. Lord knows he won't tell me anything."

I shrugged. "Maybe because there's nothing going on."

Constance chuckled. "Please. For the first time in a long time, I hear happiness in his voice. Not the 'work is going great' happiness I've been listening to for years, but the 'life is good' happiness a mother craves for her kids."

I tried not to smile, scrunching my face to hold it back. "You think?"

"I know. But you don't sound the same. Did he do something? Do I need to whoop his ass like I did when he was smaller than me? I'm not sure I could anymore, but Gracie would help. She's always been a little tougher because of hanging around all these boys."

I shook my head, owning my mistakes. "No. If anyone's at fault, it's me."

"But you're here to fix that, it seems. That takes courage." Constance took a drink of her lemonade, her eyes on the flowers in the window box. We were quiet for several minutes, both of us lost in our own worlds. Mine orbited around the things I'd done wrong, the guilt I felt at treating Easton the way I so hated to be treated. But there was fear there as well. A pervasive worry that he might not forgive me. That I'd killed whatever was between us before it even had a chance to truly breathe.

She looked to the street as a car door closed nearby. "Looks like my wild one is home."

Gracelyn Cole—a girl I'd once tutored in math and who'd played the clarinet in the orchestra with me—opened the screen door, smiling but looking cautiously from her mom to me. "Hey. What's going on here?"

"Hi, baby." Constance lifted her face as Grace came closer, accepting a kiss on the cheek from her daughter. "Violet and I are just chatting. You know Violet, right?"

"Yes, of course. It's nice to see you again."

"You too. It's been a long time." Ten years since I'd run, eleven or so since I'd spent any real time with the girl.

Grace nodded, looking me over as she said, "Easton's been trying to reach you, you know."

Crap. I yanked my phone from my pocket and brought the

screen to life. Missed calls and texts, ones I'd been ignoring all day. Ones I'd forgotten to check once I'd pulled up at the trailer. "I was with my grandma most of the day then decided to take a drive. I should have looked—"

"Sometimes a girl needs a day to herself. No harm, no foul for that." Grace leaned against the side of the trailer, her eyes locked on mine, her flared skirt climbing her thigh as she raised a foot. Colors and patterns peeked from under the fabric, a tattoo of something leading up her thigh. Something I couldn't help but stare at. At least until Constance reminded me why I was there.

"How about you call him, baby?" Constance said to Grace. "Tell him to get his butt home right now. But don't tell him why."

"Yes, ma'am." Grace grinned and pulled her phone from the neckline of her dress. She typed something, then turned away, stepping inside so we couldn't hear her, I assumed.

"You don't want him to know I'm here?"

Constance grinned. "Nope. That boy has been a workaholic since his dad left us high and dry, always trying to earn that extra money he thought would give him some stability. He'll be mad having to leave work, especially if Gracie won't tell him why. She knows just how to wheedle her way under that boy's skin. Seeing you will clear all that irritation up, though."

If only that were true. "I doubt it. I really screwed up this morning."

"I figured you were feeling guilty about something. Don't worry, honey. Easton's too smitten to stay mad for long. He'll come around."

I could only hope.

CHAPTER EIGHTEEN

EASTON

Violet was sitting on my front step when I pulled up to my trailer that night. It took me about ten seconds to believe my eyes and another twenty to figure out what to do. When Gracie had called, she'd said I needed to get home or I'd be pissed, and she was right. But I wasn't ready for this. As much as I'd chased down Violet all day, I wasn't ready to see her. Wasn't ready to hear her say she was leaving for good.

I couldn't leave her sitting on my porch, though, so I turned off the truck, took a deep breath, and manned up. She stood when I finally opened the door, looking so damned nervous. But I couldn't fall for that. The girl had some serious talking to do. We both did.

"Hey," she called.

I slammed the truck door, still not moving toward her. "Hey yourself."

She fidgeted with the skirt of her skirt, having a hard time keeping her eyes on mine. "I...hope you don't mind that I just showed up like this."

I shook my head and took a single step in her direction. Drawn to her but holding myself back. "I don't mind, though you'd better have something to say after today's disappearing act."

She sighed and closed her eyes for a moment before bracing herself as if for a battle. "I'm sorry I ran from you this morning. I should have stuck around so we could talk about things."

I blew out a breath and ran my hand through my hair. "Okay."

"Okay?" she asked, looking at me as if I'd gone crazy. And maybe I had, but there was a finality to our relationship. Something I could see coming but refused to avoid. As bad as it would be for me, I just wanted to spend time with her. To dig down deep and see if there was any way to help her. To convince her to stay. If that was fixing her, as Gracie and Brogan thought I was doing, so be it. She was here, she was talking, and to be honest, that was enough for me. For the moment.

"Yeah," I said with a shrug. "Okay."

"That's it?" She stepped closer, looking completely confused. "Just okay?"

When she was close enough, I wrapped an arm around her waist and pulled her against my chest. Needing to touch. To feel. To know she was still here. "Yeah, just okay. I accept your apology. We can talk this shit out when we get inside. I'm just really fucking happy you're standing on my walk and not halfway to Chicago by now."

Her face fell. "I thought about it."

Those words of hers nearly shattered something inside of me. I knew she had, could have guessed it, but hearing her confirm that fact sent everything I was trying to build crashing to the ground. There really was no future with her, not how I hoped. But I still wasn't ready to give up. Not yet. Not on something as good as I knew she and I could be.

"How far did you get?" I asked, keeping a chokehold on the churning in my gut.

"Jackson. Then I went north for a while. But I came back."

Ninety minutes. That's how far west she got on what would be a five-hour drive. Not even halfway. I could work with that.

"Good. Because I'm not ready to let you go, though I don't want to play that game again. No more disappearing on me—you're upset, run to me, not away."

She gripped my arms, those green eyes I'd been dying to see all day looking a little red-rimmed and watery. "I'm sorry. Running away was a crappy thing for me to do."

And yet something I should have been expecting. She was a runner, not a fighter. And she'd run again. So I did the only thing I could do in that moment, the only thing I wanted to. I kissed her hard, refusing to give her time to think. I had her back. No matter how bad things were going to get when she finally left, I had to take advantage of what she was willing to give me. Needed to.

She lifted her arms, wrapping them around my neck, pulling me to her level. I went willingly, wishing we were already inside so I could strip her down. I knew we needed to talk more, knew we had some things to say still, but tossing her ass in my bed seemed like a much better idea.

Maybe she wasn't the only one of us who was hiding.

But as the kiss turned heated, as my hands gripped her ass over her flirty little skirt and pulled her against where I was already so hard for her, our night was interrupted.

"Might want to take that inside, Easton." Dalton stood on the sidewalk, giving me a smile that was far too smug.

Sighing, aching to get my girl alone, I took a step back from Violet. Gave us both a little room. But I kept my arm around her waist and started pulling her toward my porch. "How you doing, Dalton?"

He grinned and cocked his head. "Not nearly as good as you are, my friend. Am I going to get introduced here?"

I laughed and shook my head. "Dalton, this is Violet. Violet, this jackass is related to another jackass you know."

"Oh, you must be Colton's uncle." She nearly tripped over the bottom step, but I held her up and kept us both moving. Not long now.

Dalton's grin took up nearly half his face. "My nephew's jackassedness precedes me, apparently."

"Today, yes." I dragged Violet with me through the screen door, ready to get her alone. "I'll talk to you later, man."

"It was nice meeting you," Violet called out as we reached the front door.

"You two behave, now. Don't make me call your mama, boy."

Jackass was too soft a term for him. "Thanks, Dalton."

"Something I should know?" Violet asked as she stepped inside.

"No, just...jackassery."

"Seems fitting."

"Trust me, it is." I leaned against the closed door, staring at her. The moonlight shining through the windows cast a silvery glow about her, making her seem ethereal. Unreal. Something not of this world. "You are so fucking beautiful."

She smiled all slow and sly. "And you're a charmer. But we need to talk."

"Yeah," I said with a sigh. "We do. Eventually." I kicked off my shoes, then grabbed her hand and pulled her behind me, heading past the living room and down the hall. Dolly ran out to greet me, but I strode by her without so much as a pat on the head. "Later, Dolly. I need a few."

Violet chuckled. "Where are we going?"

"Bedroom." I pushed open the door and walked in, immediately yanking my T-shirt over my head. I dropped the shirt in the laundry basket and unzipped my work pants. She watched me from the doorway, her eyes following my every move. When I let the jeans I'd been in all day fall, I heard her breath catch.

"Easton, I thought we were going to talk."

I closed the distance between us and grabbed her hand, pulling her as I backed into the bathroom off my bedroom. "We will. But I've been working in a sweatbox all day, and I stink. I need a shower."

"Oh." She blinked as I turned on the water, though she didn't pull away. Not physically. "I can wait in the other room."

"Nope." I stepped into the shower and let my head fall forward as the hot water pelted me. "You can either stand right there or get in here with me. No hiding."

"I'm not hiding."

"Not anymore, and I'm not about to let you start again." I shampooed quickly, afraid she was going to bolt if I took too long. To my surprise, she didn't. She stayed right where I'd left her. Fidgeting and nervous, but there. And when she did finally move, it wasn't to escape to the bedroom. It was to pull that sassy sundress over her head and push her little panties down her legs. I wanted to sigh, wanted to sag with relief that she was staying, but the sight of her naked in front of me, of her being so daring…no part of me was going to be sagging any time soon.

"Scooch over," she said as she opened the glass door to the shower stall. I stepped back with a smile, my hands automatically going to her hips. Pulling her closer. Needing to touch her.

And perhaps she needed to touch me as well. She grabbed my bar of soap from the holder and ran it over my arms and chest. Rubbing the lather into my skin. Her touch set me on fire and calmed me at the same time, something I'd never experienced. Something that made every part of me long for more of it. My hands shook where they gripped her, my heart pounding so loud, I could feel it in my ears. This was it—my girl. The one I'd drop everything for. Naked and in my home. The things I'd do to keep her here, the things I'd give up. If only she'd give us a real chance.

Her hands slid lower, down to my abs and over my hip bones. Teasing me with her touch. Enticing me with her affection.

"Violet," I whispered as her wrist brushed over the head of my hard cock.

"Hush," she said, keeping her voice low. "Let me take care of you, and then we can talk."

God, those words sounded so good. My knees locked, my muscles clenching as she stroked over them. Her hands slid down my thighs all the way to my knees, and she followed them, dropping into a crouch before me to rub soap all over my calves. I bit my lip, trying to think of anything but her kneeling in front of me. Of her mouth on me, her lips wrapped around my cock as she stared up at me with those soft, green eyes. Damn it, she had me ready to come in a heartbeat.

And then she kissed the tip.

I fell back against the wall, my legs shaking. Groaning as sparks of arousal fired up my spine. But she didn't stop, didn't even pause. She leaned in, gripped my cock, and licked the length of it.

"Fuck, Violet." My hands landed on her head, not controlling, just...there. Touching. Feeling the reality of what she was about to do.

She didn't answer my expletive, simply kept licking from base to tip, running her tongue along the head and squeezing her hand in time with her motions. I was in such a state of hell. The pleasure too good to want to stop her, the need to settle things too fresh to not. But when she wrapped her lips around me and sucked me down, I gave in to the devil known as desire. I fisted my hands in her hair and moved with her. She grabbed my hips and took me in deep in response, seeming to like it when I directed her. And thank every deity known to man for that, because I was seriously ready to fuck that pretty mouth of hers. She felt so good, looked like such a naughty fantasy as she got comfortable on her knees before me. I could have died right there and been happy with the life I'd lived, all because Violet Foster had my dick in her mouth.

"Such a good suck." I moaned as she pulled off with a pop

before sliding back down. "That's it. Let me slide in there a little deeper. Fuck, your mouth feels so good, baby."

I thrust shallow and slow, keeping my eyes locked on her face. She was so beautiful, so ridiculously sexy. I wanted to grab her and throw her ass in my bed, fuck her all night long in every position possible. I wanted to curl up beside her and fall asleep. I wanted to keep her safe and do whatever it took to make her happy. I wanted anything and everything with her, including more than just today. Hell, I wanted her...completely.

"Violet, I'm gonna—"

She hummed around me...*hummed*. Like my dick was some kind of lollipop. The sound flipped my switch, the vibration definitely helping. I came with a grunt, gripping her head and thrusting deeper than I'd planned. But Violet took it all, swallowing what I gave her without complaint. Leaving me limp and exhausted with a fucking smile on her face. The tease.

"Jesus." I had to lean against the wall. "I don't think my knees work."

She laughed as she stood, rubbing her body up the length of mine like a cat and placing soft kisses against my chest. "Am I going to have to carry you out of here?"

"Maybe." I chuckled and pulled her against me, kissing her long and deep while I ran my hands all over her naked back and ass. Teasing her with soft strokes of my fingers between her legs. But the distractions needed to end before I went too far. Once I got inside her, the talk we needed to have would be forgotten. I wasn't about to let her get away from me so easy. "Discussion time."

She frowned up at me. "You don't play fair, getting me naked and then wanting to talk."

"I never claimed to be fair, and I'll use any trick I can to get what I want." One more kiss, a soft one. Sweetening her up. "How's your grandma?"

"The chemo makes her sick, but she has good and bad days.

Today was a good one. She and Mary spent the day playing some online video game."

"Video games?"

"They have a bit of an obsession. Always have."

"Huh. I never would have guessed it." I tugged her closer, pressing our bodies together. "How is it having Dahlia home?"

She shrugged. "Good. She works a lot—Pilates instructors have weird hours."

"And pastry chefs work the old nine-to-five?"

"You got me there."

I had her everywhere. Had her body wrapped up tight in mine. I wanted to keep her there too. But first… "Time for a tough one. You ready?"

She took a deep breath. "Maybe."

That would have to be good enough. "Why didn't Jace ever defend you after the video came out?"

She took a deep breath but couldn't look me in the eye. "It's a long story."

I wanted to argue, to hold her there until she told me everything, but the tremble in her body drew me up short. This wasn't just avoidance—there was fear in her answer. Something about that time scared her. I couldn't see forcing her to answer a question that made her tremble the way she was.

Pushing aside what I knew we needed, I turned off the water. "Okay. I'll back off this once." I reached out of the shower and grabbed a towel, drying her with deft hands. "I've always got time for you, you know. Whenever you're ready to talk, I'm here."

She bit her lip, her eyes cautious. "Can we not right now? I know we need to, but not tonight. I'm already exhausted from this day."

I swallowed hard, biting back the need to demand she talk about it right then. To make sure she didn't hide from me again. But in the end, I nodded and let her get away with silence. She sighed and sagged against me, still not speaking, still trembling and clinging to me as if afraid. Something I hated with every inch of my being.

"Hey," I said, forcing her eyes to mine. "I mean it. I won't push you again, but I want to understand what happened. Before you head back to Chicago."

Her green eyes seemed watery, as if she was fighting back tears. Whether over her past or at the thought of walking away from us, I had no idea. I hoped the latter. Still, she nodded. Agreeing. And that was enough for me. It had to be.

When we had dried ourselves and each other off, both of us rubbing our hands over one another to touch as much as possible, she pulled me into the bedroom. I picked her up halfway across the room and kissed her, squeezing my eyes closed. This was what I wanted. So much so, I was willing to take whatever she'd give me in the hopes that I could get it all. It was risky and probably stupid, but I couldn't resist her.

When my knees hit the mattress, I fell with her still in my arms, dropping her down and catching myself. Hovering over her for a moment. Those green eyes of hers stared into mine, open and honest and so fucking pretty, they made me hurt.

"Stay," I whispered as I dragged a blanket over top of us. She wrapped her legs around my hips, pulling me against her. She didn't answer, but her lips met mine in a sweet kiss that quickly turned heated. Naked, warm from the shower, surrounded by soft cotton and darkness, we fell into one another without hesitation. There was no need for words or questions. We knew each other's signals at that point, knew when to break to draw things out and when to come back together. Within moments, we were full-on fucking, our movements slow and heavy, our arms wrapped around one another. Pressed close, refusing to break.

"Stay," I whispered again as she closed her eyes and tossed her head back.

"I'm here." She clawed at my shoulders, pulling me deeper. Moaning as I thrust harder inside her sweetness. "I'm right here."

Violet cried out, squeezing me from within, her entire body jerking under mine. Setting off my own release with the feel of hers. After a little time to come down and a quick cleanup trip to the bathroom, I fell asleep to the sound of her heartbeat under my ear, to the feel of her hands stroking my back and her legs wrapped around my hips.

But when I woke up hours later to an empty bed and a small note with a simple *had to go* written on it, I was struck by the fact that she'd never promised not to leave. I had two choices: walk away from her with my heart intact, or...

Or.

Or was going to hurt like a bitch and might break something unfixable inside me, but there really was no other choice. I cared for her. Hell, I might have been falling for her. I was all in on the "or" plan.

CHAPTER NINETEEN

VIOLET

I parked my car on the street and hurried through the night toward the house. It was late—or maybe early was the right term for the hour. The only lights in the neighborhood were from the streetlights overhead, and the only noises those of the insects out and about. Dawn would be breaking soon.

I rarely stayed out all night, but I hadn't been able to leave Easton right away. We'd fallen asleep together, his big arms holding me close, me wrapped around his body and in his blankets. I slept better than I had in months like that, but reality had sunk in around three. I didn't want his neighbors to see me walking out the door, and I didn't need Grandma waking up and looking for me when I wasn't there. I needed to leave. Easton was probably going to be upset that I'd only left him a note, but I hadn't wanted to wake him. He needed his rest to work in the heat the way he did. Plus, I didn't want to have to deal with him trying to convince me to stay, because I wasn't sure I could resist him. One word, and I probably would have cuddled right back up against him and let the chips fall.

I'd snuck out, and now I was sneaking in.

Grandma's door made only the quietest of noises as I closed it, but it was enough that I cringed. Also enough for me to get caught. It didn't help that Dahlia was already up and in the kitchen.

"She returns." She took a sip of what had to be tea, her eyes bleary and her hair a mess.

"Are you up for the day already?"

"Couldn't sleep. I started having nightmares about back injuries and the arrogant dickhead at two in the morning. Figured there was no coming back from that, so I got up and made some tea. Want a cup?"

The long night made my eyes heavy, and I could practically feel my bed calling me, but resisting wasn't something I was up for. "Yeah, I'd love one."

I sat at the counter as she poured what smelled like a cinnamon blend. She even added a sugar lump, knowing how I preferred my tea on the sweet side. When she was finished, she picked up her cup again and leaned her hip against the counter. "I'm officially on vacation starting today. I can be here more, and you can run off and do whatever it is you and Easton are doing." Her voice sounded light and casual, but there was an edginess to it. A jealousy. Or perhaps I was imagining it.

"We're just…friends."

"It's three in the morning. You have sex hair and swollen lips, so don't tell me you two were playing euchre or something."

I licked my bottom lip, remembering the feel of Easton against it. Remembering his taste and the way he shook when I teased him with my tongue. A card game compared to that? No contest. "Nope. No euchre."

She laughed as I took a sip of my tea. "Well, good for you. I always did like him. His taste in friends is suspect, though."

The warmth of the cup in my hands soothed me, and the darkness of the house seemed to cut off the rest of the world. The kitchen felt safer somehow, more intimate than ever before. And though we'd talked a million times before that moment, we hadn't had a conversation about high school in years. Not really.

Perhaps it was time. "Why'd you go out with Wyatt in the first place?"

Dahlia stiffened, probably not expecting that question. But as her shoulders relaxed, as she sank deeper into her slouch against the counter and shrugged, she almost seemed to shrink into herself. To lose the front she put up every day and become just Dahlia. The little girl with the big heart, stirring her tea and staring into her cup. "He was cute and funny, and I'm not going to lie—his drive and ambition in regard to his dream of a career in hockey was something I loved. He was super nice to me at first. Very attentive, really into spending time with me." Her voice grew softer, a tinge of pain still there even after all those years. "He told me I was special."

"You are special."

"Ten years, no serious relationships, and countless other men always finding something wrong with me have proven you wrong." Her lips turned up almost sarcastically. "Not special enough anyway."

Her obvious pain hit me hard, her self-deprecation uncomfortable to hear. Dahlia was beautiful—bright and lively, with a personality that could set a room on fire and make a nun blush. She was so much more than I'd ever been, but she was struggling. A fact I'd never realized.

Because I hadn't been there for her.

"And that still bothers you?" I asked, leaning in. "That Wyatt was the only one who said you were special?"

"Because of how much of a lie it was, yes. Because he did it for years and never meant it, absolutely. I never would have asked him to give up his dream, but the way he walked away as soon as the first scout showed up without even attempting to make our relationship work gutted me." Her gaze met mine, harsher than before. On the offensive. "Does your history with Jace still bother you?"

Sometimes truth blew through like a wind rippling in the treetops, barely more than a whisper as it skated across the land. But sometimes truth was a chainsaw knocking the same tree to the ground with vicious teeth and a powerful thrust.

"Yes," I whispered, my throat tight. "It kills me that I hurt him, but I'm still so fucking angry about how he handled it all."

She sighed, her shoulders softening, her aggression reined in. "Anger gets you nowhere."

Eyebrows up, I cocked my head and threw her a halfhearted smile. "Is that directed at me or you?"

"Fuck if I know anymore." She shook her head. "Man, aren't we a couple of saps? All these years later, and a couple of immature boys still drive us to make really bad decisions."

"My decisions aren't so bad."

"So, you're staying this time?"

I couldn't recoil fast enough. "I never said that."

"Exactly." She held my gaze, refusing to let me escape. "Easton's not Jace. In fact, he's not like Jace at all. Maybe it's time for you to move on before you miss something amazing."

I set my cup down and rose to my feet, ready to call an end to the conversation. "You move on from Wyatt, and then maybe you can tell me what to do."

"Yeah, sure. Just one small difference between those two scenarios, Vee. Jace didn't cheat on you, did he?"

And just like that, the happiness from the night with Easton vanished, popping just like some delicate balloon floating through the air.

I pushed past her, heading for my bedroom. "Thanks for the tea."

But there was no sanctuary in the pink and tan room. No peace to be found. I paced over the plush carpet and worried my lip, wishing I were back with Easton in his bed. Wishing I were back in Chicago in my own bed.

Wishing I were anywhere but here.

Jace didn't cheat, did he?

No, he hadn't. That honor fell completely on me.

Dahlia's words spun through my mind, loud and bombastic. But underneath the noise, setting a rhythm I couldn't quite pin down, were Easton's words from the night at the trailer park. The ones that had filled me with shame and dread. The ones about his cousin…and his friend Dalton.

My cousin cheated on him, so we sort of took his side.

Easton had walked away from family because of cheating. Had hated it enough to side with the one who'd been cheated on. We'd been dancing around each other and spiraling closer for weeks, but he still didn't know. He had no clue the true history of Cowgirl Vee and the sex tape. And that fact, that truth told so late in the game, had the potential to ruin whatever I might possibly have with Easton.

Good news wasn't exactly what I'd been expecting the next morning. "What do you mean, you feel better?"

Grandma shrugged, scrubbing the kitchen sink as if her life depended on it. "I feel better. I think I'm over the worst of the adjusting to the chemo."

Dahlia and I met eyes, her looking about as unsure as I felt. "Okay," she said, stretching the word out to fill several seconds. "But you have chemo later today, right?"

"No, I meet with my oncologist this afternoon, though." Grandma rinsed out the dish sponge and set it back in its holder, still focusing on tasks instead of us. Still…hiding.

"I can take you," I offered, wishing for anything close to solidity beneath my feet.

"Mary's going with me," Grandma said as she grabbed her scouring pad from under the sink before heading to the stove. "You two girls can do other things."

"Not happening." I joined Dahlia, the two of us standing as a unit. A confused but wary unit. "What the hell is going on?"

"Nothing." Grandma tried to laugh, but there was no humor behind it. Not truth.

"Don't lie to us," I said.

That caught her attention. Grandma sighed and turned around, clutching the edge of the counter as if she needed a lifeline. "I don't want to upset you girls."

Dahlia flicked her eyes in my direction before refocusing on Grandma. "Why would you upset us?"

Grandma wiped off the counter and set her pad down, all with slow and precise movements. Stealing time. "I want you to understand that I've thought a lot about this."

A knot formed in my stomach. "About what?"

Her pale eyes met mine, then slid over to Dahlia. "I'm not going through with the chemo."

The clock in the family room ticked altogether too loud as the seconds passed. No other noises infiltrated the space. No other interruptions. It was as if we existed solely to count down those seconds, to dread each break in the silence. Each moment that we grew closer to losing the woman who seemed to be surrendering to death.

"No," Dahlia said with a shake of her head. "You can't just give in."

"I'm not giving in."

"Then what do you call it?" I asked, the pressure in my head growing with each infernal second marked off by the clock. "The doctors gave you good odds with chemo."

"Good odds to extend my life a little, not to make a recovery." Grandma sighed and led the way into the dining room, where she sat at the head of the table. She waited until

Dahlia and I sat as well, giving us time to get settled before she sat up straighter and took a deep breath. "Girls, the chemo is hard on me."

"We knew that was likely to be the case," I said.

"True, but I didn't know how bad it would be." She gave us a small smile. "I don't want to spend my last months so sick that I can barely make it out of bed."

Dahlia sniffled and reached out to hold my hand. "But if you stop the chemo—"

"Don't," Grandma interrupted. "I die either way. There's no medical intervention to stop that. The chemo was only going to delay the inevitable."

I sat in silence, staring at the woman who'd raised me. The one who'd loved me through every second of my life even when I didn't deserve it. I'd known when her diagnosis had come in that she'd be leaving us sooner than I'd like, but I'd hoped for the impossible. For more time than her body was willing to give us. That hope died right there at the table.

"How long?" I asked, knowing she'd already had this discussion with her doctors if she was so solid in her decision.

Grandma hesitated for only a moment. "Six months to a year is a solid estimate."

My cheeks grew wet, and my eyes burned as tears I didn't want to cry fell. Six months was nothing. It wasn't enough time to pay her back for all she'd done for me. It wasn't enough time to show her how much she meant to me. Hell, it wasn't enough time for me to figure out how to say goodbye to her. But it was enough time for her, and there was no way I could take that decision away from her.

"Okay," I said as I wiped the tears away. "Okay."

"That's it?" Dahlia asked, looking ready to do battle. "Grandma throws in the towel, and you say okay? This is so not okay."

"Dahlia—"

"It's her choice," I said, interrupting Grandma. "We don't have the right to tell her how to live her life or at what point she's had enough. She gets to decide that."

"So, you're just going to give up?" Dahlia turned her angry eyes on Grandma, making me want to jump in between them. "You're going to be like Vee and run away when things get tough?"

"That's enough," Grandma said before I could even respond. Before I could get over that particular knife to the back. "This is my life, my body, and my decision. I'm not giving up, but I'm also not going to suffer through my last days just to give myself more suffering. And that has nothing to do with what Violet does or does not do in her life, Dahlia Marie."

Dahlia wilted, glancing at me out of the corner of her eye. "Sorry, Violet. I didn't mean to throw you into the middle like that."

And though I nodded, though I accepted her apology without a word, the hurt still bloomed harsh and bright in my chest.

"Good," Grandma said. "Violet, I'd love it if you could stay a little longer. Even if you're not here to help me, I've missed you and would like to spend some time with you."

"I... Yeah," I whispered, my voice rough and broken. "I have a couple more days before I need to get back."

"Good. And, Dahlia? I'd like for you to spend a little more time with me. I don't want to get in the way of your work, but I want to take advantage of every moment I have left."

Dahlia sagged, tears running down her face already. "Of course. Anything you want."

"Good. Now, I'm going over to talk to Mary for a little bit. Maybe you two should take a moment to make sure we're all on the same page here because I won't be changing my mind." Grandma headed for the door without another word, leaving Dahlia and me at the table. The silence grew heavy, thick with tension in a way it hadn't before. Even that infernal clock couldn't break the moment.

But I could. "I'm sorry I ran away the way I did."

Dahlia looked up at me, her eyes wide and surprised. "I never thought you'd actually say that."

I shrugged. "It needed to be said. I can't regret making a life where I felt comfortable after everything that happened, but I can be sorry I missed out on more time with Grandma."

"Yeah," she said with a sigh. "Me too."

"But you're here—still. You live with her."

"But I work too much. Maybe if I'd chosen a different job, I'd have more time for a personal life."

I huffed and sat back. "We're a couple of real winners, aren't we?"

"Totally."

"What do we do?"

She lifted one shoulder. "We do what we can to make sure her last days are the best they can be."

Hours later, after many more tears and moments of despair, while the sun made its final show before tucking itself away for the night, I lay in my childhood bed and thought over Grandma's decision. She wasn't running from death or her cancer, but she was choosing how she wanted to go out. Choosing how she wanted to live before that choice was taken away from her. I longed to have that level of confidence, that strength within to say screw it and do exactly what I wanted to do. I wasn't brave enough, wasn't sure of how to move forward half the time. But she was, and it was inspiring.

In a moment of pure guts, I grabbed my phone and sent a message to the one person I wanted to talk to. The only one who could help me make sense of what was in my head. I reached out instead of running, and though the moment was fraught with fear on my end, it was also oddly empowering.

Grandma's stopping her cancer treatment. She doesn't want to spend her last days sick.

Easton came back immediately, as if he'd been waiting for my text.

She's a strong woman. What can I do?

Nothing. We're okay, I just wanted to—

I waited, my fingers over the screen, knowing what I should type to finish the message: *I just wanted to let you know. I don't need anything. I'm fine.*

But I wasn't fine, and I wasn't going to be fine anytime soon. There was no sense in lying about it. I erased the message I'd planned to hide behind, and I told him the truth.

I can't handle this alone.

I pressed send and held my breath. Asking for help wasn't something I was used to—hell, it wasn't something I had ever thought I'd be willing to do—but then came Easton, and all my old rules went out the window. Still, I couldn't bring myself to ask for anything. I could only throw him my own version of an SOS signal and hope he understood.

I rolled onto my side and waited as the bubbles that indicated he was typing appeared. Would he get it? Would he figure out what I needed? The message wasn't exactly clear.

But I never should have doubted him.

I'm coming. Give me fifteen minutes to wrap up, and I'll be there.

I gripped my phone as more tears fell. Almost happy tears this time. Relieved ones. I'd reached out, and he'd answered my call. He was a good man, one I didn't deserve. One I wished I'd found in so many different places and situations. But that was an impossibility. Easton was as Downriver as they came, and I was going to have to figure out how to handle that.

I'll be waiting.

CHAPTER TWENTY

EASTON

"Why do you suddenly look like your cat died?" Colton asked as he strolled into the office.

"What?" I glanced up from my phone, still stuck on the fact that Violet had sent me that message.

"Your face. It seems broken. Everything all right?"

"Yeah. I just…" I huffed a breath, trying hard to resettle myself. "Violet's grandma is stopping her cancer treatment."

"Shit," he said, leaning against the desk. "How's Violet taking it?"

"She said she doesn't want to be alone."

Colton's eyebrows flew up. "Well, that's unexpected."

"Yeah." I jumped out of my chair, the reality of what Violet had just done adding heat to my fire. She'd reached out instead of running. Without so many words, she'd asked me for help. I still had about fifty things to do, and that damn Land Rover still sat in one of my bays, needing to be finished, but work would have to wait. For once, I wasn't putting my business before everything else. Violet needed *me*. There was no fucking way I was failing her. "Can you close up for me?"

"Sure," Colton said, following me into the garage. "Anything else I can do?"

I grabbed my keys and looked around, unable to see the disarray of a shop in busy season. Unable to force my mind away from anything but my girl. "Finish that crappy engine rebuild for me."

"Yeah, not really possible, my friend."

"I figured. Finishing that brake job and closing up will be enough."

"Then, go. I've got this."

"Thanks." I was out the door and running to my truck seconds later. The engine thundered when I started it up, and the tires squealed when I popped the clutch and slammed the gas pedal down. Fuck speed limits and railroad tracks that could bust a suspension system faster than anything else—Violet needed me.

The front door opened as I pulled into the driveway, and Violet appeared. She looked wan, sad and pale and altogether not right. I threw the truck into park and jumped out, nearly running across her driveway. I didn't even give myself time to speak, couldn't figure out what needed to be said. All I could do was grab her, pick her up, and carry her back toward my truck so I could get her alone. I needed her safe and with me, someplace where I could focus solely on her to make sure she was okay. I craved it.

And the cab of my truck was going to have to do.

"You okay?" I asked as soon as I slammed the door behind me. I'd pushed Violet across the seat, barely giving myself room to climb up. But once we were tucked away inside, once it was just her and me, I reached for her again. Pulled her tight. Clung to her. "Talk to me, Violet."

She shook in my arms, her breaths coming fast. My shirt growing wet with her tears. "She doesn't want to live her last months sick from the chemo."

I ran a hand over her back, tangling my fingers in her hair at times. "I'm sorry."

"Me too," she murmured. "I feel like I wasted so much time."

I closed my eyes and pressed my lips to the top of her head, understanding that one all too well. "Yeah, I don't think that ever really goes away."

We stayed like that for what felt like forever, the two of us wrapped around each other. Not talking, not needing to, barely even moving as we simply existed together. The reality of the situation heavy between us. Violet would have to watch her grandma die, knowing with every day that her time was growing shorter. Wondering if every cough or headache was a sign that her time was drawing to a close.

A living hell for sure.

"Was it hard?" she asked suddenly, pulling me from the thoughts I'd let myself be distracted by.

"Was what hard?"

"Losing him…when your dad left. Was it as hard to get used to him not being there?"

I took a deep breath, letting myself remember. "Yeah, but it was a different situation. I had a lot of anger at how he left us."

She nodded and sniffled, still clinging. Still shaking. "I lost my mom when I was just a toddler, but I don't really remember, you know? I'm not sure if I should remember. It could be that I forgot because I was so young when it happened, or I might have blocked it out along the way to protect myself."

"Yeah, it could be either."

"I won't have that luxury this time."

I yanked her closer, forcing her into my lap as I adjusted my position so I could hold on to more of her body. "No, you won't. But you won't be alone either. I've got you."

And I did. I'd do anything for her, including reminding myself of the worst point in my life to help her through this. That moment was all I needed to know that I'd lost my grip on my restraint. There was no more holding back, no more bullshit *friends* lie to myself. Hell, I doubted I'd be able to hide it another second.

God help us both, but the girl was mine, and I was going to do whatever it took to keep her with me.

CHAPTER TWENTY-ONE

VIOLET

It took me close to an hour to calm down again. An hour that Easton spent being a quiet, calm, and soothing force. I so didn't deserve him.

"Thanks for coming for me." I sat in the middle of the bench seat, staring at Grandma's porch light glowing in the darkness and not wanting to leave the safety of Easton's truck. Not that the house wasn't safe, but it wasn't…Easton safe. There were memories inside that brick building that haunted me, smells and decorations that brought back the days when Jace would come storming through the door or sneaking through a window. Add into that the last few weeks of Grandma being so sick, of telling me she was giving up any hope of extending her life, and I was through. That house would never again be my home because of the ghosts inside, and it certainly wasn't where I wanted to be right then.

I hadn't realized I'd been crying again until Easton wiped his thumb over my cheek to collect my tear.

Without a word, he pressed his finger under my chin to force my eyes to his, peering at me. "What's wrong?"

Everything. "Nothing."

His lips tightened even as his brow furrowed. "You're sitting here like you're about to go to the guillotine. What do you need?"

I stared, my heart racing, words battering about in my head. Seeking answers to a question I hadn't been prepared to hear. Had anyone asked me about my needs before? Had anyone cared enough to stop everything and come to my aid? Anyone who wasn't family, at least? I peered at Easton and let words and wants and base needs cycle through my head until finally, I opened my mouth. "I don't want to be here."

Easton leaned closer, holding my head up with his fingers as his thumb brushed over my lips. "Here as in Downriver, here as in this house, or here as in with me?"

"This house. I don't want to remember..." I closed my eyes. *Damn it.* My entire life seemed to be wrapped up in that house. All the memories of my life there came flooding in, and they wouldn't let go. The good and the bad, the joyful and the ones that hurt. Like an anchor, they dragged me down, slowly drowning me. Pressing against my chest until there was no room for anything else. And I just wanted to breathe.

Without a word, Easton threw the truck into gear and backed out of the driveway before heading toward town.

"Where are we going?"

"Someplace else."

Oddly, that answer was enough for me, because Easton was holding my hand. I liked it, liked feeling so connected to him, liked the vibration of the engine transmitting through the bench seat and his hand. I liked everything about being in this truck with him. But when he turned into the lot at the ice rink, all that like turned into something closer to confusion. "What are we doing here?"

"You came here with Jace."

"Yeah," I replied, still not getting his point. "And you probably came here with girls you dated."

He parked the truck all the way in the back, in one of the darkest spots, before turning in his seat to face me. "I did."

"Okay." I glanced around the near-empty lot, still not putting the pieces together. "So then why are we here now?"

"We're taking your mind off everything and making new memories."

Easton grabbed me and pulled me against him, pressing his lips to mine in a blistering kiss. I melted in his arms, so thankful to be touching him again. But Easton wasn't going to let me be passive. He gripped me hard, sliding me underneath him as he angled his body across mine. And when his lips moved down my chin, his teeth finding sensitive spots along my neck to tease, I clutched him just as strong but with my knees around his hips.

"I'm not going to let you go," he murmured, breaking my heart with the need in his voice. He didn't mean right then, didn't mean physically. He was looking for more...more time, more of me, more of us. More of things I had no idea if I could give him. But right then, as he lifted my shirt and pulled the cup of my bra down, as he whispered words against my skin and held me so strongly, I wanted to believe. Wanted to cling to him, to never let go. I wanted to stay.

"Don't let go." I worked my hands between us, under my skirt, quickly shoving my panties down one leg. "Easton, please."

He dropped his head to my chest, his mouth finding my nipple and sucking. So hot and wet. An enticing little mix of pleasure and pain as he bit down. I arched into him, wanting his hands on me. Wanting so much more than we could get in that old truck. The seat burned my skin, the angle making my ribs ache a little. Too much.

I shifted toward the door, spreading my legs and placing a foot on the dash to inch myself back. Easton dropped one knee to the floorboard, and all those teenage fantasies of the things we could do in this truck suddenly spun through my head. Some were about to become more than just fantasies, and I couldn't wait. God bless bench seats and the days before consoles were created.

Easton groaned as he took me in, his light eyes practically sparkling as he saw how I'd bared myself to him so blatantly.

"Is this a hint?" He gripped my ankle, holding my leg against the dash. Almost pinning me in place. He lifted my other leg, bringing my calf to his shoulder. "You feeling greedy, baby?"

I bit my lip and nodded, shivering as his fingers trailed down my inner thigh. Unable to speak past the haze of desire blanketing me. I wanted him. His hands, his lips, his tongue…just him. All of him. And I wanted him now.

"Keep your dress covering most of you, just in case. I only need that pretty pussy to work with." Easton edged closer then sank between my legs, teasing me with his mouth on my hip bones. Lower still, biting his way along the seam of my hip. I fisted his hair as he inched lower yet, licking a trail down to where I was so hot and wet for him.

And, oh God, his mouth.

He didn't tease or go slow, didn't warm me up with something soft and easy. No, Easton wasn't that type of guy. He dove right in, attacking me with his tongue. Going from zero to sixty in a single breath. The shiver of desire that ran through me made me shake all over. Easton gripped me harder, pulled me lower on the seat. Groaning. The vibrations sent me spinning, had me jerking and clenching even as he continued his torturous ways.

When he sucked my clit between his lips, when he made sparks appear behind my eyelids with his tongue, I arched right off the seat and practically screamed. So much sensation. So much wet and heat and pressure and everything. Easton gripped my hips, pulling me toward him as he grew more aggressive. As he licked and sucked and bit at me, each exquisite action driving me toward the moment we both knew was coming. Lips, tongue, teeth…he treated me to an experience I wouldn't soon forget.

Every brush had me seeing stars, every warm breath against my skin was something to treasure. And when he slid two fingers inside me, when he sat back on his knees to watch as he fucked me with his hand, I lost all control. Writhing, groaning, tweaking my own nipples through my dress, I chased that sensation of completeness I knew he could give me. I raced for it.

"That's it," he whispered, keeping his hand moving. "I feel you, baby. You're so wet for me. I want to see you come like this. With my hand inside you, with my tongue on that pussy I can't stop thinking about. Give it to me."

He licked me again, all the way around his own fingers. So fucking filthy with his mouth. My legs shook as he came back to my clit, as he surrounded it with his lips once more. He gave it a flick of his tongue before sucking. Before knocking me right out of the race.

With a stuttered gasp of his name, I fell. Jerking, shaking, cursing, I came with an explosive power that took me completely by surprise. But not Easton. He was ready for me. Before I was over the aftershocks, he slid up my body, kissing me deeply as soon as he could. The taste of myself on his lips was sexier than I'd ever thought possible. Something to truly take note of, an intimacy I'd never shared with anyone else. And when he pulled back with a groan and a roll of his hips, I knew we weren't quite done.

"God, I want to fuck you so bad right now." He thrust forward, rubbing himself against me. "I'm so hard for you, Violet."

"Do it, Easton."

He shook his head, pulling my leg over his shoulder and sinking his teeth into my knee before coming back to me. "Not here. Not like this. I won't let anyone see you so wild. Won't risk you. I want your body all for me."

I nodded, something inside me warming at the idea that he was looking out for me, for us. There were a few things we could do, though. A few tricks I had hidden up my sleeve. I pushed his shoulder and reached between us. Grabbing his dick and wrapping my fingers around it. Sliding them up and down in a rhythm he'd taught me well already. Pulling him against where I was so hot and wet for him. Where he'd just spent so much time.

"Violet, what—"

"Hush." I tugged harder, inching down the seat to bring us even closer. "Let me see you come. I just want to see you."

Easton could only nod, his eyes closed and his head hanging as he thrust into my hand and against my folds. Every few jerks, he'd open his eyes and look around outside, checking for privacy, making sure we were still alone, it seemed. Taking care of us. Each was a moment of sweetness in a debauched sort of situation. And they were perfect. Everything felt so darn perfect.

The way he held me down, controlling most of my body with the sheer mass of his, should have put him in the power position between us. And yet, my hand on him put me in the driver's seat. He gave that to me, let me take him where I knew he needed to go. Let me lead him even as he played protector and guarded us. And that was so hot.

It didn't take long before Easton began to shake, his eyebrows drawing together. "Close. Fuck, baby. A little harder. I want to be inside you so bad, so bad."

I nodded, tightening my hold, biting my lip as he ran his dick against my overstimulated clit over and over. Shit, he was going to make me come again if he didn't stop soon. He felt so good right there, felt so hard. I wanted him inside me, wanted to pull him up on the seat and let him pound me right into the door. But we couldn't...not here...not now. So I held him in my hand and against my pussy, and I made sure he got what he needed.

"Come on me," I said, leaning forward to press my lips to his jaw. "Mark me as yours. I want it."

His groan may as well have been that of a wild animal, deep and long and so very sexy. It fed my own desire, made my body shake with the feral quality behind it. A few thrusts, and Easton came all over my hand with a grunt, curving into my touch and locking down every muscle. Such a sexy image. Completely out of control, surrendering to what I could do for him. And it was exactly how I wanted him to be. Exactly what we both needed…almost.

"Want to be inside you," Easton whispered as his body relaxed against mine, biting my collarbone while pushing me into the seat with his mass. "Let me take you home with me, Violet. I don't want to leave you yet."

I wrapped my legs around him and held him tight, knowing I should say no. That I should tell him I was heading home in a few days, go back to Grandma's house, deal with what was coming, and pack for Chicago. I still hadn't mentioned that I was leaving soon for a catering job, but I didn't want to. Not right then. I gave in to the utter temptation that was Easton Cole, even though I knew how hard it would be to crawl away from him later.

"Yes."

CHAPTER TWENTY-TWO

EASTON

The moonlight made the kitchen seem almost bright as I stood in the midnight shadows. Violet slept in my bed down the hall, peaceful and quiet. I couldn't sleep, though. There were too many worries flying around my head, too much anxiety. With her grandma dying, Violet would have every reason to run again. If I couldn't help her see how good we were together and how much this place could be home for her, she'd get spooked and disappear. Not because of something I'd done, but because of something she was. I'd given myself over to the "or" plan, knowing how it could go. Knowing how bad it would hurt when she left.

With Dolly purring at my feet, I poured a glass of water and grabbed my phone from the charger. Thirteen texts. Colton, Brogan, Gracie…all checking to see if everything was okay, if Violet was okay. If I needed backup in some way. And while I loved them for their concern, there was nothing they could do. Not for me, and especially not for Violet. They didn't know her the way I did, didn't understand how skittish she could be. How guarded. When I had her wrapped in my arms, she was so calm and sweet, so *there*. That was the Violet I was falling in love with. The one I was beginning to think about a future with. The one who could and probably would destroy me.

The sound of feet padding across the wood floor greeted my ears moments before her soft voice did.

"Hey." She wrapped her sleep-warm body around mine, her arms coming across my chest. I grabbed her hand and brought it to my lips, kissing the back. Clinging to her the only way I could.

"What are you doing up?" I asked, knowing the answer might be leaving. Dreading it.

"I needed some water. Hey, Dolly." She let me go only long enough to pet my cat, something I found endearing. Or maybe it was just the fact that I was so far gone over this girl and, for the moment, she wasn't leaving.

I set my glass and phone on the counter and turned, wrapping myself around her. She was wearing one of my Second Gear T-shirts, a threadbare, black thing that barely covered her ass. Something that made the caveman in me quite happy. My clothes, my girl. Not that I could ever say that, but I could think it. I teased the edges of the shirt, lifting the back to slide my hands over her naked flesh. To squeeze her even closer.

She smiled up at me, her tousled hair making her look so much younger in the shadows. "Did I tire you out?"

"Definitely, but I'm not complaining."

Her lips were warm and soft when I kissed her. A perfect combination I'd become addicted to. I flicked my tongue against hers, the heat that always flared between us growing brighter. Stronger. But I let it fade, let us go back to our comfortable snuggle. It was late, and I was already shocked she'd stayed this long. I had no doubt she'd leave before the sun came up. And I hated that thought.

"I need you here, Violet," I said, more honest than I may have ever been. Knowing that made me more vulnerable.

She sighed as I placed my forehead against hers. "I know."

"Stay," I choked out, ready to fight for her. Ready for the disappointment when she told me no.

"I don't think I can."

"You can. I'll be right beside you." I squeezed her in tight, closing my eyes and wishing like I've never wished before. "We'll figure it all out. I promise."

She clung to me, shaking. Her voice weak as she said, "I wish I could go back and make different decisions."

"I know, baby. But there's no going back. We can only move forward. And I want to move forward with you beside me. Please."

She shook her head but held me tighter, the two of us rocking back and forth in the middle of my dark kitchen. Dancing together, the only music the sound of our hearts beating in time.

As the moon lost its light, as clouds began to roll in from the west, she whispered one single, impactful sentence. "I want to be with you always."

And fuck, didn't those words sound good? I kissed her forehead and sighed, ready to take her back to bed so I could rest my weary mind. Those words were what I needed, were what I was desperate to hear from her. The start of a promise. The possibility of tomorrow.

"That's all I can ask."

I took her back to bed, spooning against her under the blankets. Holding her in my arms the way I was desperate to. But again, I couldn't sleep. Reality refused to let me go. Words were good, they were a start, but Violet was a runner. Words wouldn't pull her back if she bolted.

It was impossible to cage a wild animal set on running away.

CHAPTER TWENTY-THREE

VIOLET

"Five minutes," I murmured, trying and failing to pull myself away from Easton's lips.

He tilted his head, kissing me deeply for a moment before pulling back with a nip to my bottom lip. "Three, or I'm coming in to drag you out."

I chuckled, kissing him again. "I need time to get dressed."

His hands gripped my hips, almost lifting me over the console of the sports car he drove. "I prefer you naked."

I finally sighed and edged back, leaving him looking all kiss-swollen and half-lidded. So fucking sexy. "Three minutes. Then I'll be back."

"You'd better."

With a last blown kiss in his direction, I stumbled out of his car and hurried inside. I was still wearing my clothes from the day before when Easton had come to my rescue. We'd spent the entire night together at his place, me wrapped up in his arms. Him holding on to me as if I was something precious he didn't want to lose. And it was everything I ever could have wanted, everything

I'd needed in that moment. As was early-morning sex in his bed, though we'd apparently scandalized poor Dolly. She'd refused to come out from behind the couch after that.

But we'd grown hungry as the day had passed, and he wanted to take me somewhere for lunch, so I needed to get dressed. Which meant heading to Grandma's house to grab some clothes.

Dahlia was in the dining room when I walked through the front door. "Well, aren't you a little harlot."

I rolled my eyes and brushed past her with a smile, heading toward my room. "Back off, cuz. I'm just here to change clothes."

"Walk of shame extended? Nice. Where are you headed?"

"Lunch." I tossed my suitcase onto the bed in my room. My hands shook as I dug for a skirt, knowing the bag was packed for a reason. For when I went back to Chicago.

Two days to go, and I still hadn't told Easton. Still didn't know when or if I'd be back.

When...it has to be when. Grandma is dying, and I need to be there with her.

"Lunch." Dahlia leaned against the doorframe, watching me.

"Yes, lunch. As in food."

"Food…with Easton."

"Yeah."

Her smile spread across her face, making every bit of her seem to light up. "I'm happy for you."

I rolled my eyes again, my stomach knotting. "It's just lunch."

"After a slumber party."

I switched my dress for a skirt, glaring at her as I pulled the cotton up my legs. "And your point is?"

She shrugged. "He showed up here like a knight in shining armor when you needed him. I told you, I'm happy for you. You deserve a good man."

"It's just lunch." I pushed past her, stopping in the bathroom to apply a bit of deodorant and perfume. God, this was crazy. When Easton had casually said "let's go for lunch," I hadn't realized how insane it would be. We'd showered at his place, which led to some amazing sex in the tiny bathroom. The man had arm strength to spare. But now…now it was settling in that we were about to go out again. To have a date in public. With me wearing one of his Second Gear T-shirts just as bold as anything. There would be no denying we were together if anyone saw us.

I shook my head and threw my hair into a messy ponytail. This was crazy, but right. It felt good. And even Dahlia's mild-mannered teasing wasn't going to make me think twice about it.

I grabbed my bag and headed for the door, ready to be back in Easton's car with him.

"Hey, Violet?"

I spun, worry knotting itself around my heart at the concerned expression on my cousin's face. "Yeah?"

"Don't let them win."

"Who?"

"Jace and his friends. Don't let them and what they did run you off from your home or keep you from someone amazing. We don't have nearly as much time as we always think we do, so don't let them take a second from you."

The answer was automatic and not necessarily true. "I'm not."

Her silence said more than any words could have. The quiet begged to be filled, and I caved far too easily.

"I'm not letting anyone win. I know you don't believe me."

"You're right—I don't. But I hope for you. I still hope that you'll find a way past everything and come home." She sighed before whispering, "I miss you so much, Violet. These next few months are going to be brutal for all of us, and we need you here."

"I know." I swallowed hard, my throat tight and my eyes burning. "I miss you too, Dahlia. We'll get through this together, I know it. I need to figure a lot of things out, but I have to go right now. Easton's outside."

"He's a good man," she said after a slight pause. "Don't keep him waiting. Grandma and Mary are playing that building video game they love, and I've got nothing but bad reality shows to catch up on."

"Good. I'll see you when I get back." I hurried out the door, chewing on the inside of my cheek. Her words hit hard, hit home in a way only Dahlia could do. I shouldn't keep Easton waiting for me. This situation—me being here—wasn't permanent. I couldn't ask Easton to leave Downriver, couldn't make him risk his business and his career on the chance of something great. Great didn't always last. Great sometimes failed. True, I'd probably be home more over the next few months as I tried to steal every second I could with Grandma, but that would never be enough. Not for him. Not for me either. And even if it were, that need to be here would end when Grandma died… Then what?

I wasn't at all ready to think about that.

Easton stood on the passenger's side of the car, waiting for me. Even though he wore dark sunglasses, I knew his eyes were on me the whole time. I could feel them. And I liked knowing he was paying so much attention. Without a word, he helped me into the passenger seat then shut the door behind me, running around the front. Once he was in the driver's seat with the engine humming, he turned to me with a serious expression. "Everything all right?"

I nodded, fidgeting with the hem of his shirt. "Yeah. Of course."

He put the car in gear, the engine growling low and strong. "Liar, but I'll let it go for now. Answer me this, though. What do you want to eat?"

I stared blankly. "Food."

"I figured that, but what kind?"

"Any?"

He pulled out of the driveway, revving the engine down the street. "Steak? Fish? Burgers? Wings?"

My stomach practically growled at the words falling from his lips. "Burgers. Definitely burgers."

"My kind of girl." He grabbed my hand with his, weaving our

fingers together while using his palm to change gears. Windows down, radio blaring, he drove us to the river then turned south, heading away from the city.

"Where are we going?"

"New joint on Biddle. A couple of the guys I know opened it. Good beer, great burgers."

"Sounds perfect."

He glanced at me, smiling. "Yeah, it does."

We drove down Jefferson, passing the shuttered steel mill and the small community golf course, over railroad tracks and through neighborhoods good and bad until we came roaring into Wyandotte. The downtown stretch was crowded with shoppers out walking on their main thoroughfare along the water. A fact that had the butterflies flying about in my gut. So many people. So many chances to be recognized.

Not what I needed to focus on right then.

Easton pulled behind a strip of buildings to a small parking lot practically filled with muscle cars like the one he was driving, only older. Bright paint jobs, wide tires, and animal-like curves made of metal and fiberglass decorated the space and stole every bit of my attention.

"Everyone driving large these days?"

Easton grinned. "This parking lot is like an art gallery of my work."

"You rebuilt these?"

"Every single one of them."

"They're…beautiful." And they were. All curves of steel and aggressive design. Paint jobs ranged from simple black to a glittery bright-blue paint with flames over the wheel wells. I pointed at the flame-covered car. "Flashy, no?"

"That's Gunner's car and Colton's handiwork with the paint. Gunner manages the restaurant, and if you think his car is flashy, wait until you meet *him*." He escorted me inside with his hand on my back. A polite but possessive move that made me walk a little taller, made my hips swing a little more. We entered through a back door, cutting down a hallway and past what had to be the kitchen on the way to the main dining area. When we turned the final corner, Easton leaned down and whispered in my ear. "Get ready."

I shivered at his breath against my skin, but the hall erupted in noise before I could say anything to him.

"Easton Cole, you filthy fuck. Get over here!" A man with wild, bright blond hair and the iciest blue eyes I'd ever seen hurried over. He smiled at the other customers like a shark, all teeth and no emotion, but for Easton, that smile went all the way to his eyes. Lighting him up, making him more stunning than anything I'd ever seen before. A fallen angel in the middle of a suburban restaurant.

"What's up, Gunner? How's business?"

"Eh, local code inspector's got my nuts in a vise over some stupid vent hood issue, but otherwise, it's good, man. I'd ask about your business, but that would mean ignoring this beautiful piece on your arm." He turned those eyes on me, almost dazzling me with the power of his attention. "How you doin', doll? I'm Gunner."

"Easy, killer." Easton put his arm around my shoulders and pulled me against his side. A not-so-subtle pissing-on-my-leg maneuver that I, oddly, didn't mind. "This is Violet, and she's here with me."

"You poor thing." Gunner's eyes practically twinkled as he leaned closer. "You get tired of dealing with this lug, you come see Gunner. I'll take good care of you."

"Okay, okay." Easton laughed. "Enough with trying to steal my girl. We're just here for lunch."

I grinned, biting my lip to try to hide it. Gunner was hard to resist in a way, not that he had a shot. I had Easton wrapped around me and calling me his girl. There was nothing that could compare to that. Even if it *was* temporary and would hurt like hell once it ended, it felt too good right then to give up.

Live in the moment, and all that jazz.

"You finally bring a girl around, and all you want to do is eat my food." Gunner winked at me. "Come on this way. I'll give you two primo seats up front."

We followed Gunner to a table by the windows overlooking the street. The restaurant was crowded even though it was a little early for lunch, telling me the food *had* to be good. It definitely looked good. My mouth practically watered when I saw all the hefty burgers on plates as we passed.

"A seat for the lady." Gunner held my chair for me and pushed it in as I sat, making Easton roll his eyes.

"I got this, man."

"Don't listen to him," Gunner said, leaning over to hand me a menu as he motioned for a waiter. "He knows a lot about nuts and bolts, but I taught him everything he knows about being a gentleman. This guy was a boorish brute when we met. It was I who smoothed those edges."

"Now that's the truth." Easton grinned, sitting back in his chair. "I had no game before Gunner."

"Damn straight." Gunner turned to the waiter. "Charlie, set them up, anything they ask for. On the house."

"Gunner, no—"

"Shut up, Easton. My treat for you bringing me such a lovely decoration for my window." He leaned over my hand and kissed it. "Miss Violet, I truly hope you enjoy your lunch. If you need anything, you tell Charlie to come get me and I'll be here."

Jeesh, those eyes were so…intrusive. It was as if he could see right through me, or at least through my clothes. "Thank you."

"You're very welcome." He smacked Easton in the head on the way past. "Put your napkin in your lap, you cretin."

"Yes, sir." Easton laughed and shook his head, but he dropped his napkin into his lap as directed.

"Soooo," I said, trailing the word until I knew Gunner was across the room. "He seems nice."

Easton snorted a laugh. "'Nice' is an understatement. He's the epitome of charm but on speed. When we played hockey together, the man gave all of us lessons on manners and how to treat women, but he did it while busting the balls of every guy on the team."

"Sounds almost terrifying."

"Try exhausting. But he means well, and he did teach me how to treat the lady on my arm."

"Yes, he certainly did."

Easton's eyebrows shot up as his lips tipped into a crooked sort of smile. "So, no complaints so far?"

I shook my head, hiding my grin behind my water glass. "Definitely not."

He nodded, smiling as he looked over the menu. "Good to know."

I took a drink of water and picked up my menu as well. The burgers crowded their section, words calling out every type of meat and topping available. And I wanted them all. The last twelve hours had brought on one hell of an appetite.

When Charlie made it back to the table, Easton glanced my way. "Ready to order?"

"Yeah. I'll have the double black and blue burger, medium, with caramelized onions on brioche please."

"Great choice," Charlie said, smiling my way. "If I could recommend a side, the truffle fries are amazing."

"How about one large order of those?" Easton said, looking to me for approval. "We can split them, that way we have room for ice cream later."

I grinned. "Sounds perfect."

Charlie took my menu. "And to drink?"

I glanced at the beer listing on the table. "How's the pilsner?"

"Light and well-balanced," Charlie replied. "Not too heavy on the hops and perfect for a hot summer day."

"Sounds like exactly the right choice."

"Yeah, it does." Easton handed Charlie his menu. "I'll have the same."

Charlie nodded once. "Great. I'll get your orders in and bring you your beers."

"Blue cheese fan?" I asked once we were alone again.

Easton shrugged. "I like a little bite to my cheese sometimes."

"You should try the blue-cheese cheesecake I make. It's savory and sweet at the same time. It sells out every time it's on the menu." And just like that, my good mood wobbled. That light, fun feeling I'd been enjoying turned darker, and my stomach knotted into something unbearable. Two days. Our relationship would change or end in two days, and he had no idea. I had to tell him. I still had so much to tell him.

Easton grew quieter, smiling softly. "I'd love to try it. I'd love to try anything you make. Cooking seems like such a passion of yours."

"It is. Which reminds me." I swallowed hard, fighting to find the words I needed to say. To find the guts to speak them. "Remember I told you about the catering job I have scheduled back in Chicago?"

He nodded and grabbed his water "Sweets table, right? What about it?"

Before I could answer, a group of people walked into the restaurant, talking overly loudly and disrupting the vibe of the place. But that wasn't why I spun, why I stared, and why my chest seized up.

Lacey Brown led the way into the restaurant. Former head cheerleader at my school. Former friend. One of the first ones to turn on me, and definitely the most vicious.

Also, Jace's twin sister.

"Shit." The vision of everything I'd attempted to build over these past weeks came crashing down. I should have known I'd run into her eventually, should have been prepared for it. Instead, I'd built a house of cards in a room with the window open, tempting fate.

Easton followed my gaze, his shoulders going stiff when he noticed the same crowd I did. "Do you want to leave?"

I glanced toward the back of the restaurant, but I couldn't see past the crowds. We were trapped. My chest tightened, my breathing turning labored. Everything hurt, every inch of me burned. I couldn't focus, couldn't speak. I couldn't—

Easton placed his hand over mine, his blue eyes calm but fierce as they stared at me. They gave me something to focus on even as a chill descended over my body. Every instinct screamed at me to run, but Easton sat tall and steady. Boosting me up. He was a man ready to fight when all I wanted to do was disappear. It was then, as I peered at the man my heart had chosen to love, that the sickening truth washed over me. I'd never be strong enough for this man. But I could try.

I took a deep breath, glancing once more at the group behind him. "I'm afraid this is going to get really ugly."

Easton nodded and squeezed my hand. "It's fine. We'll go."

He waved for Charlie, but the motion was also noticed by the crowd at the door. By Lacey. And when her eyes met mine, I knew that house of cards was about to come crashing down.

CHAPTER TWENTY-FOUR

EASTON

I waved for Charlie, watching as Violet's face went white. Shit. I'd brought her all the way down here without thinking about the clientele. The restaurant was popular with people from our area because Gunner was a sort of local celebrity. He'd been on television a hundred times, had helped emcee a parade or two, and he hosted a radio show about the food scene in Detroit. He was a draw for the restaurant, but I hadn't even considered that. And because I'd been an idiot, Violet was sitting across from me looking as if she was ready to sprint all the way back to Chicago. Where the hell was that waiter?

"Vee? Is that really you?" Lacey Brown walked up to the table, her fake smile a little too cunning for my liking.

"Hi, Lacey." Violet looked sick, though she sat with her back straight and her head up.

"I heard you were back in town. Where have you been hiding?" Lacey caught a look at me, her eyes widening a bit. "And out with Easton Cole. What a…surprise."

Violet had been right—this was going to get ugly. It was time to get Violet the fuck away from Jace's sister.

I rose to my full height, towering over Lacey. Making sure she got a solid look at my glare before heading around her. "C'mon, Violet. We should get back."

"Everything okay over here?" Gunner appeared out of nowhere, his manager smile in place. Thank fucking Christ.

Violet's arms shook under my palms as I helped her out of her seat. "Yeah, but we were thinking about getting our order to go."

Gunner looked at each of us in turn, his eye twitching just slightly when he focused on Lacey. "Of course. I believe you parked in the private lot, correct?"

I nodded, hoping like hell Violet could hold on for just another minute. And that Lacey could watch her mouth for that same time.

"Why don't you two come back with me?" He grabbed Violet's elbow, looking like the perfect host helping a lady to her feet. But I knew him. Knew he was holding her tightly, that he was directing her. Gunner was good with people. He had to see how badly Violet needed to escape. I was so thankful for that knowledge, too.

Once Violet was on her feet, Gunner stepped between her and Lacey, giving me the opportunity to take his place at my date's side. Which was good, because all I wanted was to touch her, to lend her my strength. To let her know I was right there with her and wouldn't let her fall.

Gunner gave me a subtle nod as I took Violet's elbow, then turned to face Lacey. "I'll have Charlie over here in a flash to seat your party, ma'am."

"Going so soon, Vee?" Lacey asked.

Violet flinched but pasted a smile on her face. "Yeah. It's time for me to get back to my grandma's house."

By now, other people were noticing our little party. Heads

turned and whispers started as they recognized me or Violet. Or Lacey.

"You should stay," Lacey said in a fake, high-pitched voice. "It would be fun."

Fun, my ass. Cruel. A cat playing with the mouse it was going to eat when it got bored. Well, fuck that—Violet was no mouse, and I wasn't about to let her be batted around for nothing.

But before I could steer her toward the back hall, Violet grabbed my hand. Clinging to it, really. "My grandma's sick, and I'd really like to get back and make sure she's okay."

"Oh well, that's too bad. Jace is on his way here right now. I bet he'd love to see you. You two haven't really talked since he found out you cheated on him with that football player from Grosse Pointe, right?" The smile on Lacey's face turned positively wicked, not that she mattered anymore. Violet had gone completely pale, her eyes almost dead as she stared at the other woman. "Too bad the cameras never showed his face. I heard he was a real looker. Though they caught you just right. Made any other pornos for my yearly rodeo party, Cowgirl? Or was that the end of your adult film career?"

All the air disappeared out of the room, and every head turned our way as my blood practically boiled. If Lacey had been a man, I would have decked him. All out, no holding back, knocked him flat on his ass. But some lessons were too ingrained not to stick, so hitting a woman was off-limits.

But words weren't.

"You're a real piece of work, bringing up stuff that hasn't mattered in ten years," I spat, stealing Lacey's attention from Violet. "Maybe we should call that basketball player from Monroe you got cozy with sophomore year. The one you gave a blow job to right under the bleachers."

Lacey's face went stiff, her emotions well hidden. "I don't know what you're talking about."

"No? You put his dick in your mouth, but you don't

remember? We could call my buddy Jude, then. I heard all about that night when you dragged him into the ladies' room at the Metro Lounge. It was your bachelorette party, if I remember how the story goes. How many women walked in and saw you on your knees on the bathroom floor, I wonder? Violet was just a kid making a bad decision. What was your excuse as an adult with a fiancé at home?"

Lacey blanched and glanced around the room at all the people staring, her mouth hanging open as if she wanted to say something but couldn't find the words. Not that anything she had to say mattered. I'd made my point. I pulled a shaking Violet past the table, quickly yanking her in front of me so I could put my body between her and Lacey. Who wasn't quite done yet.

"You'd better watch yourself, Easton. She's a liar and a cheater, though I don't know why I'm warning you. I'm sure she told you what really happened at the bowling alley."

Violet stumbled at Lacey's words, grew even more pale, if that was possible. I held on tighter, trying to keep her on her feet, but that only made the situation more obvious.

Lacey spotted that moment of weakness and pounced, using that damned singsong voice to do it. "Aw, did the poor cowgirl forget to tell her latest fling the truth? C'mon, Vee, you've played the liar card too many times."

"Lacey," I spat, pulling Violet as quickly as I could toward the back. "Give it a rest."

Violet tried to pull her hand from mine, but at the same moment, Gunner pushed his way through the small crowd that had gathered. He pulled Violet and me along with him, heading for the back of the restaurant. Just a few more seconds, and I'd have her out of the fishbowl the restaurant had become. Another minute, and she'd be in my car. I needed to keep calm, stay focused, and not hit the woman following us.

The one who wasn't done torturing my girl yet.

"I thought Colton Bearn was the manwhore of the trailer park quartet, him and his brother, Wyatt. I heard he had a number of women in his bed while Dahlia Foster sat at home waiting for him to take her on the road with him. Isn't that right, Vee? Those Bearn brothers have reputations almost as bad as yours. I would have guessed one of them would have been the one to try to hit on Cowgirl Vee, not you, Easton," she said as we finally made it through the throng of people clogging our way. Would she ever shut her mouth? "Guess Colton passed that video around your shop. Did you need to see for yourself what it was like to have the cowgirl ride you?"

"Fuck off, Lacey!" I yelled, unable to hold my tongue or keep my voice down.

But some people didn't know when to quit. "Oh, I see. You're not just passing the video around. You're passing the cowgirl around too?" She laughed, the sound wicked and cruel. Fake. "Jesus, Vee. Did you really go from bowling alley bimbo to garage floor whore? That's a big step down—from Jace to the trailer park kids. You an *employee* of Second Gear Auto Repair now?"

I spun, my hand clenched in a fist, ready to say fuck every rule I'd ever learned, but Gunner slid right in front of me.

"Enough," he said. "Let me handle it. Violet doesn't need you going to jail right now."

It took a second, but I finally nodded, my neck stiff. That woman, that fucking beast, didn't deserve my attention. Violet did, and it was time to take her home. As Gunner headed for Lacey, I threw my hand in the air, offering Lacey a one-finger salute as a parting shot.

Violet, on the other hand, stayed silent. Eerily so.

"You okay?" I asked, rubbing my hand over her shoulder.

She flinched, taking a step away from me. Something that sent a blade of ice slicing across my chest. But this wasn't the time or the place to discuss what had been said.

"C'mon, baby. Let's get you home." I directed Violet through the back hallway, too fucking furious to dare pausing. Too worried about her non-reaction to even take a breath. So many things suddenly clicked, pieces of the past finally falling together. Jace's refusal to help Violet battle the gossip once everyone found out, the guilt she continued to wear like a shroud. Her refusal to call Jace out for being an ass. She'd cheated on Jace. She probably felt like the one to blame, as if she deserved to be treated like trash for a decision she'd made as a kid. We needed to talk about all of it…and quick.

Gunner caught up with us by the kitchen, though. "You two okay?"

"Fine," Violet whispered, refusing to look up from the floor.

Gunner peered at me over Violet's head, a pained expression on his face. Fuck, I needed to get her out of here. Especially now with Jace showing up any minute.

"Gunner," I whispered, holding on to Violet's arms. "I'm sorry about the food, but we need to go."

Charlie appeared as if summoned, handing me a paper bag with thin rope handles. "Your burgers."

"Thanks, man." I reached for my wallet, but Gunner put a hand on my arm.

"I got it."

The noise from the restaurant grew louder, and a voice I was pretty sure was that of Violet's ex-boyfriend joined the din. As much as I wanted to argue with Gunner and pay at least the tip, I needed to get Violet the hell out of here.

Still, I made sure to hold Gunner's gaze as I promised, "I owe you."

"You owe me shit." Gunner waved us down the hall, he and Charlie stepping behind us. "Go take care of your woman. I've got a party to ban from my restaurant for good."

There were a lot of reasons I called Gunner a friend, and that decision was one of them. I'd owe him for this. Big-time. But that would be handled another day.

I directed Violet to the door, leaning past her to open it. The humid air was a slap in the face when we stepped outside, and the sunlight burned my eyes, but that didn't even faze us. Violet strode for the car, not pausing, not looking back. Silent. So fucking silent. The sort of quiet that always foretold bad news.

Sick to my stomach, I held the passenger door as she slid inside, then set the food on the floorboard next to her feet. Once she was settled, I shut her door and rushed to my side, silently praying she wasn't crying when I hopped inside.

She certainly wasn't crying.

"Violet?"

Her face was slack, no emotion there. Nothing but dead eyes staring my way.

"Baby, are you okay?" I reached for her hand, but she pulled away and turned to look out the front window.

"I'm fine."

My stomach knotted. She was about as far from fine as she could be. "Okay," I murmured, starting the Hellcat and throwing it into gear. "It'll be okay. Let's get you home."

I gripped the wheel tight, my foot pressing hard on the gas as I pulled onto Biddle. The engine responded, rumbling to life under the hood. We whipped past businesses and restaurants, past the golf course and the abandoned steel plant, but I made a quick right onto a street far earlier than I'd planned. And apparently, that small change in what was expected was just enough to wake Violet up.

"Where are we going?" she asked, sounding a little more alive than before.

"Home."

"This isn't the way home."

I sighed, hating the detached coolness of her voice. "There's more than one way home, Violet."

Her face was still slack, her eyes focused on something too far away for me to see. The sick feeling grew in my stomach. We needed to talk. I needed to make sure she knew Lacey was full of shit about everything. I also wanted to know what Lacey meant about the other guy and how he'd played into the release of the video. And I had a feeling Violet wasn't going to want to talk about that at all. In fact, I knew she wouldn't. She'd run instead.

She'd already started.

I drove the rest of the way to her Grandma's house, holding her hand on the stick shift. That was the one small concession she allowed—her hand—though it sat lifeless under mine. She wasn't giving me anything.

When I pulled into the drive, I didn't jump out right away. I didn't even turn off the engine.

"You okay with what happened back there?" I asked, bracing for the worst.

She shrugged. "No. But what can I do?"

"You want to tell me about what Lacey said?"

"No reason to." She turned her head toward me, still leaning it against the headrest. Her eyes were flat again, almost lifeless. Her voice matched them. There was no denying what was happening here—she was done.

"Violet, I want to talk about—"

"I'm leaving tomorrow to go back to Chicago," she said. No hesitation, no working up to it. Just dropped a bomb on me without consideration for how it would make me react.

That girl was running hard.

I clenched the wheel tighter, doing my best not to yell out a refusal. "So suddenly?"

She shrugged. "I meant to tell you but never got the chance. I have commitments that I need to fulfill."

"Commitments." I chewed on my lip, my leg shaking. "Is this because some girl talked shit at the restaurant?"

"No," she said with a shake of her head. "It's about my life. It's about going home."

I waved my hand at her grandmother's house, the place she

grew up. The place where her family still lived. "Violet, you *are* home."

She stared for a moment, her face hard, silently regarding me. Her expression sent chills down my spine. There was nothing there, no Violet. All that was left was the scared little girl putting on a show, hiding behind a mask of indifference. One I had no idea how to break through.

Without a word, she opened the door. And she ran.

"Shit." I threw the car into park and hurried out the door. She was already halfway up the driveway, walking fast with her shoulders back and her head up. Running from *me*.

"Violet, wait." I hurried after her, leaving the car idling behind me. "Don't go like this."

"Like what?"

"Mad."

"I'm not mad." She shook her head but turned, that damn vacant expression back in place. Her mask unbreakable. "I'm not mad because you want things that aren't realistic."

"Not realistic? How is us together not realistic?"

"Downriver…Chicago. There's three hundred miles between them. It's not feasible."

The hairs on my arms stood on end, my body going cold. This was the end. Whether I liked it or not, she was running. But I wasn't ready to give up just yet. "You don't know that."

"Yeah, I do. Long-distance relationships don't work."

"We might."

She stopped moving away, staring at me with an expression of hurt on her face instead. "Are you willing to give this all up? Leave your family, walk away from your business, and move to Chicago to be with me?"

Somehow, I hadn't expected that question. I couldn't speak, couldn't answer her. There was no way I could just go. My entire life was here, the business I'd built and bled for, all the responsibilities that fell squarely on my shoulders were right *here*.

She knew that. But still, the very thought of walking away from her made my heart feel as if it were being ripped from my chest. I wanted both—my girl and my life here. I just didn't know how to manage that.

Violet shook her head as she began to cry. "That's what I thought. You want me but only if I'm local, and that's not going to work for me."

She turned to leave, but I lunged for her. Not willing to let her go. Needing another minute to think. "Baby, don't do this. Give me a chance to figure this out."

"There is no figuring needed, Easton. I'm not something broken you need to put back together. I'm just a girl with a life I'm not willing to give up."

"You…you're hiding again." I pointed at her, my voice growing louder as the reality that she wasn't going to try crashed into me. "You don't want to tell me the truth, so you're avoiding the conversation. You're running away even after you told me you wouldn't."

"No, I'm not running away. I'm going home." She leaned up on the balls of her feet to give me a small kiss, then turned toward the house. "Goodbye, Easton."

My heart fell into my shoes. "That's it? A kiss on the cheek?" I asked as she headed for the front door. Leaving me behind. Leaving us behind. And I still wasn't ready to give up. "Violet, don't you know how much I love you?"

The words were out before I could stop them, before I could even think them through. And though they were the truth, I knew I'd royally fucked up. Violet wasn't ready to hear that yet. She wasn't ready to admit her feelings for me either. I'd just pushed her even further away without meaning to.

"You don't love me, Easton. You can't—I'm not worth it." She glanced over her shoulder, giving me a look that froze my heart into a ball of ice. "I'm done being the butt of every joke."

The slam of the door was like a gunshot to the chest. My heart cracked, shattered, disintegrated as I stood in her driveway staring after her. As my world crumbled around me. I waited there for minutes, maybe hours, just staring at the house. Wishing she'd come back outside. Wishing for all the things I'd just lost.

"Easton?" Dahlia walked up behind me, placing a hand on my arm. "Everything okay?"

I licked my lips, still staring at the door, having no idea when Violet's cousin had pulled up. "No, Dahlia. Everything is about as far from okay as it can be."

Dahlia glanced from me to the door and back again. "Something I can do for you?"

"No." I turned for my car, stopping just before I reached the door. "Actually, yeah. Tell her...tell her I'm sorry. Tell her I'll be at the shop when she's ready to talk."

I climbed into the driver's seat, ignoring the confused look Dahlia shot me. Finally, she hurried up the steps and into the house, leaving me alone once more.

"Stupid, stupid motherfucker." I slammed my fist against the steering wheel, wishing I'd just opened my mouth when she'd asked me about moving to Chicago. That I'd told her...something. That I'd been able to think of a way to compromise, to make this work. To meet her somewhere in the middle.

But I hadn't, and now she was gone.

CHAPTER TWENTY-FIVE

VIOLET

I barely made it through the door before the tears started. No gentle crying for me this time, no sir. This was a full sobfest filled with gasping breaths and knees that no longer worked. I stumbled twice, clinging to the wall as my world shattered, before finally falling to the floor.

You're not just passing the video around. You're passing the cowgirl around too?

Did you really go from bowling alley bimbo to garage floor whore?

I curled into a ball in the middle of the rug, unable to process his words against hers. Every person in that restaurant had heard all my dirty secrets. Every one of them had watched as Lacey—

I couldn't even think her name without wanting to vomit.

And Easton…sweet, kind Easton with the manners and the charm. Would he have lied to me? Would he have told me one thing, then gone and laughed about it with his friends later? It certainly didn't seem like him, but apparently, I'd been had before.

Don't you know I love you?

My heart broke over and over again, shattering within me

with every breath. Why did Easton have to say *those words* at that moment? When my past had torn a hole right through the middle of us, when the woven pattern of lies and deceptions had finally begun to unravel in his presence? Easton couldn't love me. He didn't know everything about me. He didn't know anything, really.

But as I lay there on the floor, feeling worse than I ever had before, the hardest thing to accept was the fact that Easton's not knowing was all my fault. Again, I'd made decisions that caused a total upheaval in my own life. And again, it had affected others in the worst way.

And I'd suffer from that knowledge forever.

"What's going on?" Dahlia rushed through the front door, zeroing in on me immediately. "Violet, what happened with Easton?"

Just hearing his name sent another stab of anguish through my gut, and I curled tighter to try to soothe the ache. This hurt. And it was my fault. All my fault.

"Violet?" Dahlia rubbed a hand over my hair, crouching on the floor next to me. "It can't be that bad. He was out there looking like a love-sick hound when I walked up, so it can't be that bad."

She was so wrong. "He said he loved me."

"Yeah?" she asked, drawing out the word.

"Lacey implied Easton, Colton, and Brogan were passing me around…like they did with the video of me in the bowling alley."

"Shit," she spat, the word sounding like a warning. Shit was an understatement.

I couldn't stay on the floor doing nothing. It was time to take control, time to move forward. It was time to go. Pushing myself to my knees, I crawled for the couch. I needed to end this, to give myself some space to deal, and to get the hell out of here so Easton could get over me and move on or quit playing whatever game this whole thing was. A thought that had me almost doubled over again. It'd be better, though. Easier for me. The pain would fade with time and distance. I'd figure out how to see my grandma more without coming back. There were other places, other areas we could meet. Ones where I wouldn't have to see Easton or his friends again.

When I finally reached something to hold on to, I pulled myself to my feet and headed down the hallway. Wobbling. Barely able to see past the tears that refused to stop. Past the boulder lodged in my gut that refused to let me breathe.

"Violet?"

I shook my head, stopping only to peek in Grandma's room. She napped soundly, looking small in her big bed. Small but peaceful, something I envied. Peace wasn't something I'd been able to find in life, and especially not back in Downriver. It was time for me to escape. I needed to go. Needed to get back home. Needed to find a place where I could think and breathe again.

I closed the door to Grandma's room, and then I hurried into my bedroom and grabbed my suitcase.

"What are you doing?" Dahlia asked, sounding awfully accusatory.

"Packing."

She stood in the doorway and watched as I dealt with the things I had sitting on the furniture. I'd never truly unpacked when I'd arrived, so there wasn't much to grab. A random shirt, a hairbrush, a few rubber bands. The stuff I hadn't tossed back into the bag over the last few days as I'd started preparing to extricate myself from this house.

Dahlia handed me the hoodie I'd hung on the doorknob, something I'd brought for sitting in air-conditioned medical offices with Grandma. Something I'd barely had the chance to wear. She was giving up, a fact that only made me want to go home even more. I needed time to process, to think, to accept. And I couldn't do any of that here.

Or, at least, that's what I told myself over and over and over again.

"When are you leaving?" Dahlia asked, leaning against the door with her arms crossed. I could hear the irritation in her voice, the disappointment. Maybe this was better. Maybe if I just left, I'd get out of everyone's way and stop dragging them down.

I finished folding the jacket and set it in the bag, avoiding her eyes. "Tonight. Now. I've got that sweets table job coming up, and I need to get started on what I can."

Her pause was long and tension-filled, and when she spoke, irritation was replaced with outright anger. "So that's it?"

I huffed and grabbed the sides of the bag, trying to keep my hands from shaking. "It's good money."

"It's not about the money, Violet, and you know it."

"Sure it is."

"No, it's about the fact that Grandma's dying."

"You're wrong."

"Really? Fine, then it's that you're in love with Easton Cole, and that thought terrifies you."

I squeezed my eyes closed, trying so hard to deny her words. But I couldn't. I did love him. Loved him more than I knew how to deal with. But there were still so many things left unsaid, so many obstacles in our way. So many questions and possible pitfalls. I just couldn't deal with all that.

"I have to go." I zipped the bag and pushed past her, refusing to meet her eyes. If I stopped, I'd stay. If I stayed, I'd just keep being forced to run into the people who'd helped ruin my life over and over, and I'd drag Easton down with me. I needed out. I needed to go back to Chicago, where no one knew me, and I could melt into the crowds. I needed to be invisible again.

I needed to get the hell away from Easton Cole and death and Downriver.

I grabbed a T-shirt off the floor that I hadn't noticed, ready to toss it into the bag with the rest of my stuff, but something about it caught my attention and made me freeze. It was big and black, softer than anything I owned. When I turned it over, the Second

Gear logo on the front made me catch my breath. I ran my fingers over the letters, letting the roughness of the printing guide me, taking one moment to truly allow myself to feel all the hurt I'd caused myself. Giving myself permission to experience the ache of loss before I had to pull myself back together again. Before I locked away every emotion I had left.

I folded the shirt with careful hands, placing it on top of the rest of my clothes and resting my palm over it for a few seconds. That was my goodbye to this place, to that shop, and to the man who ran it. I couldn't do more. I took one final look at the shirt before closing the lid on both my emotions and the suitcase.

It was time to go.

"Slow down," Dahlia said when I picked up the bag and moved for the hallway. "What the hell is going on? Why are you running?"

"I'm not running. I'm going home."

She stood taller, her expression going flat. "Home? As in not here."

"Yes, home as in not here. As in Chicago. As in where my job and my life are." I sighed, trying hard not to start crying again. This wasn't how I wanted things to be. "I'll be back in a few weeks to spend time with Grandma. Tell her I—"

"I'm not telling her anything." Dahlia glared for a moment before letting out a breath and stepping closer. "Fine. I'll tell her you're a stupid chickenshit who needs a swift kick in the pants. She'll probably agree."

I let myself have one hug, allowed myself enough time to curl into her for comfort, wrapping my arms around her. Being in her hold made the hurt flare bright and hot, though. Made me remember all the things I was leaving behind. Again.

"I have to go." I braced myself to separate from her, to shutter all those emotions back beneath the surface. To tuck that pain away until a time I could better deal with it.

"You don't, but I know you think you do." Dahlia pulled back, holding me in place by my shoulders. Refusing to let me go. "What about Easton?"

Her words should have hurt, should have made me feel something like guilt or pain, but they didn't. Couldn't. I was dead inside, completely emotionless as I walked out the front door and headed for my car with Dahlia on my heels. The first time I'd left this place after graduation, I'd sobbed halfway to Kalamazoo. Not this time. I wouldn't let the pain overwhelm me. Wouldn't let the guilt get in my way.

Still, the words felt like broken glass in my throat as I said, "Easton deserves better than what he'd get with me."

I wasn't even half a block away when I pulled over and grabbed my phone from my bag. I couldn't leave without a word to him. Not after everything. I typed out a quick text, giving myself over to my tears for that one painful moment. Once I hit send, though, I turned the phone off, took a deep breath, and readied myself for my drive. No pain. No crying. No...feeling. This was what needed to be done.

It was time to go back home. Alone.

CHAPTER TWENTY-SIX

"Put the fucking phone down." Brogan smacked his hand on the table, interrupting my daydream of the damned device actually making a sound. I slid my finger across the screen, reading the last words Violet had sent to me for the hundredth time.

I'm sorry. I know I said I'd try, but I'm not ready for something like this. I'm not ready to be back in this place.

Fuck, those words still killed me. I'd sent a ridiculous number of texts since I'd received that message, all met with silence. Just like right then. Brogan was right—I needed to let it go for a night, but that didn't mean I'd tell him that. I set the fucking thing down and glared some more. Brogan didn't flinch, though I hadn't expected him to. This wouldn't be the first time he'd caught me obsessing over my phone since Violet had left me standing in her driveway.

Brogan sat next to Gracie on the other side of the booth at Moose McGregor's, both of them staring at me. Pitying me. It'd been three days since Violet had sent that fucking text message. Three days since she'd run. Three days of me wishing for a redo on so many things. Brogan had dragged me out to our usual dive bar just to get me to leave the shop, not that I was feeling much up for socializing. How Gracie had ended up with us I still didn't know, but I didn't care either. I didn't want to be there.

"She won't answer me," I said, looking from my phone to him and back. "She's gone completely silent. How can we fix things if she's silent?"

Gracie glanced at Brogan before shooting me a serious frown. "What if you can't fix this?"

And goddamn, wasn't that a bucket of cold water? I wasn't ready to go there yet. Wasn't ready to give up. I sat back and shook my head, knowing I was being stubborn but too far gone to care. "No fucking way. And don't even give me that look, Brogan. This isn't some random need to fix people's problems. This is Violet. *My* Violet. This is fixable."

Brogan sighed. "Not if she doesn't want it to be."

I grabbed my beer and downed it, wishing for some kind of pain relief. For some kind of way to clear my head enough to figure this thing out. When I hit the bottom of the bottle, I slammed it down, eyeing the room like a panther on the hunt. Though I was hunting for a waitress, not a meal. "I need another."

Gracie scowled. "Right, like you need another hole in the head."

"Fuck you."

"Hey," Brogan spat, sitting up in his seat and leaning across the table. "You don't get to talk to her like that."

"She's my sister. I can talk to her however I want."

"Stop it, both of you," Gracie said, looking more irritated than ever. "Easton, I'm not the one you're angry with, so quit being a jackass. And Brogan, I'm a big girl. I can take care of myself."

Brogan grunted his displeasure, but Gracie wasn't one to back down. She winged that eyebrow up and kept a firm frown on her face until he conceded defeat. It took some time, probably longer than it would have taken me to give in to her, to be honest, but she held firm.

After a couple of awkward moments, he gave her a head nod and broke the staring contest they'd been having. "Fine. But I don't like it."

"I appreciate the concern." Gracie put her hand on his arm, and he smiled. The two were sitting a little too close for my tastes, leaning toward each other in a way that wasn't their norm. Without Colton here to round us out, it probably looked to the other patrons like Brogan and Gracie were on a date while I was some loser third wheel. Shit, that wouldn't do.

"You two want to find a room until Colton finally gets his ass here?"

Gracie spun toward me looking like a viper ready to strike. "You want to worry about your own failed love life, brother?"

Yeah, I probably deserved that. Still hurt, though. I sighed, putting up my hand in surrender. I knew to give up when Gracie got mean. That temper of hers was too strong to fight against. At least for me.

I grabbed my empty beer bottle, signaling to a passing waitress to bring me another. "I probably shouldn't even be around people tonight."

Brogan caught the waitress's eye and made a motion for another round, then dropped back against the booth seat. "We're celebrating you finishing that time-suck of a Land Rover rebuild. How you got that thing running again without missing Rick's deadline, I have no idea."

Yeah, neither did I. But spending all day, every day in the shop had given me enough time to finally get the beast of an engine purring again. Okay, not purring—more like chugging along after decades of a two-pack-a-day habit. Whatever, Rick was off my tail, and that piece of crap was out of my shop.

"Besides," Gracie said as she pointed my way. "You shouldn't be wallowing alone. It's not good for you."

She had a point. "I just want to talk to her, you know? Make sure she's okay."

I ripped the label completely off my beer bottle, unable to sit still. Unable to forget every second of the scene with Lacey at Gunner's. Unable to stop hearing every word she'd said. The ones against Violet, the ones against me and my friends. Against us as a business. It was all so fucked up.

I'd almost forgotten about one particular comment—about Lacey calling Violet Cowgirl and saying something about her yearly rodeos. I still couldn't figure out what that meant. Of course, I'd been too pissed off about the accusation of passing Violet around between us to focus on something that seemed so small. At least, I had been for the first two days. This morning, I'd woken up with questions ringing in my head—what were these rodeos Lacey hosted, and why the fuck would Violet have anything to do with them? I'd figured it would be easy enough to find out, so I'd called Colton right away. That guy knew everybody's business—plus he'd screwed around with some of the girls in Lacey's circle. He had to know. Fucker hadn't answered me, though. Ten calls, even more texts, and still…nothing. The longer he avoided me, the more my temper frayed too. It was a bad fucking day all around.

"I'm going to kill Colton when he finally finds his nuts and returns my calls," I said as I pressed the home button on my phone to light up the screen. Still nothing. From either of them. I really hated being ignored.

"No, you're not," Gracie said, smiling up at the waitress as she brought over our next round. "You're going to get Violet to listen to you so you can stop sulking over her."

"How do I do that?" I tipped the bottle, gulping down the beer. I was too far into the night to be able to count how many I'd had, but by the way my head was starting to swim, I'd guess at least five or six. I was going to be pissed at myself in the morning.

Gracie shrugged, looking at her own bottle with a frown. "No clue."

"Fix the shit you can, and let go of what you can't," Brogan said, sounding way more let down than I would have expected. He lifted his beer bottle, taking a few long gulps before setting it down again. "Or obsess over the things you can't do anything about, and suffer in silence like the rest of us."

His words had an air of personal knowledge about them, enough so that even Gracie turned to stare at him with wide eyes. I would have asked—maybe, if I'd cared enough to at that moment—but right then, Colton came strolling into the bar with Dalton at his side. Both looking far more serious than I would have expected. Not that it mattered.

"Yeah, okay," I said just before I polished off my beer. Suffer in silence? Not my style. I wiped my mouth with my wrist and slammed the bottle back down on the table. "There's something I can fix, all right."

I jumped up and stormed across the bar, greeting Colton with a hard shove to his shoulders. "Where the fuck have you been?"

He stumbled, looking as if he had no idea why I was so pissed. As if he hadn't gotten all my voice mails and texts. "Yo, man. Go get your dick sucked so you can calm down, then we can talk."

The room went red as fire blazed through what was left of my control. Was that a shot against Violet leaving? It sure felt like it. Without another word, I dipped down and swung hard, my fist making contact with his face. He fell back, only keeping his feet when he knocked into a table behind him. He didn't stay down, though. Can't say that I expected him to, really. We were scrappers, both having been in enough fights to know how to win. No, he didn't give up from one hit. He popped up and rushed me, ducking low to wrestle me to the ground. My back slammed into the floor, my breath rushing out in a single groan, and then it was on. I didn't know how long we fought or who threw how many punches, but before we were done, Dalton was shoving us out the door as the bar owner threatened to call the cops. A sobering moment for sure.

"Damn it, Easton," Colton said as he stumbled away from me. He wiped the blood from his chin and spat on the concrete once the door closed behind us. "What's gotten into you?"

"Why haven't you been answering my fucking calls?" I yelled every ridiculous word, knowing how I sounded, too deep into my anger to care. The rage inside me had become a physical thing. It pushed and scratched, wanting to be let out, wanting to hurt someone else. Even if that person had been my best friend since we'd been in diapers.

"I'm not Violet, man. I wasn't ignoring you." Colton put both hands up and took a step back as I lunged for him again, this time being stopped by Dalton. "Hang on. I had shit going on today, and then I figured I'd get an answer for you before I bothered calling you back."

"Guys. Stop," Brogan said as he hurried out the door. Always the peacemaker, always trying to get in the middle.

But I wasn't having it tonight. I shoved him out of the way, earning a curse from Gracie but not caring. This was between Colton and me, no one else.

"I'll stop when he starts talking." I managed to get a palm against Colton's shoulder and shoved him again, still too wound up to care about anything but causing him enough pain to match my own. "Violet ran away from me because of something to do with Lacey and those fucking rodeos. I need to know what they are."

Dalton jumped right in my face, blocking me from Colton, no fear in his gaze. "Don't go attacking my nephew, son. Violet ran because she was afraid. You know what makes a woman afraid?"

As much as I burned for some sort of retribution, I couldn't take that out on Dalton. He'd never done a thing to me, had never pissed me off in the slightest. I'd watched him struggle after my cousin had cheated on him, watched him fall apart and pull himself back up.

The first crack in my temper—the first bit of calm and quiet—appeared inside my mind, growing larger as Dalton kept looking at me with those gray eyes of his.

"Don't know," I finally said, forcing myself to take a step back. To get out of his face. "Your naked ass in the morning?"

Dalton didn't back down, even though his lips turned up just a little into one of his off-center smiles. "No, you jagoff. Not knowing whether their man has got their back is what makes them afraid. Violet ran not because of what some girl said, but because she assumed you couldn't handle the truth."

My brow tightened as I tried to make sense of his words. "What truth? What are you talking about?"

Dalton didn't even flinch, looking me square in the eye when he said, "She cheated on that boy she was with."

"I know that," I spat, pulling away, hating that her secrets had to be laid bare like that. "I figured that one out already."

It was Colton who answered. "Charity was at the bowling alley the night Jace and Lacey got even with Violet. The night before the video went screaming through the school."

The night I'd picked Violet up on the side of the road—her tear-stained face and dead eyes staring back at me. Lacey, Jace… they would have been looking for revenge, and that bitch was just plain cruel. Everything in my body tightened, and my voice came out as more of a growl as I asked, "What did they do to her?"

"From what Charity told me, it was an ambush planned by the sister," Colton said, shaking his head. "Fuck, even I'm not as much of an asshole as that Lacey chick."

"Could have fooled me," Dalton murmured from where he stood next to Brogan and Gracie.

"Fuck off, old man." Colton huffed, facing me down. "They set Violet up, told her it was a party, but really, they were watching her video on the overhead screens. All the screens. It was nothing but naked Violet all over that joint."

"Fuck me." I ran a hand through my hair, tilting my head back and growling at the sky. "That's why she was in the rain the night I picked her up. She'd walked into a viewing party of her having sex."

"But that was years ago," Gracie said. "What does that have to do with now?"

With a gut weighted down by dread and a throat tightened by rage at a situation I couldn't control, I let the pieces fall together. "Yearly rodeos."

Gracie still looked confused. "Not finding the connection."

"Cowgirl Vee," I spat, the words foul. "Lacey hosts yearly rodeo parties."

Gracie's eyes went wide, and her mouth fell open. "Oh my God, those sick bastards still watch the video together."

"Motherfuckers." I kicked a garbage can, not taking pleasure in the crash as it went rolling across the lot. I plopped my ass onto the concrete, leaning against the wall and putting my head in my hands. Colton sat down beside me, followed closely by Brogan and then Dalton. Even Gracie slid down the wall, the five of us sitting beside each other on the concrete. For a good few minutes, there was nothing but the sounds of music from inside and the traffic rolling by out on Telegraph. Nothing but the swirling thoughts in my head and the suffocating sense of failure blanketing me. I'd lost her. And I had no idea how to get her back.

Finally, Colton sighed and pulled his phone from his pocket. "You heard from her yet?"

I grabbed my own phone, sinking deeper into that failure as the screen showed no new messages or calls. "Nope."

Colton sent a quick text to someone, then pocketed his phone again. "Given up yet?"

I thought about it, flipping my phone from one hand to the

other. Had I given up? Was I ready to? Was finding solace again worth more than having Violet in my life?

The answer was a lot easier to come to than I would have thought. "Nope."

"Good." Colton bumped my shoulder. "Don't give up on the right one, man. You'll always regret it."

"I don't plan on giving up, but she might. It's just such a mess." The alcohol in my stomach burned, my gut twisting at the thought of those fuckers watching that...still. "I'm sorry I hit you."

"Yeah, well—you're missing your girl. That shit makes us all do crazy things."

But his words hit me in a way he probably hadn't meant, and as much as I hated to admit it, I had to. "She's not my girl anymore."

Colton shrugged before hopping up to his feet. "You'll get her back."

"How?"

Brogan stood, helping Gracie to her feet and dragging Dalton with them. The four of them stared down at me, waiting. Watching.

Finally, Colton shrugged. "Fuck if I know, man, but you gotta have some sort of faith."

I practically snorted as they watched me lumber to my feet. "I'm gonna need more than just faith. I think I'm going to need a miracle."

CHAPTER TWENTY-SEVEN

VIOLET

Michigan Avenue on a warm, summer day was a level of hell I sincerely despised. Why were there always so many people? And how could they think it was okay to stop in the middle of the sidewalk to look up at a building? Every delay, every tourist more attentive to the latest overpriced fashion accessory in some store window instead of the hundreds of locals trying to get to and from work, only made my blood boil hotter.

Or maybe I was just in a rotten mood.

I pushed my way through the crowds and headed south. My feet ached from standing all day, and my hands were raw from all the time spent washing fruit, but my shift was over. It was still sunny out, which was why even the stretch south of the Magnificent Mile was so busy. Chicago in late summer was never quiet or peaceful, that was for sure. Too many people visiting from all over the world, too many street performers out to make a quick buck, too many locals soaking up the summer sun. And then there were those of us who worked all day, just trying to get home at a decent hour so we could take off our pants, curl up on the couch, and pretend our heart wasn't still broken in a million pieces.

As I turned west at Grant Park, my phone rang with an actual call. Something that made my heart jump. For a split second, I hoped it was him. That Easton was reaching out to me again. Not that I actually expected him to. After I'd received—and left unanswered—about fifty texts and ten voice mails, I'd blocked his number, no longer wanting to see his name on my screen. A decision I'd been regretting more and more as the days passed.

But he wasn't the only person important to me. I smiled when I saw who was calling and swiped to accept. "Hey, Grandma."

"Let me get this straight. You'll only talk to me over the phone. What…do I smell?"

I laughed, the first real laugh I'd had since I'd torn out of Downriver and headed west. "Sorry, I know it's crazy, but I really needed to go after the whole…thing."

She hummed, probably not buying my line of bullshit. "Whatcha running from this time?"

Yep, totally not buying it.

"I'm not running," I said, my voice too soft to be convincing, even to my own ears.

"Sure seems like it. You disappear for days to your secret zombie-proof lair in Chicago when you weren't supposed to leave yet. And now you're not coming back when you said you were. Why? This can't be because I'm dying—we're all dying eventually."

How she could be so morbid, I had no idea. I eyed the traffic as I entered the Loop, looking for a way across the street without having to be trampled by the crowds of tourists on every corner. "It's complicated."

"Well, uncomplicate it. Tell me what's going on with you and Easton."

God, just the sound of his name sent pain shooting through my chest. I rushed across State Street, swallowing down the tears

I knew would eventually come. "What do you know about me and Easton?"

"I know he's about as handsome as a heartbroken guy can be. I know he showed up here last night hoping to find out how to reach you since you won't even talk to him. And I know Dahlia seems almost as sad as he does."

Well…that hurt. He was still looking for me? I came to a stop, tucking myself into a doorway to avoid getting run over by foot traffic. "That's not fair."

"Oh, it's fair," Grandma said, sounding angrier than I thought possible. "Now tell me what's going on."

"Nothing," I lied, closing my eyes against the need to lay everything out for her to dissect. Wishing she could solve all my problems and tell me what to do, but not willing to let her try. "Honest, there's nothing going on."

But Grandma wasn't stupid, especially when it came to me. "Lies."

"Look, I just got…swept up," I said, once more on the street and heading home. "I needed a few days to get my feet back underneath me, but the restaurant is busier than I'd expected, and my dessert offerings are flying out the door. I'll be here a couple more weeks—probably until the tourist season slows down—then I can come home for a bit to see you and Dahlia."

Grandma didn't reply, probably noticing how I'd said nothing of seeing Easton. Because I wouldn't, couldn't. If I saw him again, I'd fall right back into his arms—assuming he'd let me. That wouldn't be good for either one of us in the long run. No, separate was better. The pain would fade with time. The need to be close to him would disappear eventually.

I hoped.

But Grandma always knew more than she let on. She sighed heavily over the phone, her voice soft and almost tired-sounding as she said, "He seems like a really nice guy, Violet."

I nearly buckled over, the pain of that truth hard to fight

against. "He is. But he deserves so much more than I can give him."

Silence came through the line, and when Grandma spoke again, her voice was far angrier than before. "You are the most stubborn child."

"I…" Okay, she wasn't lying, and I had no rebuttal for that. I took a deep breath, turning south for the final few blocks of my walk home. "I'm not trying to be. I want what's best for him, and that's obviously not being involved with me."

Grandma's voice was calm and soothing but sure when she finally spoke. "Maybe what's best for him is being able to make his own decisions."

"What does that have to do with anything?"

"You just did the same thing to him that's been done to you for years. You took away his right to decide how his life should go without consulting him. Seems a little hypocritical, doesn't it? Did you even ask him for his opinion on what might be best for him?"

"No," I said, my voice quiet.

"Shouldn't you?" she asked just as I reached my building on Printer's Row. I stood in the doorway, watching the cars go by as I turned her words over and over again in my mind.

"I don't know," I finally said, a sense of uncertainty making me itch to do something. To reach out. I sat down on the stoop and leaned against the brick wall, watching as the sun began to disappear behind the buildings to the west of me. "What does it matter?" I asked, a sense of hopelessness coloring my words. "It's not like he'd be willing to move to Chicago for me. He has his business there, and I won't ask him to give that up."

"Maybe meeting Easton again was fate's way of telling you to get your ass back home."

I rolled my eyes. "Doubt it."

"That's your problem, Violet," she said. "You're always too full of doubt."

Hours later, as I lay in bed staring at my phone, Grandma's words played back again and again. I hadn't really given Easton a chance to talk to me. To tell me how he felt about me and a possible future—not once I realized we were definitely more than just friends. I'd barged into his life and made demands without giving him a single reason to meet them. I'd assumed things from the very start, never really talking about them with him. Never telling him the whole story so he could make decisions on his own. Or so we could make decisions together.

I'd acted in the worst ways.

Surrendering to my need to reach out at least a little, I unblocked his number. The hopeful side of me wanted to see that screen light up, to see a message come through right away. To know that he was still thinking of me just as much as I was thinking of him. But nothing happened. The phone sat quiet and still in my hand long after I gave up hoping.

CHAPTER TWENTY-EIGHT

EASTON

EASTON

Weeks. I spent weeks sending daily texts to Violet, wishing every time for some sort of response. I got nothing. Over a month of me laying my heart bare to her and getting absolute zilch in response. I was the losingest loser who'd ever lost, and my so-called friends refused to let me forget it. Which was why I was spending a quiet Sunday evening at my trailer instead of at the shop or the bar. If I had to hear them ribbing me one more time, I'd snap.

People already thought I was trash—no use proving them right by going to jail at this point in my life.

"C'mon, Dolly. Let's have a snack." The orange ball of fluff followed me into the kitchen, weaving between my feet as I opened the cabinet where I kept her food and treats. "You hungry, girl?"

Her responding meow might as well have been a rebuke for starving her for the past—I looked at the clock—four hours. Greedy little thing.

I tossed a few treats her way and grabbed a beer from the refrigerator. I should probably do some laundry or go cut the grass. Maybe run the street sweeper for the park before the sun went down completely. Something to keep myself busy and stop my mind from wandering to green eyes and dark hair, to healthy curves and a smile that made my heart ache.

Dolly certainly helped, wrapping herself around my ankles again and meowing for more treats and attention.

"Whipped," I said, leaning down to pat Dolly's head and give her an extra morsel or two. "I am definitely whipped by the women in my life."

I got a full stretch and a few claws in my jeans for that one. The purr when I rubbed those orange ears was worth it, though.

A knock sounded at my door, so I left Dolly behind with a couple more treats and made my way across the trailer. It was too late for a random visitor or salesman—not that many came into the park—so it had to be someone I knew. That didn't bode well for me.

I didn't even get the door all the way open before the attack began.

"You'd better have a good reason for ignoring me, Easton Cole." My mother swept in, some sort of casserole dish in her arms and a heavy frown on her face. I knew the woman well enough to know exactly what was coming and how much I was going to have to hear from her before she'd feel she'd made her point. Great. Dinner and a show, apparently.

"I haven't been ignoring you, Mom."

"Bullshit. I call, and you do everything you can to get off the phone. I stop by, and you basically kick me out. You don't come over, you work ridiculous hours, you hole up in this trailer whenever you do take some time off, and you're avoiding the entire neighborhood. You don't even stop by to torment Gracie anymore. I can't do that job myself—it's hard work to keep that girl's ego in check. Why do you forsake me, child?"

If I hadn't been afraid of getting a wooden spoon upside the head, I'd have rolled my eyes. "You're being way too dramatic."

"No, I'm being honest. And maybe a little dramatic. I've spent the past few weeks with Gracie instead of my son. It was bound to happen." She scowled my way, sighing when that look didn't break me. "I made goulash for dinner. Eat with an old lady."

"You're not old."

"I'm older than you."

"Well…yeah."

"That makes me an old lady. You should get some bowls and spoons out. Napkins would be nice too."

It sucked to feel sixteen all over again while standing in your own home. "Yes, ma'am."

Two bowls, two spoons, and two healthy servings of goulash later, we sat side by side at the kitchen counter. Both quiet. Both eating dinner *not* alone. A definite change for me over the past few weeks.

"This is nice," I said as I scooped another spoonful. "Thanks for forcing your way into my place to feed me."

"You're welcome. I worry about you, son."

"No need to."

She sat silent for a few minutes, still eating. Her shoulders stiffening with every bite until she finally got to the point of this visit. Attack mounted.

"Heard from Violet yet?"

Direct hit. I tossed my napkin over my bowl, appetite gone. "Not yet, no."

"Still trying to get in touch with her?"

"Yeah, though I don't really know why."

She hummed, grabbing our empty bowls and heading for the sink. "A broken heart is a hard thing to get over. Trust me—I know."

I'd never really thought much about my mom's love life after my dad left us. Never wanted to think of her *like that,* I guess, but I suddenly found myself curious. Wondering if I'd missed something along the way.

"Did you ever date anyone after Dad?"

"Wow, way to pay attention to your old mom there, Easton."

Seriously, eye rolls were getting harder to resist. "I pay attention to you, but you're wily like Gracie. You keep a lot close to your vest. I don't remember you having a boyfriend…or girlfriend."

"If you're fishing, my preference is for the male of the species." She chuckled as I groaned. "But to answer your question, no. I've not gone on a single date since your dad walked out on us."

Huh. "Why the hell not? I mean, not to be creepy, but you're sort of hot."

"Sort of?"

"In that mom way." I huffed and scowled. "Don't make me think of you in that way, woman."

"But it's so much fun to see you this uncomfortable. I like it." She laughed and shrugged, turning on the water and soaping up my dish sponge as I moved in beside her with a towel to dry. Growing serious quickly. "Are *you* ready to date again?"

"No." The answer almost exploded out of me, my chest tightening to a level close to torturous at the very idea. "I'm not giving up on the idea of us yet."

"Well, there you go."

Oh. "You still love him."

She shot me a look and took a deep breath, rinsing the bowl in her hands. "Sometimes. There are days when I remember the good times and miss the friendship we had, the partnership we grew. Others, I think about how hard those first couple of years without him were, and I want to find him so I can wring his neck." She held out the now clean bowl. "Emotions are weird like that."

I took the wet bowl from her hands, wiping it with my towel as I let my mind wander back to a time I tried really fucking hard to forget more often than not. "He left us without a word of goodbye or good luck or…anything. Not a single reason for packing up and disappearing."

She nodded. "He did."

"With nothing. He literally left us with nothing."

"Yup." She turned off the water and handed me the second bowl, drying the spoons on the end of my towel. "I'll never forgive him for putting us through what he did when he left, especially not because of how it affected you and your sister. But there were a lot of good times before the bad came. Those, I miss." She shot me a crooked, sad little smile. "Besides, my heart doesn't care about the details. It wants what it wants."

"That's..." *Green eyes. Dark hair. Curves. The sad look in her eyes. The way she trembled in fright at times. The way a single text from her made my heart race that much faster.* I couldn't help but take a deep breath and blow it out. "Yeah, that sounds about right."

"I figured." She took the towel from my hands and hung it up. Taking care of me as always. "Your heart is just like mine."

"Stupid?"

"Pretty much." With a laugh and a true, wide grin she rose onto the balls of her feet and pressed a kiss to my cheek. "She seems like a really nice girl."

"She is." The goulash turned to lead in my stomach, the words I'd already said coming back to force their way out. "And I'm *not* ready to give up on her yet."

Her eyes sharpened, pinning me in place. "I hear that, but what are you going to do if she *does* come back?"

"What do you mean? Because what I'd do if she showed up tonight isn't something I want to talk to my mother about."

She *did* roll her eyes—the benefit of being the parent, apparently. "Mind your manners, son."

"I'll try."

"Good. Now, back to the topic of what you'll do if your Violet comes back. She lives in Chicago, but your life is here. What if she refuses to come back here? Are you willing to move for her? To start all over again somewhere else?" She gave me a saucy sort of pout that looked way too much like an expression Gracie would wear. "Are you prepared to abandon your old mother to a life of loneliness without you walking distance away?"

"Nice guilt trip, lady."

"Answer the questions."

I took my time, covering the casserole dish in plastic wrap and putting it away in the refrigerator before even considering giving her an answer. Letting the options percolate in my mind. And though I couldn't say the words outright because the idea of hurting my mom—the woman who'd stepped up and dealt with all the bullshit after my dad left—just about killed something inside of me, my intentions were clear.

"I would call you every single day to make sure you and Gracie were okay and had what you needed."

She nodded, smiling but suddenly looking ready to cry as well. I couldn't stop myself—I grabbed her thin shoulders and pulled her into my chest, hugging her the way she'd hugged me when I was smaller. With her entire body and with the abandon of someone who truly cared for the other person.

I hugged her with all of me, exactly as I sensed she needed to be hugged. "He never deserved you, Mom."

"You're such a good man, Easton," she whispered, patting me on the back. "I hope she does come back to you. *You* deserve a little happiness in this life."

She pulled out of my arms, shaking her head and backing away until it was obvious she was headed for the door.

I wasn't ready to watch her leave, though. "That's it? You come, you insult me, you eat the food you made for me, you almost make me cry, and then you leave? You could stay for a movie or something."

"No way. I've spent enough time with my progeny today. Besides, I've got plans tonight."

"You don't date."

"No, but I play poker. And tonight, I'm feeling real lucky."

I walked her to the door, standing on the porch and watching as she headed toward home. Needing to talk to her for one more moment before she left. "Hey, Mom."

She turned right there in the middle of the street, suddenly looking so much older than I knew her to be. Sadness pulling out every wrinkle and sign of age even as she tried to smile through it. "Yeah?"

"If you're right and you win big, send some of that luck my way." Luck for me, for Violet, for us coming back together. I'd take anything I could get.

My mom's smile lifted just enough to make her glow. To bring truth to the expression. "I already have, son. Be patient. And when you no longer have to be patient, be strong. Nothing's ever easy in life, and sometimes you need to wait for actions instead of words. Remember that."

I watched her walk all the way home and then headed back inside to find Dolly in my favorite chair.

It had been a night with the women in my life.

Sans one.

And man, I fucking missed her.

"Soon, pretty girl." I picked up my cat and sat in her spot, rubbing her head as we got comfortable. "Hopefully Violet will be home soon."

No matter where that home was. Chicago, Downriver, somewhere in between. Wherever we ended up, home would be there because she'd be beside me.

If I was lucky enough to get her back.

VIOLET

Five weeks. I'd left Michigan five weeks ago and hadn't been back. What had I been thinking? The longer I stayed gone, the more I wanted to be there. To go home. But Easton hadn't contacted me.

Not that I should base my life and decisions on a man, but he was a big reason why I wanted to go back. If he didn't want me there...

I couldn't blame him a bit if he didn't want me there.

The "L" rumbled through the Loop, heading south along the tracks. Work had been hard, and my legs were too tired to walk all the way home. The train was a quick way to shortcut some of the crowds, though it would take me a bit out of my way. Still, it was a nice break in routine, and it gave me time to stare at my phone and think about the man I kept trying not to think about. The one I was too weak to avoid much longer.

I swiped my phone to life and opened my texting app. Maybe if I sent Easton a message. A simple text. Something to initiate contact. But what would I say? *Hey, sorry for freaking out and running away from you? Hey, I didn't mean to humiliate you in front of a crowded restaurant? Hey, I miss you but I'm afraid?*

No. Those wouldn't do. And sending him a message begging him to come to Chicago would be all sorts of wrong. We weren't even talking, which was entirely my fault. I couldn't demand he come to me to fix things. If they could even be fixed.

I shook my head and slid my phone back into my pocket. An act that was getting harder and harder to do as the time went on. One of these days, I'd break and call him. I knew it. I just wasn't quite there yet.

I rushed off the train at my stop and trudged down the stairs to the street level. I had a six-block walk ahead of me, plenty of time to stew and daydream about what I could or would or should do. There was a large crowd on my normal side of the street, so I crossed to avoid them. As I passed a storefront I'd never noticed before, a sign in the window caught my eye. It was so simple, so ordinary, but out of place considering the venue. In between mannequins dressed in wild colors was a black chalkboard with pretty script writing on it.

Forgiveness is a virtue of the brave. –Indira Gandhi

I must have stood and stared at that sign for minutes,

dissecting every delicate swirl of handwriting. Memorizing every dotted I and crossed T. The city quieted as I absorbed those words, and the people rushing past disappeared. All I knew, all I could focus on, was that sign and the message it bore.

I desperately wanted to be brave.

I wanted to forgive myself for the mistakes I'd made in my past. Did I deserve a second chance—or third, or fourth—to fix what I'd done so many years before? Did I even have the right to ask Easton to forgive me? Maybe he'd consider it. Maybe he'd accept my apology if I told him I was an idiot who'd acted without thinking and then settled in to wallow in the grief those actions caused instead of pulling myself up and fixing them.

Maybe it was time to be brave and ask for forgiveness before I lost something so very vital to my heart.

Without thought, I plucked my phone from my pocket. My hands shook as I typed a message to the man who'd been my obsession for five long weeks.

I'm sorry I ran. I miss you.

I swallowed hard, my finger hovering over the send button. Was this it? Was this me being brave? Or was this another cop-out? Should I call him? It was a workday and too early for him to have left the shop. I'd probably interrupt him. But a text was easy. A text could be read when convenient.

A text was a lot better than silence.

I hit send, tucked my phone away, and strode the rest of the way to my street. I refused to look at the screen, refused to even think about what I would do if he answered. If he told me to fuck off, like I deserved. If he told me to come home, like I was afraid he'd do. And I was absolutely terrified that he wouldn't answer at all, having given up at some point in the weeks when I hadn't been brave at all. I could only hope for more than just silence, even if I didn't deserve it.

My phone stayed silent through the rest of my walk, through my climb to the third-floor apartment I called home, through a quick session in the kitchen where I warmed up lasagna I'd brought home with me. It stayed silent all the way until I was getting ready for bed.

And then it pinged.

I set down my toothbrush and padded into my bedroom, wary. Maybe it was Dahlia. Maybe it was one of the few friends I'd made in the city. Maybe it was—

I'd never know if I didn't look.

So, I looked.

And my heart nearly stopped when I saw Easton's name on my screen.

Actions speak louder than words, baby. Prove it.

Prove it. Prove how sorry I was. Prove that I missed him.

I didn't even give myself time to think twice about how to do that. With shaking hands, I switched from the texting app to my contact log, scrolling past screens of numbers until I found the one I was looking for. I pressed call without even bothering to think about the time.

Time to be brave again.

CHAPTER TWENTY-NINE

EASTON

Violet never texted me back.

I should have seen that coming, but I'd hoped. I'd really fucking hoped. I'd given her the time she needed, no matter how hard it'd been to resist driving out to Chicago every day of the last five weeks. But last night…last night she'd finally reached out and told me she missed me. That had to mean something, right?

"You going to get to work soon or what?" Gracie leaned out of the office door, giving me her standard smartass glare. "I don't have all day."

"Fucking numbers," I mumbled, earning me a look from Brogan. "I know—it's a business. Numbers are important. They still suck."

"I can't say I disagree with you." He went back to the oil change he was doing on Gracie's thirty-year-old Chevelle. Apparently, it was time to get to work and quit worrying about my phone. And Violet. Which really wasn't possible. All the *what-ifs* and *should-haves* refused to let my mind settle. I couldn't shake the feeling that I'd lost an opportunity last night. If I'd been smart, I'd have gotten into the truck and driven my ass to Chicago the second she'd texted me. Caught her when she was still reaching for me. No matter how much I knew she was the one who needed to do the trying, the one who needed to remind herself what we were together, it was hard to not give in and run to her. But five weeks was a long time to wait for her to finally crack. Too long.

By the time I headed toward the office, I could hear Gracie speaking to someone. Typical. I walked away from the one thing that could keep Violet off my mind, and my sister was too busy to deal with me.

"Yeah, he's right here," Gracie said just as I breached the doorway. Assuming the he was me wasn't hard to do. I almost stopped and called for Brogan to handle whoever was in there—I wasn't in any mood to deal with customers—but I figured I'd probably already been seen. Hopefully whatever they wanted could be handled quickly so I could get done with Gracie and go back to work. Stay busy. Stay focused.

Maybe plan my drive west.

But when I finally looked up, all thoughts of drives and focus and work fell away. It wasn't a customer standing by my desk. Not really. It was Violet. A thinner, exhausted-looking version of my Violet. When did she get so pale?

My mouth moved before my brain could. "Jesus, what the fuck happened to you?"

Violet ducked her head, looking more nervous that I'd ever seen her.

Gracie practically growled, that eyebrow winging hard into her bangs. "Way to be an ass."

Yeah. I deserved that.

"Sorry, I just meant…you look tired." Understatement, but that would have to do for the moment.

Violet glanced from Gracie to me, looking skittish and wary.

The last things I wanted her to feel around me. Okay, maybe not the last. If she felt nothing, I think my heart would turn to fucking dust. I could work with skittish.

"I had to work overnight to be able to take time off so I could come out here," she said, her voice a little scratchy. "I haven't slept in like thirty-six hours."

Okay, that explained the exhaustion, but not her presence. "What are you doing here?"

Gracie groaned as if I'd just said something epically stupid, grabbed her purse, and headed toward the shop floor. "I think it's time to leave you two alone. I'll make Brogan take me to lunch and put up the closed sign so the shop will be empty. You two can…talk." She paused before disappearing, smiling softly at the woman who'd most recently ripped me to shreds. Traitor. "It was really good to see you, Violet."

"You too." Violet glanced at Gracie as she walked out, then went back to staring toward my desk, her eyes avoiding mine. My sister didn't give me a break, though, mouthing *don't fuck up* before closing the door behind her. The brat.

Once we were alone, I had no idea what to say. No clue how to start off a conversation. I was too focused on the fact that Violet was *here*. Standing in my office and smelling so good, I wanted to grab hold of her and never let go. The moment was practically a dream, a fantasy come to life. If only I could—

"I cheated on Jace."

That wasn't at all what I was expecting to hear. "What?"

"At the bowling alley. That's why I could never really defend myself about the video and why Jace and Lacey are so brutal about the whole thing." She shrugged, moving to the computer and bumping the mouse to bring it to life. "It wasn't just me having sex. It was me having sex with someone who wasn't my boyfriend."

"Violet, I know—"

"Here, this one. It's one of the more popular cuts." She turned the monitor my way, her voice flat. Her eyes locked on the screen where a younger her gyrated on top of…someone. Jesus fuck, my heart crashed, and my stomach knotted. What the hell was she doing? "They zoomed in on the action to get more attention, though I think a few things got lost along the way. He was grabbing my ass—can you tell? Hard to with the angle. Hard to see who it was I was with, too. Isn't it?"

I licked my lips, unable to speak. Unable to look away from the monitor and yet wanting to throw the thing through the wall. That video was why she'd run, why she'd left town the first time and me the second. That video had destroyed her in so many ways.

Without waiting for me to pull myself together, Violet pressed a few keys on the keyboard to make the image go full screen. "Marcus Knight, quarterback from Grosse Pointe High. We met at an ice-skating rink, of all places, a few weeks before this was shot. He was nice."

"Violet—"

"Everyone always assumed it was Jace, and he did nothing to stop that idea. Of course, neither did I. I was already being called a whore because of the video, God forbid I make it worse by admitting it wasn't even my boyfriend I was having sex with in it." She shook her head, pressing keys on the computer until she tracked down another clip, this one from farther away. Her head was thrown back, Marcus' hands covering her breasts. Throwing the monitor was seeming like a better idea with each second. "That one's the one that gets the most shares. You can see my face clearly, can't you? Trust me, people can. They recognized me from that clip. They still do."

My mind roared, anger burning me up from the inside. Not at her—no, never at her. Anger at life. At Jace and Lacey. At the judgment this town had thrown at her. At myself for not stepping in earlier. "Turn it off."

She didn't, though. Of course not, because Violet was doing what she needed to. She was finally confessing. "Do you know why I cheated on Jace?"

I could hardly shake my head, and I definitely couldn't speak past the rage building in my throat.

"Neither do I. I should have ended my relationship with him a long time before that night. He was such a…jackass. But he was handsome and popular, and he charmed me right out of my pants. It took me over a year to figure out how he was controlling me. Tiny statements, little decisions that ended up being big ones. He picked where we were going to college, he picked where we went every weekend, he picked when and where we had sex. He picked everything, and I followed him around like a puppy. Until I decided not to be a puppy anymore."

She ran a finger over the screen, right along the curve of that guy Marcus' arm. "Marcus was different. He was kind and funny. He kept telling me how much of a jerk Jace was. Kept trying to seduce me. That night? That was right after the spring snowball dance. Jace had dropped me off at home early, even though I'd wanted to stay out. He'd said I should get some sleep, but I knew. I knew he was going to meet up with his friends and probably hang out with some girl. Things were super rocky with us—I assumed he was as unhappy as I was, and I wanted to pay him back for being such a dick to me for so long. So, I called Marcus, and we went to the bowling alley Jace's dad owned. I knew how to get in, knew the alarm codes. I knew everything except that they'd installed three cameras the week before."

"Did Jace know about the cameras?"

She shrugged. "I never asked him. From what I understand, Jace's coworker was the first one to see the video. It was totally an accident. He was trying to figure out the new security system and stumbled on clips of Marcus and me walking in. He called another friend, then another, and finally, they called Jace. Once it got back around to me, Jace was…oddly calm about the whole thing. Lacey, on the other hand, wasn't. And that's where the problems started."

"That night," I whispered. "When I picked you up in the rain…"

"Jace convinced me to come to the bowling alley. His dad was letting him and Lacey have friends out to bowl after hours. Perks of being the owner's kids, you know." She shrugged, her eyes unfocused as she stared at the screen. "Jace came and picked me up. I didn't want to go—didn't want to see him—but I had to." She looked up, and the expression on her face—the pain there—nearly knocked me over. "I was going to tell him. I swear, I was going to break it off for good with him. I was so over everything, and I just wanted to be rid of him. Plus, the guilt from being with Marcus when I was still technically with Jace was too much. I felt like a liar and a fraud, and maybe I was, but Jace and Lacey were worse. They had the video playing on every screen in the bowling alley when Jace walked me inside. The entire football team was there. The cheerleaders. Half the basketball team. All of them sitting around and watching it. Critiquing me."

My stomach lurched. "Jesus, Violet."

Her eyes were rimmed in red and looking way too close to watery, but she held my gaze. My little warrior. "The people I thought were my friends ambushed me, but I felt as if I deserved it, you know? Like it was penance for cheating. That humiliation was my pound of flesh, and I accepted the punishment. I was willing to pay that price because I really had been wrong. But see, those guys didn't just watch the video. They downloaded it. They posted it online as different forums became available. They spread that video far and wide, all while perpetuating the lie that it was Jace and me having sex. You couldn't see Marcus's face, and he had a haircut similar to Jace's, so it worked. Marcus disappeared, too afraid he'd be named as the guy with me, not that I can blame him. But Jace was oddly proud of it. He let that lie spread everywhere. And everyone believed the legend. I got called a whore in school, had boys I barely knew assault me in the hallways, had people on the street glare and look away when they noticed me. The community basically excommunicated me while Jace earned some kind of weird guy street cred for the whole thing. Some kid I'd never met would grab my ass and call me a slut with one breath, then high-five Jace and cheer him on with the next." She cocked her head, finally closing out of the window on the computer. Making that damn clip disappear. "I became everyone's favorite victim, even though I never wanted to claim that title."

Every word, every breath made me long to hold her more. Increased my need to comfort her. "I'm sorry. I should have been there—"

She brushed off my words with a wave of her hand. "You had your own tragedy to get through. I was just so grateful when you picked me up that time. That was the night. I'd run out of the bowling alley in tears and started walking home, but then the storm had rolled in. I'd kept walking because I didn't know what else to do."

Shit, neither had I. I still didn't. "You were so sad that night."

"I was. I thought my world was crashing down around me, though I didn't know to what extent at that point. Still, you made me feel better. Just talking with you at the pizza place made me feel normal for a moment, gave me something else to think about besides the fallout from that tape. Even then, that night—as you talked about your dad leaving you without a word—I knew things would get bad for me. Not as bad as they were for you, though. My problems seemed so much smaller in comparison." She choked on a sob, and I reached for her. Unable not to. Thankfully, she sank into my hold and didn't pull away.

"It wasn't a contest. Your pain and fear were just as valid as mine, even though the sources were different." I held her tight, every muscle in my body relaxing at her softness and warmth. Even breathing felt easier with her in my arms.

Violet snuggled close, taking deep breaths as I held her and waited. Because as much as I dreaded it, there was more to hear. More for her to tell me. Her story didn't end that night in the rain. It didn't even end with graduation.

"That night, you told me it was okay to want to escape. Do you remember?" She looked up at me, her brows furrowed, so fucking beautiful even as she fought back tears. "When I said I just wanted to leave, you convinced me that the idea wasn't wrong, even though that's what your dad had done, that leaving was an option when things were too hard. I clung to that. Through those last few months of school when things were so hellish, I held on to the knowledge that I'd leave the second I graduated, and it would all be over."

There was that feeling in your stomach when you were about to race—that tension of knowing the next few seconds would determine your fate. Fear and excitement, adrenaline maybe, rushed through your body and heightened your awareness. That was me in that moment. Knowing we were about to get to the rest of the story—finally putting the motor to the test and see if we could control the ride.

And just like when I raced, I closed my eyes, popped the clutch, and held on. "But it wasn't the end."

"The internet is forever," she mumbled, reciting the words we'd all heard a thousand times from Mrs. Michaelson when we were in school. "I was at freshman orientation at Western the first time someone recognized me from the video. He stared at me from across the dining hall for like twenty minutes, which I thought was him sort of flirting. I was such an idiot, but I didn't know how far everything had spread then, so it never occurred to me to be worried. Finally, the guy walked up and asked if I was Cowgirl Vee. Said he recognized me from the internet and wanted to know if I'd sign something for him. I had no idea what he meant. It didn't take me long to figure it out."

"Wasn't there something anyone could do? Some way to get the videos taken down?"

"Oh, sure. I could spend all day searching for GIFs and clips and send takedown notices, but that wouldn't do anything except take up my time. The video was literally everywhere, including on international servers." She pulled out of my arms and dragged a hand over her face, meeting my eyes again. Almost seeming to brace herself. "It still is."

Her words felt like a warning, though I wasn't sure why they would be. "What are you saying?"

"I'm saying people will find it. Customers of yours, friends, people we meet. If you're with me, this video will shadow you just like it's shadowed me all these years. I'll never get out from under the stigma of Cowgirl Vee, whether I live Downriver or somewhere else—though Downriver is worse because that story is practically legend here. Hell, Lacey still hosts those porn rodeos with my video as the feature."

"We'll call a lawyer," I said, everything tightening back up as I thought about Lacey and that day in the restaurant. I should have said fuck it and punched her right in the face. "We'll get them to make her stop."

"Easton, you don't see it yet. She doesn't even matter anymore. She can have a hundred parties, and it won't be a drop in the bucket of viewers compared to the number of people who see it online." She ran her hands over my chest, trying to calm me even as I held her up. As I wished there were some way to make everything disappear. As my entire body vibrated with the force of my rage. "I'm not worried about her anymore, except in relation to how her bullshit affects you and your business. Because it could, and I'd never want to be responsible for making things more difficult for you in this town."

My heart jumped. Her worries meant she was thinking of a future together, which was all I wanted—chaos be damned. But she didn't look quite right as she talked to me. In fact, she looked small and sad. I fought the urge to drag her out of the office and take her to my trailer. To block out the world and keep her safe and warm in my home, in my bed. To hide her away until she felt like mine again. We weren't there yet. We still had a few things to discuss, but I was ready to get that shit out of the way.

It was time to hit the gas a little harder.

"So, you cheated on Jace."

CHAPTER THIRTY

VIOLET

Oh God. He dove right in, didn't he? No easy questions, no hedging around the discussion. Just...that. I'd never wanted to hide more.

"Violet?"

"Yes," I said, the word thick and hard to push out. "I cheated on Jace. I shouldn't have, but I did. And I'll own that mistake."

His silence scraped at my already raw nerves. What was he going to say next? He'd walked away from a cousin because of cheating. Would he be able to see past that fact for me? Would he not? There were so many more important things to deal with—the legacy of that mistake. Would he—

"Did you cheat on *me* when we were together over this past summer?"

My head flew up, my mouth moving before my brain even caught up. "No."

Easton didn't blink, didn't give me a hint of what he was thinking. "Will you?"

"Hell no," I said, shaking my head. "Never. I'd never cheat on you, Easton. I…I know that I should have said it sooner and that I'm an idiot for how I reacted when you said it, but I love you. I'd never want to hurt you that way."

He shrugged, the picture of casual while I sweated out every microsecond. "Then none of that shit matters."

"You don't know what you're saying," I said, inching closer, needing to have his hands on me. Finally feeling something other than hurt and loneliness. Feeling something that reminded me a lot of what hope used to be. "That video will always be around—people will always know me from it. The internet is forever."

He didn't even flinch. "We'll deal with it."

"Lacey and Jace will always try to get a rise out of me. Especially her."

"I'll punch them in the face."

"You'll go to jail."

"Worth it."

"Easton," I said, trying so hard to make him be serious for just a minute. "Being with me will just bring…chaos. Every time my past cycles through, there will be a mess to clean up."

Another shrug, this one less casual, more…aggressive, if that was possible. And apparently, with Easton Cole, an aggressive shrug was a thing. "I grew up in a trailer park and still live in one. My dad left us with nothing, like some sort of bad country song, and most of the town judged me for using government aid to keep food on the table instead of having a little empathy for a family destroyed. Who gives a shit about chaos?"

But I couldn't be flippant. Not with him, not with us. "I do. And you do too. At least, you should."

"Well, I don't. I just care about you." Easton grabbed my arm and tugged me closer—not demanding, giving me the option to touch or not. And I wanted to touch. Needed to, so I went with his direction. I surrendered to his pull and let my body meld into his, because it was what I needed. What I craved. His touch was the glue holding me together.

He continued moving me until I was pressed against his chest, our eyes still locked, his hands sliding down to grab my ass in a possessive yet oddly comforting sort of way.

"Easton, I—"

"Will you stay?" he asked, his words soft, his fear plain as day in his tone. "Will you let me help you fight that past instead of running away from us?"

Such a hard question but one with an easy answer. At least for me in that moment. I'd sinned, I'd confessed, and I'd paid my penance. It was time for my redemption, even if it was only to the boy who'd taught me that running could be a good thing...until it wasn't.

"Yes, Easton. I'll try to stay and fight, even if it hurts." I ran my nose along his, letting our lips brush in the softest of touches as I whispered, "My God, have I missed you."

His lips covered mine before I said the last word. His kiss set my soul on fire, so deep and strong, it practically overwhelmed all my senses. I gave myself over to the kiss, clinging to him so I could return it with as much passion as he was showing me. Trying to tell him without words how desperately I wanted him. I'd missed him so much. I hadn't even realized exactly how much until he was back in my arms again. And I was never letting him go.

When we finally broke apart, Easton pressed his forehead to mine. "I'm so sorry about that day in the restaurant. I didn't understand what Lacey was implying. Colton finally told me what that viewing party meant, and it all clicked. I've never been to one of those watching parties, and Colton only knew about them because his friend Charity had been to one. We—me, Brogan, Colton—we'd never do something like that to you. We'd never celebrate your betrayal like that."

I kissed him again, unable to resist. "I know, and I never assumed you'd been to one. I was just so surprised by her and embarrassed that you'd heard all that. I was an idiot to run without at least talking to you first."

"No, baby, you weren't. Yeah, you shouldn't have run from me, but you were scared. I get it. But this whole thing isn't your fault. You deserve to hold those moments as private, not have to endure the whole world watching them for years on end."

"It's not going to stop, you know."

"Yeah. I know. And I hate that, but not because of my feelings. Because of yours." He ran his nose along mine and kissed my chin. "You should be able to walk into any room and not worry if the person there has seen you naked. Unless it's me. I've seen you naked and would really like to again sometime."

I chuckled, my heart pounding so hard and so loud, he had to hear it. "We'll have to see about that."

"Can we see soon? Because it's been a long five weeks without you." He grabbed my ass again, kneading it, pulling me closer so I could feel just how much he wanted me. And hell, I wanted him just as much. Was desperate for him to touch me, to kiss me. To let me back into his life. He was all I'd never known I wanted, and I'd come so close to losing him. So close to walking away from what could be the best thing that had ever happened to me.

I was an idiot, and he was still able to steal my breath with nothing more than a look.

"Missed you," I whispered, unable to hold it back. My throat too tight to be any louder. Thankfully, Easton never did need me to be loud.

"If you hadn't shown up here today, I'd probably be on my way to Chicago right now. I was barely holding on to my resistance, especially after that text."

Oh God, those words were just what I needed from him. I nodded, one hand on his chest, the other holding him around the neck. Needing to touch. Not wanting to let go for a second. "I'm only here for two days."

He shrugged, his eyes locked with mine. "Can we spend them in my bed?"

"I should probably go see my family."

"I'll give you two hours for that."

I laughed, unable not to. "You're ridiculous."

"No, I'm a man in love. I told you I don't want to live without you. I meant it." He kissed me again, soft and deep and filled with such a sense of hope. A kiss made up of promises.

I pulled away, though, for once putting talking above all else. "What about your work?"

I'd meant the question in terms of the next few days, but Easton took it a whole other direction. "Gracie and the guys can run the shop on their own while I figure out how to make a living in Chicago. I'm ASME certified, so I can work on cars anywhere." He pulled me close again, kissing along my jaw to my ear. "As long as we're together, I'll figure out the rest."

"Easton, no. You're not leaving this town," I said, my voice almost too soft to hear. I ran a finger over his cheek, ready to cry. Unable to say all the words he deserved to hear. My God, he was willing to give up everything. His family, his business…all to come to Chicago on the chance of us. On the hope that I might not run away again.

Good thing running was the last thing I wanted to do at that moment.

I pulled out of his arms, holding on to his hand as I backed toward the door. He watched me with a confused look on his face.

"Where ya going?" he asked.

I grinned as I closed and locked the office door. "Did you really miss me, Easton?"

He shot me an almost arrogant smirk, purposefully looking me up and down as he murmured, "Yes, I missed every single hot little inch of you, baby."

I giggled, then turned to close the blinds on the door so no one could see in. Just in case. "Dirty boy."

"You like me that way," Easton said, stepping up behind me and pressing his hips into mine. So right in his words, so amazing in his touch. He stayed close, trapping his erection against me. Showing me how much he wanted me with his body. His hands roamed, devouring every inch of me, becoming reacquainted as they slid over my stomach and up to my breasts.

"You're wrong," I said, closing my eyes and arching into his touch. So needy for him, I could barely speak. But I would. I had something important still to say. "I don't just like you that way. I love you that way."

Easton moved fast, spinning me and pinning me to the door. His eyes were bright as they met mine, heated and wild. "Damn, that sounds good," he said, pressing his lips to mine in a fiery kiss.

I pulled away with a gasp, unable to stop my hips from rocking against his. To keep from showing him exactly what was on my mind. "We have two days together."

"Minus two hours." He bit my neck as he squeezed my breast, stealing a gasp from me at the incredible pleasure-pain of it all. "And what will we do after the two days?"

I spun, pulling him down to me. Kissing him hard and long, clinging to him. The man wanted time—wanted me. And for once, I wasn't going to run away from that. It was my turn to get something real, to have someone to support me. It was my turn to plant my feet and stay still for a while, even if still meant living two states away.

"We'll figure it out," I said, confident in our ability to beat the odds. Knowing we were both strong enough to fight against the powers that would try to tear us apart. We'd each been through hell already... At least now, we'd have each other to commiserate with. "We'll talk and text and video chat. We'll stay together while we work out the details."

He grunted but returned the kiss, stroking my tongue with his for a few languid moments before pulling away again. "What kind of details are we talking about here?"

I dropped my hands to the waistband of his blue work pants,

unfastening them without a single fumble. "The details of how to manage a long-distance relationship…while we make plans."

He sighed and reached down to grab my ass. "I like the sound of plans."

"Me too."

"So, are you saying you might be willing to come home with me someday?" He licked his lips and pushed his pants down his legs, standing naked before me in more ways than one. That question couldn't have been easy to ask, and it was definitely not easy to answer. But I had to. This was Easton, and he deserved my truth.

"Who knows?" I stripped off the rest of my clothes, needing to be just as bare as him. Fighting past the wall of fear I'd built to give him the real me. "Forgiveness is a virtue of the brave, and I'm not sure I'm that brave…yet." My voice cracked, my words stuck. And still, I reached for him. Needing his weight, his strength. His support. Needing him.

Easton pushed me back onto his desk, bringing my knees up and over his shoulders, spreading me wide so he could fit between my thighs. "Don't worry about that. There's no end date on love, Violet. We'll focus on the now."

I nodded, falling back, not giving a care to the papers and things falling to the floor. "I'm trying to do that."

"Thank fuck." He kissed me again, rolling his hips into mine as he did. "I want to be with you, baby. No matter where we go, we'll be okay so long as we're together."

But I had to say the truth, had to make sure he completely understood. I had to give him everything. "It'll never end. There will always be someone who calls me Cowgirl or says they recognize me from the internet. And I…I've spent a lot of time turning away from that."

"Running," he whispered, pressing his lips to mine on the tail of the word.

"Yeah. I run away when that happens."

He gripped me tight, pulling my upper body to his, surrounding me with his strength. "Run to me, baby. I'll take care of you. Just run to me instead of in another direction."

I groaned as he nudged his way inside me, still clinging to his shoulders. He was right—so long as we were together, we'd be okay. Location didn't matter, not really. Because no matter where we lived, Easton would be my home. My safe place. My anchor. And I wouldn't risk losing that again. I would run toward something instead of away from everything. Toward him.

VIOLET

"Fucking Brogan's MIA again, Wyatt's being all cryptic about his rehab, and Colton can't be bothered to respond to a text. I swear, those bastards are all keeping secrets about something, and it's getting on my last nerve." Easton walked out of the bathroom with a towel slung low around his hips, his handsome face turned down in a frown as he tossed his phone on the dresser. "What the fuck was that?"

"Zombie." I grabbed for another handful of popcorn, barely even looking away from the screen. I mean, I had to for a second. Mostly naked, wet Easton Cole wasn't something I passed up on very often. Or maybe never would be the better term there.

"I get that, but what kind of zombie?" He stretched and dropped his towel, knowing exactly what he was doing to me. This wasn't his first attempt at distracting me from a movie in a hotel room.

Ignoring his blatant nakedness, I shrugged and went back to watching the screen. Faking disinterest to push his buttons a little.

"A dead one." I giggled as Easton pounced on the bed and rolled me underneath him, totally blocking my view. "Hey, I was watching that."

"Watch me instead," he said before pressing his lips to mine. But that kiss didn't last nearly long enough for me. I tried to chase his lips with mine, to no avail. Instead, Easton moved down my neck, over my collarbone, and along my sternum. Licking, biting, and sucking a path he knew well. I fell back as he pulled up my Second Gear T-shirt to expose my breasts to his lips, as he mumbled into my skin, "Love when you wear my clothes."

He sucked a nipple into his mouth, making me arch in pleasure. Easton had quickly discovered that he could tease me relentlessly with his tongue and teeth in this way, so he took advantage of it whenever he could. Which was not nearly often enough, in my opinion.

"Easton," I groaned, shifting enough so he could lie between my legs. He rolled his hips into mine, rubbing his already hard dick against me. My panties were no match for the feel of him, for the heat we shared, though they were certainly annoying. I wanted to be naked with him. Again. Now.

But he had other plans. Plans that included sliding his hand into my panties and teasing me where I was already wet and wanting.

"What time do we have to leave?" he murmured against my breast.

I sighed and lay back, surrendering to his speed. This time. "Checkout's at noon."

He glanced at the nightstand. "Three hours. I can work with that."

I giggled as he yanked me down so I lay flat on the bed. With his lips attached to my nipple once more, I tugged the T-shirt over my head. Easton lifted off my nipple with a pop and slid down the length of my body, kissing a path from my waist to my knee as he did. Watching me the entire time. But I was greedy and wanted all of him. His weight, his body pressed to mine, the solidness of him —I needed it. So, I reached for him, and he grinned as he gave in to my demand.

"One more month," he whispered as he rested his body weight on top of me.

I wrapped my calves over his hips, tugging him into my hold. Clinging to him with every inch I could.

"Four weeks," I replied.

He huffed and ran his tongue along my top lip. "Twenty-eight days."

I dropped my head back, sighing as he took the hint and kissed his way down my throat. "Technically, twenty-nine."

He bit the side of my neck a little harder than a nip, making me jump. Making me claw at his back as I begged for more without words. "Today doesn't count, because I've had you," he said, his voice muffled against my skin. He rocked his hips into mine. "And I'm about to have you again."

I laughed and pulled his face to mine, kissing him deeply, loving the way his tongue tangled with mine so naturally. "You always have me," I whispered when we broke apart.

He rolled forward, rocking his way inside me as I gripped his shoulders. "But in twenty-eight days, I'll have you every day."

"Yes," I hissed, closing my eyes to the delicious stretch of him sliding inside. I was already a bit sore from having so much sex over the last three days, but I'd never tell him that. He'd stop if he knew, and I didn't want to stop. I wanted more. I wanted to make memories that would sustain us through the lonely nights coming up.

Twenty-nine more nights.

Easton set a rhythm that was slow and deep, letting my body build toward its climax as if there were no time frame. No deadline. The way he always did when he knew we were close to parting once more. We'd been renting hotel rooms outside of Kalamazoo—the midpoint between us—for months. He'd spent time with me in Chicago, and I'd spent a ton of time with him in Downriver so I could be with Grandma, but our hotel weekends were my favorite. We would order takeout and watch movies and just *be*. Usually the naked-and-in-bed kind of being. The best kind.

But reality had fallen upon us like a jackhammer. We'd missed each other too much in between visits, and at some point along the way, we'd decided it was time to make a move. For one of us.

Lids heavy, sweat dripping down his hairline, Easton flexed and groaned and fucked me until I couldn't see. Until my eyes closed and my back arched and my body gave in to the need to simply feel. Until he pushed me right over the edge and left me shaking and gasping and begging him to come with me. A few more thrusts, and he stiffened on top of me, pushing deep, coming with a moan that almost made me jealous. Made me want to do naughty things to him just to hear it again.

Made me anxious for the next twenty-nine days.

"Love you," I whispered as he slid out of me, the two of us still connected from shoulders to toes.

"Are you sure?" he asked, rolling to the side and taking me with him. Snuggling me close.

It was a question he'd been asking every day since we'd chosen our current path. *Are you sure?* He'd offered to move to Chicago a hundred times. Hell, he'd offered to pick a whole new city, find a place for the two of us to start over. But Downriver was his home, and deep down, I wanted it to be mine too. I wanted to be close to Grandma for as long as I had her. To help Dahlia care for her as the end neared. To be there as she slowly said her final goodbye. I wanted to help the old lady in the trailer park plant the flowers in the spring and stop by Dalton's trailer to say hi to him and his dogs. I wanted to get to know Easton's mother and his sister, to learn what it was like to have roots so deep and to have survived such loss as that family had. I wanted dinners with Dahlia and shopping on Eureka Avenue and all the things I'd left behind.

Basically, I wanted my life back.

I'd resisted that truth for a long time. Had been okay with Easton giving up his life and us spending time together elsewhere. But there'd been a particular moment that had sparked my acceptance of coming home. A morning with Easton in Downriver after one of our whirlwind weekends. We'd spent the evening playing board games and drinking lemonade with Grandma before heading back to his trailer for a night of not sleeping. The next morning, bleary-eyed and exhausted, we'd stumbled into The Little Spoon Diner to grab a quick breakfast before I headed west once more. Easton had been paying at the counter as I'd returned from a trip to the restroom.

It hadn't been a big thing that caught my attention, more of a feeling of being watched. A whisper of a snicker from a table a few feet away. When I'd turned, there'd been three high-school-aged boys staring at me. Whispering to one another with their phones in their hands and their tablets sitting on the table. And I'd known.

Cowgirl Vee.

"That's her," the biggest one had said as he'd looked me up and down. I'd nearly frozen, my heart thumping and my body going into a state of panic like it always did. But then I'd looked up, and Easton had been watching me. He'd smiled my way, and that had been enough for me to remember who I was and what I had to lose if I let people who had no place in my life overwhelm me.

"You got something to say to me?" I'd asked, glaring at the boys with my eyebrows up.

"Yeah," the biggest one had said, nudging his smaller friend with his elbow. "What's your hourly rate?"

I'd glanced over at Easton again. He'd flicked a glance at the boys with worried eyes, looking ready to fight if need be. His presence had given me strength, given me confidence. Given me bravery. "Oh, honey," I'd said as Easton'd started my way. "I didn't do that stuff for money. I did it because the guy knew what to do to get me excited. I still can't be bought."

"Everything okay here?" Easton had asked as he'd wrapped an arm around my hip. Supporting me. Not pushing me behind him or jumping between us, just giving me the backup he'd known I'd needed. Letting me stand on my own two feet.

"Yeah," I'd said as I'd winked at the boys in the booth. "These kids were just wondering how to get with a girl like me."

Easton had looked them over, his eyes lingering on all the electronics they had with them at their table, and then he'd shrugged. "Get off the computer and try being a human being now and again. Works like a charm."

We'd left without another word, with smiles on our faces. And that day, as I'd driven back to Chicago across the miles separating us, I'd known I could do anything so long as I had Easton with me. Including coming back and dealing with being Vee.

Easton kissed my lips softly, pulling me from my memories with the feeling of being adored. Of being cared for. Of us. There was nothing I wouldn't do for him, because I knew he felt the same way about me. We were a team, a partnership, and we'd have each other's backs no matter what.

"Are you sure you're ready for me to live *with you*?" I asked, smiling. "Your bachelor lifestyle could take a serious hit."

"Don't care," he said, rubbing his scruffy chin against my chest.

"Dolly might."

"She'll adjust," he murmured, moving up to kiss me once more, holding my face like it was something precious to him. Like *I* was something precious to him. And I was, I knew that. He made sure I knew it every minute of every day. "Will you? Adjust I mean—the bakery in Flat Rock isn't like those fancy restaurants you've been working at."

"It's not, but it'll be good for me and give me a chance to save for my own patisserie."

"And you've got Gunner's business."

Yes. That alarmingly charming restaurateur had jumped at the chance to serve some of my desserts once Easton had taken him a slice of my blue cheese cheesecake. Gunner's projections wouldn't be enough for me to quit the day job and cater to the local restaurants, but it was a start. A fresh one that I'd needed for a long time. Plus, Gunner knew everyone—if I could make him a happy customer, I had no doubt he'd toss my name out to his peers. So long as I kept some special treats just for his restaurant.

Going back to the scene of the crime had never felt so right.

I reached up, smiling at Easton as I ran my fingers over his jaw. "I'm really coming home."

"No more running," he whispered, his confidence strong. His words sure.

I shook my head. "Nope. No running."

His grin may have been bright and beautiful, but his wicked little smirk looked even better. "Well, there is one reason I'd be okay with you running."

"And what's that?" I rolled him onto his back and threw my leg over his hips, settling myself into a straddle on top. Wanting one more go before we had to separate for a month. Before I spent my very last weeks in Chicago packing and pining and missing him like crazy.

Easton smiled up at me, his hands going to my hips. Holding me in place. "If you're running toward me."

I grinned and leaned down to kiss him, taking advantage of my position to rub my breasts over his chest. "I love you."

Easton looked up at me in wonder, the same way he always did when I said those three words. That expression never got old—whether in person or on Skype, during sex or just a random afternoon snuggling together. We made sure the other knew how we felt, kept up our communication and didn't hide our feelings. Which was how I knew that he loved me just as much. How I could be so sure that moving back was the right decision.

Easton loved me enough to show me the way home, and I'd never let anything come between us again.

"Love you too, baby," he said. "One more month."

"Twenty-nine days."

"Twenty-eight."

ACKNOWLEDGMENTS

My eternal thanks go out to Lisa Hollett of Silently Correcting Your Grammar. With every book, she holds my hand, props me up, and works to make my words shine. Thank you for helping me write the book of my heart.

A chance internet conversation brought me Esher Hogan, and I refuse to let her go. Ever. Thanks, Bitch™ for always being there when I need words of advice. You're the bestest.

My dog is a big ball of love, my kids are amazing, and my friends hold me up when I can't stand another second. I'm so thankful for all of them.

Violet's Amazing Rice Cereal Bars

A rice cereal bar is a rice cereal bar…right? Wrong! When Violet Foster makes rice cereal bars, she goes all out. Here's the recipe for the bars Easton loves so much.

INGREDIENTS

2	Tablespoons Unflavored Powdered Gelatin (or 2 packets)
1	Cup Cool Water, Divided
2	Cups Granulated Suga
⅛	Teaspoon Cream of Tartar
1-¼	Teaspoon Vanilla Extract
⅛	Teaspoon Salt
5	Tablespoons Unsalted Butter
½	Box Butter Cake Mix
5-7	Cups Crisp Rice Cereal

1. Melt butter and set aside to cool.
2. Line 9" square baking dish with tin foil, grease with cooking oil spray, and set aside
3. In small bowl, combine ½ cup cool water with gelatin powder. Mix then set aside to allow gelatin to absorb the water. Once the water has been absorbed, transfer mixture to bowl of stand mixer (or larger, heavy bowl if using hand mixer).
4. In medium saucepan with candy thermometer on it, combine remaining ½ cup water, sugar, and cream of tartar. Whisk to combine. Cook mixture over medium-high heat until it reaches soft ball stage (about 240°). Remove from heat and pour carefully down the side of the bowl containing the gelatin mixture. Whisk carefully to combine, then allow to cool slightly (I let mine sit for ten minutes).
5. Add vanilla and salt to mixer bowl. Using whisk attachment (or hand mixer), beat on medium-high speed until white, thick, and glossy (about ten minutes or so). The mixture should be thick enough to run off the whisk or beaters very slowly. This is your marshmallow fluff.
6. Add melted butter and cake mix to your fluff and beat on medium speed until well combined.
7. Remove bowl from stand mixer or set aside your hand mixer. Spray a silicone spatula or wooden spoon with cooking oil spray. Things are about to get sticky.
8. Add 5 cups of rice cereal to the bowl. Stir well to combine. You can add more cereal until you reach your preferred level of gooiness. The cake mix makes the marshmallow fluff a little drier than usual, so don't over add cereal or you'll end up with bars that won't stay together.
9. Press mixture into pan well, then refrigerate for 15 minutes to set up.
10. Slice and serve. Store in an airtight container (if there are any left).

* Want to try something different? I've made this with all kinds of cereal—Cocoa Puffs, Cinnamon Toast Crunch, Fruity Pebbles, etc. You can also add small marshmallows, chocolate chips, or a little melted peanut butter to the recipe to charge things up.

ABOUT THE AUTHOR

Kristin Harte started off as a chemistry major in college but somehow ended up writing romances featuring ex-military heroes and the women who knock them to their knees...literally and figuratively. She likes drinking in the shade, snuggling under a warm blanket on a cold evening, and researching how to blow things up. Her children know nothing of what she writes, and her husband just hopes he's not at their Chicago-ish home the day the government shows up to confront Kristin about her Google search history.

When not writing good men doing bad things, Kristin can be found writing paranormal romance as Ellis Leigh or co-writing naughty novellas as London Hale.

www.kristinharte.com
Kristin@KristinHarte.com